Back Home to Vegas

This book is a work of fiction. Names, characters, organizations, business, places, events and incidents are the product of the author's imagination or are used fictitiously. Any resemblance to actual persons, living or dead, events or locales are entirely coincidental.

ISBN: 1-4196-2363-X

To order additional copies, please contact us.
BookSurge, LLC
www.booksurge.com
1-866-308-6235
orders@booksurge.com

C P KAZOR

BACK HOME TO VEGAS

A Story of Deceit and Murder, Vegas Style

2006

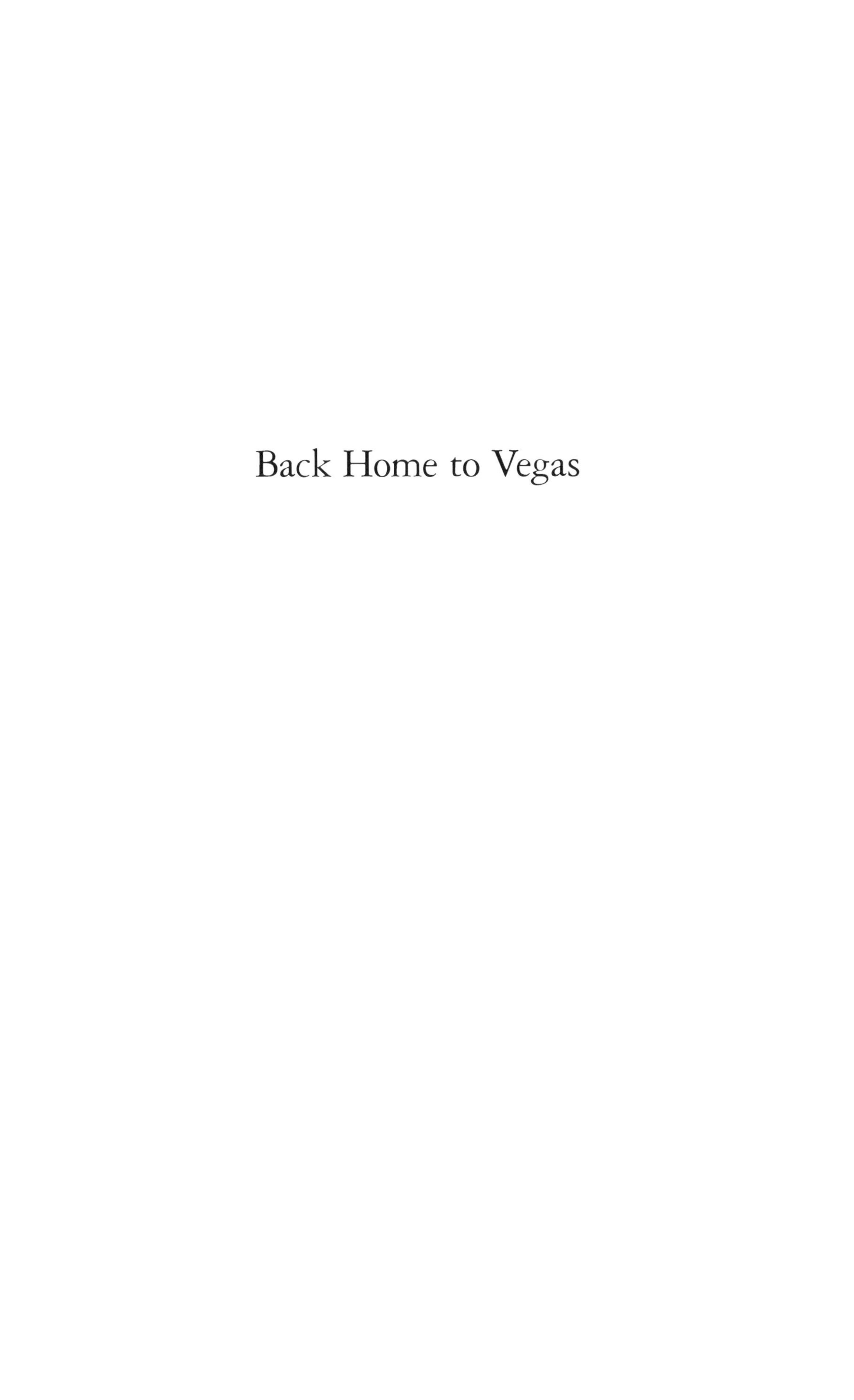

Back Home to Vegas

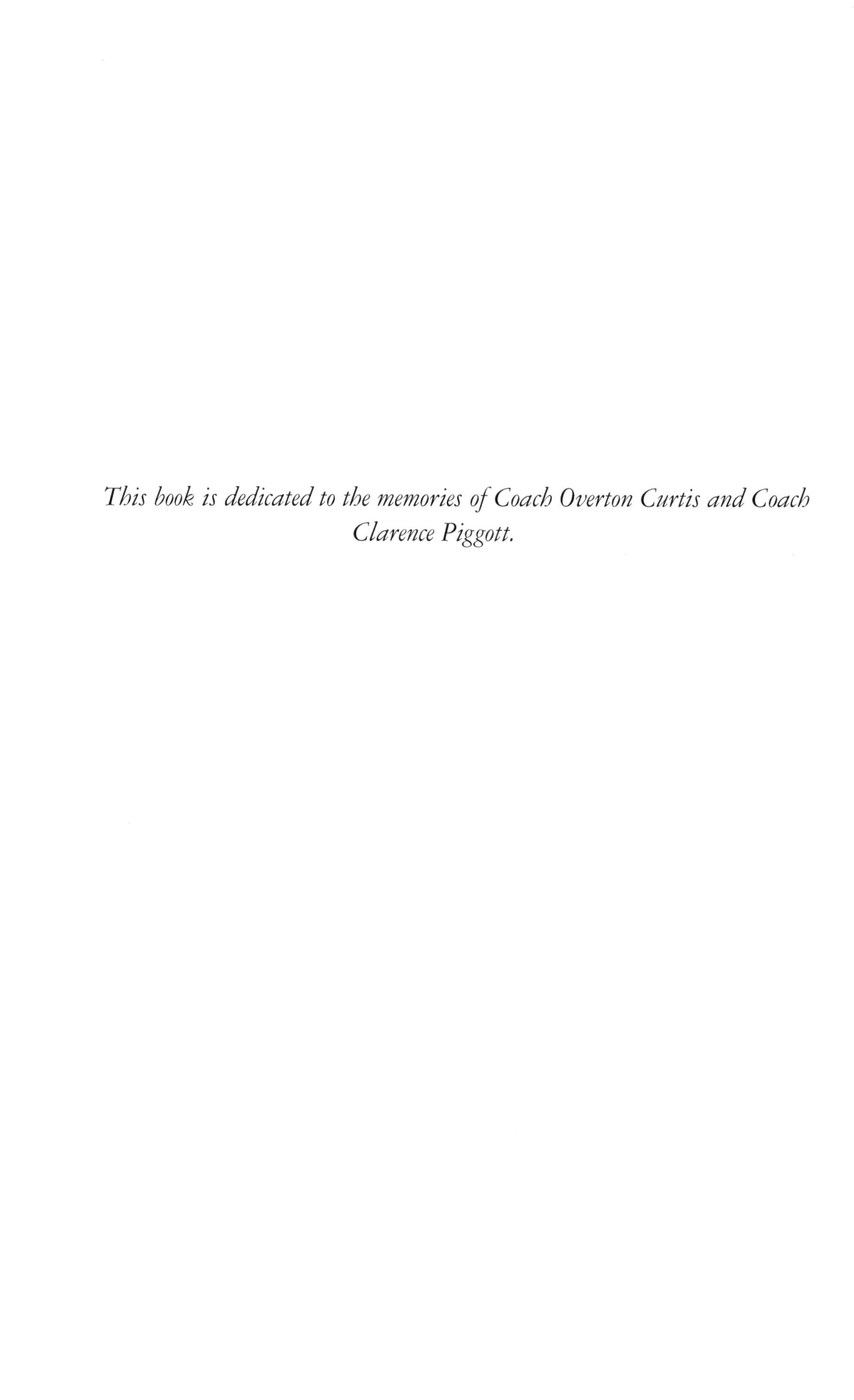

This book is dedicated to the memories of Coach Overton Curtis and Coach Clarence Piggott.

SARASOTA, FLORIDA
Thursday Morning, 1:17 A.M., April 30, 1987

The digital clock by my bed told me in its bold red illumination that it was 1:17 A.M. On my sleepy street in Sarasota, Florida, where I was a lone minority—a non-Mennonite—I heard a car pull up in front of my home. Mennonites are not party animals, and this was definitely in the middle of the night for those folks. No one is up on Ingram Avenue this time of the night, after what had happened. Was this someone trying to kill me?

The knee that I was icing, which had been throbbing with excruciating pain, stopped hurting for a moment. I heard my longtime friend Tim Floyd call for me in a loud whisper.

I rolled out of bed and peeked out of my bedroom, across the living room, which was illuminated by a lamp that was on a timer set to go off at any minute. I saw Tim standing, holding two guns. As I leaned up against the doorjamb, taking the weight off my left knee, Tim gave me a signal. Then he rolled across the room to take cover behind the couch; as he did so, he tossed me his Glock 26, a small, compact 9-mm that was quite effective.

It was amazing. I caught that gun and, in one action, turned off the safety and positioned myself.

We waited in silence as we heard someone trying to get in the front door.

It was hard to believe that until just about a week ago, I had never even fired a gun.

It was hard to believe that just about 72 hours ago, I was fighting for my life. And it was hard to believe that just 72 hours ago, I killed two men.

My knee was now starting to throb again. I leaned, putting all my weight against the doorjamb, and wondering how this all had happened.

Ten days ago was a bright gorgeous day in Sarasota—Paradise, Florida. I was working in the Penter building; a big glass building that overlooks Sarasota Bay and Marina Jack's, a great seafood place and local landmark.

SARASOTA, FLORIDA
Monday Morning, 7:20 A.M. April 20, 1987

I work for Great International Global Life and Casualty. It was such a venerable company when I started, but with new "young," aggressive management, the company name was being besmirched. What a shame, my mentor would say. Chris Bear, well, he was one of the greatest guys in the world and I was still mourning his death of just a few weeks ago.

I had inherited his book of business, and was trying to familiarize myself with it. Pressure from management was unbearable; they wanted us to sell product, by, well, let's just say not fully disclosing. I even noticed a few questionable things in Chris's book, very questionable since some of the documents did not bear his signature. They were mine, and very bad forgeries at that.

Well, it was Monday morning—time to start a new week of bullshit. I ran across the street to get a cup of Denny's coffee to take up stairs. I loved Denny's coffee when it was Pure Kona. Now it's not "pure" Kona anymore, but it is still a passable cup of Java.

I went up to the tenth floor and just got a glimmer of the fabulous view of the bay, since I worked in an inter-office that I shared with Kurt Elwood. Kurt was a piece of work, and really my best friend. He was Ying and I was Yang. And he most definitely was the good looking one, Kurt was born with a silver spoon in his mouth, as they say—real old Florida money, and most of his clients were "friends of the family." He worked some huge estate preservation cases, but Kurt did not have to beat the bushes like the rest of us. Mommy or Daddy just made a phone call. I could trust him with anything: my finances, my love life or, I should say, lack of it. Kurt was always there. Most folks thought he was an asshole, and at times he was, but I knew the true side of him, and we were real friends.

Hell, right now with Chris gone, my mother passing a few months back, and my dad gone for several years. He died of cancer, possibly from working at the Nevada atomic test site for many years. Kurt was about it for friends and family.

Yep, it was Monday and time for our "rah rah" shit, and the pledge on just how much of it we were going to sell the public.

It is 1987, and all the insurance companies were coming out with these great innovative products—a lot of smoke and mirrors, with just enough smoke to blind the public. The meeting was a typical one: good old Tony Lopez, who was maybe one-tenth Spanish, just enough to get a quota position as manager, and sweet Alexandria Butterfield, his personal assistant who just recently had store-boughts installed.

Tony ranted and raved about our top producers, and sure enough mentioned those at the bottom of the list—the very bottom—"and rounding out the bottom of the scum line is Cliff, Cliff Zavitch." Tony then got a party horn and blew it, you know, like the raspberries. How original.

I sucked down my last gulp of Denny's and started to file out of the conference room with all the other sheep when, yep, Tony called.

"Zavitch, Zavitch—my office."

Oh, damn, is this it? I really don't need this, but he had an office with a view and it was almost worth getting yelled at to see the view.

Tony stood behind his desk; Alexandria shut the door behind me as I entered, and stayed in the room. Oh, God, I had a crush on Alexandria, sweet Alexandria. But it was well known that she was fucking Tony and even gave him blowjobs early in the morning under his desk to get him going.

"Zavitch. Sit," he commanded like he was giving direction to his dog.

"Naah" I replied in the most sardonic tone I could muster.

"Fine; suit yourself." He sat, I didn't, and Alexandria stood behind him. It was a bit strange, almost as though she was encouraging him to call me on the carpet.

"Your production sucks."

"Gee Tony. Why? 'Cause I can't bullshit enough old ladies to piss away their life saving on a variable life policy that they have no reason to be in?" I shoot back, and he was not expecting it. Alexandria put her hand on his shoulder and set him back in his chair, and she took over.

"Clifford, you do have an attitude problem and, sir, you are in no position to have one. I have been investigating your book of business and have come across several irregularities," she said as she walked on the side of Tony's desk and put her gorgeous behind on it.

"Specifically?" I queried

"I really am not at liberty to..."

"Bullshit," I cut her off in mid sentence. "While Christopher was alive, you could not do shit because he had too much clout with the home office. OK, he is gone and you guys are going to try to trump up some crap to get me out of here. Well, it is just not going to happen"

"Easy Cliff," Tony answered with a soothing tone. He went on, "Cliff you need an attitude adjustment. Chris's death was hard on all of us. We want you to take a few days off and we will have Nelson cover your clients."

"Nelson? Why not Elwood? Am I suspended?"

"What?" Alexandria piped up. "We are trying to avoid that, and we are trying to protect you."

"No, I am sticking around."

"No, you are not," said Alexandria, speaking for Tony. "Either take vacation or personal days. Come in this office tomorrow and you will be suspended. Finish whatever you must finish today and get out of here for a week" Her voice changed again to a soothing tone. "Cliff, you are taking this all wrong. We want you to take it easy."

Tony just shook his head like a bobble-head doll on her dashboard.

With that, I left the office.

CHICAGO, ILLINOIS
Monday Morning, 6:00 A.M. CST, April 20, 1987

Silas was a chameleon. His job was to blend in and he did it well. He had been plying his trade for almost twenty years now and he liked his work. He had an agent whom called him from time to time and kept him busy. For the first ten years, he used to keep track of all his assignments. For a while, he even kept newspaper clippings, but now realized how stupid that was. He had matured in his profession

Silas loved his job. The money was good; he got to travel a lot; and he had become a legend in his field. The best word to describe Silas was "average." He has a forgettable face, a body not too muscular, just average, no tattoos, and a very soft, unassuming voice. Silas was the kind of guy who would ask you for directions, and you would forget about it. If asked, it would be impossible to describe him. That's how he liked it.

His agent did a good job keeping him busy, and his last few assignments were becoming high-profile cases. Silas was best at "subtlety," nothing spectacular—just accurate kills so that no one even suspected foul play—clean and accurate kills.

Silas had never met his agent, which was pretty typical in his trade. He would get a page and call the number, which was always different. That number would give him yet another number to call from a "safe phone," a pay phone in a bank of public phones; the more phones the better. When he called that number, he would be given a place to be in no more than 24 hours. There his agent would give him his assignment.

He was told to be in Tampa to check into the Plaza hotel on the corner of Kennedy and Dale Mabry. All would be set. He was to check in as a Mr. Charles Mc Millen. The Plaza was, after all, a five-star hotel, which met with his approval. Silas was first class all the way, nothing seedy.

Once in his hotel room, his job was to wait and relax. At some point, there would be a knock at the door and a brown envelop would be slid under the door. This envelop contained the terms and details of this contract.

Silas opened the mini bar and prepared to relax.

SARASOTA, FLORIDA
Monday Morning, 9:30 A.M. April 20, 1987

I had to get away for a few minutes, and it was a good time to get out of the building and go for a coffee run. I caught Elwood's eye and he met me at the elevator and handed me my pager I had left on my desk.

"Damn thing has been going off of every twenty minutes, so I put it on vibrate. Bad news?" he asked as he pointed to Tony's office with his chin?

"Yeah," and I explained the situation to him as we went for coffee.

We returned to our office after our coffee run when the pager gave me another reminder vibration. Kurt laughed, "Would you find out who that is?"

I have always been a gadget person, I had a very sophisticated answering machine, it was state-of-the-art for 1987. It would get a message and then call a preprogrammed number, my pager—

Probably a telephone solicitor. I will catch it later on. Besides, I had a lot of other fish to fry with Tony and Alexandria. I tried to tie up some loose ends, postponed appointments, but my head just wasn't in it. Maybe I should just pack it in. It was obvious that I was being set up for something.

About 3:30, sweet Alexandria came by our office, getting ready to leave for the day, Tony had already left the office and I could only imagine their planned rendezvous—just a quickie.

Alexandria was sweet, but just for a moment. She shut the door and her sweet demeanor became venomous. She sat down and crossed her legs. "Tony and I have big plans for this office. You have no idea how much we can make if everyone is on board with our programs."

As much as I wanted to keep my eyes on her, I forced myself to stare off into oblivion and responded, "What you guys are doing is bullshit. You are training agents how to con folks who just don't understand the shit you are pulling."

"You sanctimonious prick. This was your last chance. You see, Cliff, you are a loose cannon. Someone like you could go to the press, start rumors like others have done. Don't you understand we will have to discredit you, crush you so if you do say anything, you will be saying it from behind bars, and no one will give a shit."

I turned to her. "You guys would go that far to frame me? For what?"

"We don't have to frame you Cliff. All we have to do is show certain persons certain documents. Even if you are not guilty, it will not matter."

Alexandria actually got up and gave me a peck on the cheek. "Think about it, dear."

She walked out the door, pushing past Kurt, who was stunned.

Kurt entered and took his seat. "She seemed like she was in a good mood," he said laughingly.

"Kurt, There is something up here and they really want me out. They want me out, literally. They want me to take a vacation or suspension, and let Nelson work my book a while."

Kurt just shook his head, it was almost four o'clock now and I turned my pager back on and got a reminder beep.

Using the speaker, I dialed my number and put in the code to replay a message, from a person whose voice I have not heard in years.

"Cliff, its Phil Irish, from the Midway Casino." There was a long pause. "How you doing, Tiger," he said. "I need your help. I need you here. Our old friend, Tim Floyd, is going to meet you and arrange transportation. Tim should catch up to you by midnight your time. Keep close to your house and I will call you at midnight your time to make sure all is OK."

And the message ended.

Kurt saw my face go white…

Kurt had only heard bits and pieces about my life in Las Vegas. I was completely confused. OK, I understand Phil calling me and saying he wants me to come back to Vegas. Hell, that could be a good thing. More than once he has wanted me to come back and work with him, but Tim Floyd?

Tim and I were best friends in high school, I did get him a job at the Midway Casino for a while, but the last I heard, he was heading for Quantico, to work with the FBI or CIA or somebody like that. The connection just did not make any sense.

Kurt finally spoke, "You seem shook up."

"More confused."

"This Phil guy? He was the one you found the $25 chip and gave it to him?"

"Yeah. Actually I started working for another group at the Midway casino. We ran the kids' games and my first job was for some guy out of New York who was trying to get the games away from Phil."

Kurt interjected, "Yeah, but Cliff, they are kids games. Come on!"

I smiled and put my hands behind my head. "Do you remember about four years ago, I went out to Vegas. Mr. Irish invited me to the opening of the "Kastle Kasino"?

"Sure."

"It was really great, made me feel like a big shot. Phil and I had lunch and he told me that if I would have stayed with the organization, this one could have been mine. He then asked me if I knew where the money came from for the $400,000,000 project.

"Sure, I answered. The kids' games at the Midway Casino." I further explained to Kurt . " The Midway Casino was the first to offer diversions in a way of carnival games so the parents could throw away their money downstairs in the casino while there children learned how to gamble by playing carnival games upstairs. Ironically the kids games made a ton of money"

"Anyway Phil smiled and told me I had learned well. And at that time, he offered me another job, which because Mom just was starting to get sick, I had to turn down."

"So you were that close to him?" Kurt asked, and continued, "I know you had told me a few stories but, Cliff, I thought that it was just bullshit."

"Yeah, it goes back to when I was 15. Like I was saying, I started working for a group who was trying to put Phil out of business. Real political stuff; a lot of money was involved. And the owner of the Midway gave half of the games to Phil and the other half to a guy named Mel from New York. Here is the bottom line—Mel was part of the, shall we say, the 'family' from New York, and Phil—" I stopped, got up and closed the door.

"This thing really has me puzzled, Kurt. Come on, I lived in Vegas in the '50s and '60s. The Mob was very prevalent, and yeah, Phil, he was connected. His associates were from Chicago." I sat back and took a sip of coffee.

"Kurt, Vegas at that time was controlled. The New York group had no love lost for the

Chicago group. Phil managed to get Mel closed down for a few days, but he had to show that he was able to man and make the carnival games work. So Phil had problems recruiting help for the carnival games.

"At the time I was the only outsider. Everyone who was working on the games were friends of Mel's. He was a new boss. Phil called a meeting of all of us, Mel's employees, in a place called "Balls and Dolls." Yeah, this was an adult carnival game. You would toss a ball, hit a target, and knock a naked women off a couch."

Now this got a stir from Kurt, who smiled and said, "NO WAY,"

"Way," I replied. "Anyway we all sat on the counter waiting for Phil. When he arrived, he started on the person to my extreme right. There were twelve of us.

"Phil looked at Eddie Gold. Now Eddie, about 28, thought himself a real hard ass. Phil said, 'Eddie, I want you to stay on with me. You can stay a supervisor, and I will pay you 20 percent more than Mel.'

"'Fuck you, you Mick bastard,' Eddie said. 'I would never work for you, you prick.' He then turned to all of us and said, 'I better not find any of you working for this cocksucker,' and walked out.

"The next person was a young lady about 26 years old named Shelley. Phil looked at Shelley and said, 'You are Shelley Mellon. I knew your father from the Old Ranch Casino. I need your help. Will you work for me?'

"Shelley quietly declined and walked out.

"Shelley was the only female in the group. Phil knew every one of their mothers or fathers, and all declined. One portly bearded man of about 25 tossed one of the balls from the game at Phil. 'Fuck you Phil. No one will work for you, and in ten days, we understand if you don't have all the carnival games open you lose them and Mel is back.'

"Soon, I was the last one still sitting on the counter. Phil looked at me and said, 'Whose son are you? I don't have a clue?'

"I replied. 'Mr. Irish, I am Cliff Zavitch, and my Dad works at the Atomic test site, and my mom works at Safeway.'

"Phil took a moment to size me up, then said to me: 'Cliff, I certainly need your help. Will you work for me?'

"Frankly I was awed—the whole experience, working at the Midway Casino for the last seven days, Mel, Phil, the meeting. I was quite overwhelmed.

"'Mr. Irish, I don't know you, and you seem like an OK guy. But it is obvious that there is a lot going on here and I really should not get mixed up with this.'

"I got off my perch and extended my hand and Phil shook it. Then, as I turned to leave, he said, 'Cliff, hold on.' He then reached in his pocket and removed about twenty-five coveted Midway Carnival passes.

'Cliff, I watched you and you are really a hustler, a real Tiger. Here, take these and come back, bring a date.'

"Now, let me tell you, the Midway carnival passes were gold, and maybe this would be the bait I needed to get Beth Downs to go out with me.

"I gladly accepted the tokens and shook his hand again, and exited the tunnel that guarded the "Balls and Dolls Game."

"I walked out of the parking lot looking for my Mom's car when I felt a tug on my left arm. As I turned, I caught a right to the jaw delivered by none other than Eddie Gold. I fell on the hood of a nearby car that conveniently caught my fall. And then Eddie made a big mistake. He grabbed me, and my four years of judo and wrestling kicked in. I grabbed his head and launched it into the side of the car I was formerly resting on."

"It did not take but a minute until Midway security had us both and we were not gently carried to the security holding room."

"It only took a few moments for a newly familiar voice. As he looked at the cut above my right eye, 'Jesus, Tiger, you got to watch those rights.'

"He then looked at Eddie and said, 'Him. I want the son of a bitch eighty-sixed.'

"'Eighty-sixed?' Kurt questioned.

"Yeah, eighty-six was a term we used in the casino business, meaning to get rid of someone and NEVER let them back in. A lot of gaming cheats were eighty-sixed from the casino."

"OK, then what?'

"Phil apologized for what had happened and dug deep in to his pocket and gave me another hand full of Midway passes. Well, after I accepted the golden ducats, I said to myself, what the hell, and asked Phil if he still needed me to work. The guy lit up and he was ecstatic. Then he asked me to have dinner with him, me a 15-year—old high school geek having dinner with Phil Irish, the leaseholder of the Midway Casino."

"I followed Phil out of the security area and onto the floor of the casino, which technically I was forbidden by age to be in. A few moments later, we were being escorted to his special table that sat on the second story of the Ringmaster Restaurant. The second floor was reserved only for VIPs, and I knew that and I was impressed. "

"Soon after we sat, we ordered steaks, and not the cheap cuts. Phil started to ask me hundreds of questions—Who was I? Where did I come from? About my Dad, Mom, and if I had any brothers or sisters. Strange, but I think he knew most of the answers before he asked the questions."

"Soon after salads, he began to explain the situation and my part in the deal."

"You know we have been watching you from the eye in the sky while you were working for Mel. And frankly, I am impressed. The way you act, your pose; I figured you for a lot older. Cliff, do you have any idea how much we make here?"

"I was bewildered. I really had not thought about it, so I just grabbed a number.

"Four hundred million dollars? I responded."

"Cliff you are not even close," and frankly I was impressed.

"Phil went on, 'I lease the Casino and the Midway from the owners, and my lease is up for renewal. One of the owners, "Mr. T," doesn't like me much. Mel is his guy and Mr. T wants him in and me out. "T" can't do it himself. I have made the partners a ton of money, so they are not too excited to get me out. But "T" has a lot of clout.

'The Midway comes up for renewal of a ten-year lease in just twenty-one days and, Cliff, If I can't run the games efficiently, I will lose the lease on the Midway, and then in January I will probably lose the lease on the Casino also. I need your help!'

"I almost dropped my fork. Here I am, having dinner with one of the most powerful men in Las Vegas, Nevada. Me, a 15-year-old and he is asking me for my help. The expression on my face must have been priceless."

"Phil continued to explain. 'We have forty Midway games. "T" gave Mel fifteen, but I got them back on a technicality, but Cliff, only for a few days. If I do not have all the games up and running for the lease renewal, I am done. Now Mel and "T" have the word out that no one who is connected with the strip or their kids are going to work for me. I need at least 15 folks like you. Can you help?"

"I contemplated the whole situation. I was always one to believe that everything happened for a reason, so I agreed. First, my cousin was in town and he had nothing to do for a few weeks. He could work. My mind started to race.

"Before I even had a chance to nod approval he added, 'Cliff, I will pay you supervisor's pay and I will give you a hundred-dollar bonus for each employee you bring who stays more than a month...and you will get a one cent override for every ten dings your crew does.'

"I agreed to help, after one of the most pleasant dinners of my short life. Phil walked me back and had security take me to my car. After the thing that happened to me with Eddy, Phil was going to have security keep an extra eye on me.

Kurt stopped me. "A ding?"

"A ding is an old 'carny' thing. The carnival games did not have any cash controls except a bell with a counter on it. So each time you received a quarter you would pull a lever, which would ring a bell and move the counter one number. Most games cost twenty-five cents so each player was one ring, or 'Ding.'

"Well, it really did not take long; I was able to bring Phil fifteen operators, thirteen guys and two gals, including Tim Floyd. He was ecstatic. Now, he didn't want to show his hand, so my 'crew' met a couple of times in the Midway warehouse off Industrial road. There were games set up just like in the casino. And who trained us? Well, real life carnys, of course. One lady—her name was Merth—got me. I shrugged; this lady looked about 90, smoked, spit, and swore. But she knew her shit; I became a project of hers. Merth was a real life grafter, a con artist, and I became her prize student. Now she was not the only one. Phil had hired a number of these folks to train us, but none of them could even step into a casino at that time, let alone work for one, because of their criminal records. I really don't know how Phil got these folks, but they loved and respected Phil. Since none of our mentors could enter the casino, which is why we had the games mocked up in the warehouse. They taught us every game, how to work it, set it up, break it down, and fix it. They taught us how to act and sound. And Merth, she taught me the game 'Fool the Guesser.' She spend hours teaching me how to guess someone's age, weight, home state, occupation, and sign of the zodiac. It really is an art Kurt"

"For four days Phil kept most of the games dark; then on Friday all fifteen of us walked in, uniformed and polished. Each knew what to do, what to say. Phil had caught all of his critics off guard. They thought he was done. The first day went without a hitch but 'T' wanted a war. The next night, friends of Eddie came in and tried to start fights at the games. Knowing I was a target, Phil had me work the machine gun game, which was fun but also afforded a great deal of protection. Even though the machine gun shot BBs, all I had to do was jump behind the booth and start to fire if things went bad. For the most part, all went well. Three of our crew were intimidated, but the rest of us all hung in there, and the rest, as they say, was history. All the owners, except of course Mr. T, were impressed, Phil had done it. He re-signed the Carnival game contract and then re-leased the Casino about two months early."

"So you made some decent money, " Kurt concluded

"Oh yeah, I was making more in a summer as a teenager than most adults made in a year. Of course I worked off of two time cards, which was supposed to be illegal. But, hey, I made a ton of money."

"Two time cards?" Kurt questioned.

"Yeah, when I was 18, I worked from six at night till two in the morning, working on the carnival games. Then Phil would have me back at nine in the morning to work till five, working CPR."

Kurt tilted his head.

And I explained, "Casino Public Relations. I really learned a lot. I would meet Phil at a crap table at nine o'clock and drink orange juice while Phil drank his coffee. We went over a lot, about the casino business and life in general."

"Did he ever get pissed with you?" Kurt asked.

"In all the years, we never had a fight, disagreement, or argument. But, hell, I knew who the boss was. There was one time that I was scared to death, though. I really didn't know what to think. It was a Tuesday night in October, a relatively slow night, and I was working a game called "Fascination." You rolled a ball under a glass plate and the ball would go through a slot. When the ball went through the slot, a light would light up. The object was to get five lights in a row, like bingo. The first player to get five in a row was the winner."

"What did they win?"

"Valuable Midway Casino Gift tokens. You know, with about a quarter million, you could win a plastic toy or something. Anyway, about 6 o'clock, a mother with two kids in wheelchairs rolled in to the game. Now in those days, things were not wheelchair friendly. I think they had Downs Syndrome. So I actually dismantled two game alleys so the wheelchairs fit.

"Because of their condition, the kids were unable to roll the balls under the glass, so I got on the games and removed the glass so they could 'lob' the balls, which was really against the rules.

We had a lot of folks playing, and after a while, the kids started to win; not every game, but they really started to win. And except for one old bitch, the other players were happy when the disabled children won a game. I didn't notice, but some Jewish lady, with the gold Star of David around her neck, left in disgust. The next thing I see is her on the house phone, with the children sitting on the ground at her feet. Well, apparently she had a lot of clout, she knew Mr. T."

"Remember, he hated me, and sure enough, 'T' was there consoling the yenta from New Jersey. No doubt she had some serious juice. And I knew it. 'T' made his way over to me.

"Hey, you clown. What the fuck is a matter wit ya, fixing these fucking games? Are you fucking stupid?"

"I just stood there and took it. The guy was nuts—fuck this, fuck that, fucking stupid—when suddenly a huge black gentleman appeared from behind me, then stood in front of me."

"Sir, I don't know who you are but my kids are here and if you speak another expletive, I frankly will shove it up your ass."

"Now T was a small guy, and his appearance was almost comical. He could have played the role of the ringmaster, short and stubby!, the black man towered over him by at least two feet. T turned around and screamed at the top of his voice, S E C U R I T Y, and with that, I felt I was in a middle of a rugby scrum. One exec to show up was Mark Karl, a longtime friend and ally of Phil. Mr. Karl spoke to the chief of security and then, in a flash, Mr. T was uplifted and removed from the scrum and Mr. Karl substituted himself in the middle of the brouhaha. Mr. Karl began to cool things down when the large Jewish yenta started to scream, 'cheat, cheat,' and pointed to me.

"From nowhere, Phil appeared and took her accusing hand by the wrist, and pulled her away. I have no idea what she said. I saw Phil nod a few times and then walk over to me. He was not happy."

"Cliff, you cheat?"

"After all this commotion, everyone had forgotten the kids. They were all talking and bonding. Phil surveyed the situation and looked at me."

"Phil looked puzzled. 'What gives?' he said.

"The mother whose handicapped children had been playing, stepped in between Phil and me. 'Sir, excuse me, but it was my fault. I will be happy to give back all the tokens the children had won and we will leave. They were having just so much fun.'

"I interjected, 'No, keep them,' and Phil shot me a look that almost scared me—me, a 18-year-old-kid answering for Mr. Irish.

"I just shrugged and motioned to the children in the wheelchairs and said, 'Mr. Irish, I took off the glass plates. Phil surveyed the whole situation and shook his head, then looked at the fat yenta who had followed him. He reached in his pocket and pulled out about fifty game passes, and reached in his other pocket and gave her about two hundred prize tokens. Then he said, 'Here, your kids would have never won this many tokens.' She began to say something and he just raised one finger and said, 'Ma'am, go away. Do not come back to this game.'"

"She said one more truncated word and he pointed and said, 'I think the odds were even at this game. Go away.' She turned and left. Phil then turned to me and said, 'My office, end of shift.'

"After the mass of people left, things got back to well, sort of normal. Folks all had a good time and no one else complained about the kids getting a little help. The mother was extremely grateful and a few folks who left stuffed a few bucks in my shirt pocket.

"I dreaded 1:30 A.M., but that time came and I closed the game and headed to Phil's office. Navigating through three levels of security, I knocked on Phil's door. What a great office! High above the casino, there was, although not visible to the customers outside, a huge plate glass window with televisions all over.

"Phil looked up at me and motioned for me to sit. I did, and nothing was said for what seemed like hours. Then Phil looked up and said 'T's an asshole. Don't mind him. Are you OK?'

"I nodded."

"'Cliff, you have a job with me for life, if you want it. Now go home.' "And that was it."

"What about the chip?" Kurt asked.

"Not much to tell. I found a twenty-five-dollar chip on the floor, thought it could be another operator's, so I gave it to Phil. He was impressed."

"Damn, you were a regular saint."

"Well, hardly a saint. Hell I use to go to the Ranches at least twice a month back in those days. I don't think a saint would do much of that. Besides, I had been told the story of *Old Charlie*"

"Old Charlie?" Kurt repeated

I smiled "Yea, after you are hired, you are under a microscope for about 60 days, then one of the Casino Dealers will tell you about 'Old Charlie'. It seems that in the Fifties when Vegas was just getting started a dealer by the name of Charlie started to cheat. Back in those days the easiest way to cheat was to just have a friend play blackjack at your table and pay them even if they lost"

I continued, "Well the management caught Charlie and took him up to "The Valley of Fire" about 75 miles north, a beautiful place full of shell rock mountains. Charlie was left on top of one of those mountains with no shoes, socks and his hands broken. After 3 days of 125 degree August heat, management went out to retrieve Charlie."

"He wasn't dead?" Kurt questioned.

"Nope, his tongue had split, his hands deformed and his feet were infected but he was still alive. When the managers brought him back to the bosses' office he fell to his knees, confessed to everything and begged for forgiveness."

"Then did they kill him?"

"Oh no, as a matter of fact the boss gave him a job for life at about $500 per week which was great money in those days."

"Gave him a job?" Kurt was now really confused.

"He was hired to be the janitor in the dealers dressing room. Anytime he heard about someone conspiring to rip off the casino he would, shall I say dissuade them. Oh and by the way, our day shift janitor's name was Charlie and had a speech impediment and deformed hands. So Kurt, yeah I gave him the chip."

"So why did you leave?"

"Dad died, and mom wanted to go back home and she was not ever well after Dad passed."

"Phil ever call you?"

"Yeah, once to work, and the other time, he called to follow up with a favor he did for me."

"A favor?"

"Yeah, pretty soon after we moved back to Mom's hometown, which I had only visited once, I was working in the restaurant business in Georgia, a chain called Fat Kid's Burgers. Well, I was one of their managers and these bastards put me in the hotbed of unions.

"There was a mother of three of the workers who was a union organizer. Well, she had two of the other managers over the barrel because they had been trapped into making advances to her underage daughters.

Me, they tried, but I think it was the old Las Vegas intuition that kicked in here. Remember, the Midway was owned, by the unions and Mr. Irish was big-time in it, so I really knew what was going on.

"I really didn't much like it—the company management style. It was theory X. I hated how they treated the employees, but it was my job to keep things cool. There was a huge union push, and union pledge cards were everywhere. Again, I would have not known what to do if it had not been for my experience in Vegas.

"I was closing the restaurant about two in the morning. I guess I was part of the problem since I was still driving my Cadillac I bought while working in Vegas. I noticed one of my tires was flat; then I noticed they were all flat, I made the mistake of not realizing what was going on, and bent over to examine the damage. I got hit with a board or something. I hit the driveway with a thud. Dazed? Oh yeah. I felt two guys picking me up. Mistake number two. I thought they were there to help me; one held me, and the other just started pounding my stomach like a prizefighter getting his prey dazed and against the ropes. I fell and they started to kick me. I rolled up in the fetal position. To this day, I have broken right ribs. I knew I was losing it and made a last effort to stand straight up, trying to use my old Greco-Roman wrestling moves. But it was just too late. The last thing I remember I was lying on my back on the hood of my disabled vehicle.

"At about five in the morning, Steve, the morning manager, found me still unconscious on the hood of my car. Steve was one of the offenders who had slept with one of the daughters of the union organizers, and guessed what had happened.

"Now back in those days, when someone was attempting to unionize your store, the attorneys warned you not to look at union pledge cards. Well, while I was out, they had stuffed about 50 in my pockets, pants and shirt, so they knew that if ever I was asked if I had seen the cards, I would have to say yes.

"Naturally Steve's concern was for himself, so he would not call the police or the medics, and was going to have one of the cooks give me a lift home. I declined and had him call one of my best friends from college, who, by some slim coincidence, was managing a competing restaurant in the same piss-ant town.

"Now, JJ and I went to college together, and although JJ was ten years older because he had served in the military, we were in the same Hotel—Restaurant classes. JJ stood about 5-foot-6 but I knew folks should never underestimate him. He took charge and, if he got mad, could take down a man three times his size.

"JJ was there in minutes after I had asked Steve to call him."

"Shit, Cliff, what the hell happened to you?"

"I quickly explained the situation and he was very concerned and drove me to the hospital. It was about six in the morning now, and I was in the waiting room of the ER, and JJ was there at my side. Since JJ had attended UNLV in Las Vegas with me, he knew my connections with Phil."

"'Cliff, what next? Shit, you have just had the crap knocked out of you, and we at Benny's Restaurants know what is going on over at Fat Kids. Cliff, these guys are badasses. They may kill you. You need to call Phil,' JJ said in a loud whisper.

"Phil Irish?"

"Yeah, Cliff. Phil."

"How can he help?" I responded. JJ just stared at me. He knew exactly how much power Phil wielded. But In Georgia?

"JJ pointed to the pay phone.

"JJ, I need some change. It is $1.85 for the first three minutes."

"I know! I will get the change." "As JJ went down the hall, I managed to get up and slowly walk to the phone. My sides were hurting and I think my right rib or ribs were broken.

"JJ soon returned with the change, and I knew the number by heart, 702 555 1717.

"The operator interceded, 'Please deposit $1.85 for the first three minutes,' which I did.

"Midway Casino," the harsh female smoker's voice said.

"I knew it was about 3:00 A.M. in Vegas and Phil would be on the floor. "Mr. Phil Irish, please."

"And I waited, holding another dollar in change in case I ran out of time before he answered the phone.

"Then the familiar voice, very brusque at first. 'PHIL IRISH.'

"Mr. Irish. Cliff, Zavitch.,

"He cut me off and said, 'Hello, Tiger, you sound upset.'

"I think I need your help. I had the shit beat out of me tonight by some union folks.

"At that point, the operator interrupted and asked for another dollar.

"Cliff, give me the number you are at and I will call you right back." I complied and hung up.

"The nurse at that point came to me and told me it was my turn to go into the ER. I declined and asked if another could go in my stead. She nodded in the affirmative and I leaned against the wall waiting for the phone to ring. I figured he would go to his office, which took maybe five minutes. And sure enough, in five minutes, the pay phone rang, startling everyone in the room except me.

"OK, Tiger, from the top."

"I started from the top and told him when I was transferred to the store, and that the managers were afraid because they were compromised.

"Phil interjected, 'See, Cliff, I told you, if you are ever betrayed, it will be the woman. But not you.'

"Right, I thought, instead of some loving, I was here in the hospital with face lacerations and most likely a few broken ribs. I did manage a smile 'cause he would always say that.

"He wanted to know everything, who the union organizer was, which union, where exactly was Gainesville, Georgia? And then he instructed me NOT TO GO TO WORK for at least a day.

"Should be no problem," I told him.

"JJ took me back to my apartment. Yep, there were a few broken ribs and I had gotten some painkiller. JJ sent me to bed, and said he would call management and tell them I would not be in. I don't know what they gave me but I slept great until about five in the afternoon when the phone broke my sleep. It was Steve, the store day manager.

"Hey buddy, how do you feel?"

"I have felt better, Steve. My ribs are really sore." Actually they were much better now, but I knew he was going to ask me to come in.

"I got a call from the hospital. What is this shit about a workers' comp claim? Hell, we know this had nothing to do with workers' comp."

"What," I said in a puzzled voice?

"Yeah, you had a fight. The company can't help that. Nevertheless, I told them to put it on your personal health insurance."

"What a cheap fucking company, I thought to myself.

"Steve went on to command, 'Come on in and we will talk about it.'

"No, Steve. I am not coming in. I am heavily medicated, and still in pain."

"God damn it, boy, get your ass in here now!"

"Sorry, Steve. I have a note from the doctor. Fuck you, and I hung up.

"I took some more meds and was out again. Later while putzing around the house, I felt like it was time to check things out at the store. I got there just in time for the show. Mars Gutierrez, the labor organizer, was there, and pulling her kids out of the store. 'Making them quit, she yelled at the top of her lungs.

"'Fuck this place, my kids will not be working here any more, Fuck you, fuck this, fuck that.' Then I caught her eye. She ran over to me. The woman was as round as she was tall, maybe about five feet. She got right up to me and looked up, and said, 'I don't know who you know, but tell your friends I am out of here. Tell them to leave me alone. I want no trouble, you hear?'

"With that, the parade was over as she marched her children out the door,with her gone,and the kids gone, Fat Kids had no more union problem. Everyone heard what she said to me and they were stunned.

"JJ called later that day to tell me that two thugs who met the description I gave were beaten badly last night.

Kurt seemed engrossed in the story.

"I was somewhat of a hero and kept managing the restaurants until one night there was a fight between a gay guy and a redneck. I was really stupid, got right between them just as the redneck pulled a gun. The gun was right at my left side just below my gut when I heard the click. Fortunately there were two cops eating pie who interceded. The cops pounded the redneck's head against the pie case until he dropped the gun."

"When things cooled down a bit, the officers gave me notice to appear at 7:00 A.M. as a witness to tell what happened."

"Great, just what I want, to be in court instead of sleeping. Anyway I went and testified, and on the way out, I saw my regular customers, the officers who stopped the fight. I looked at them and said, 'Good thing the gun wasn't loaded.' They both smiled at me and one gave me their report to read. The gun was fully loaded it mis-fired. I was done with the restaurant business.

Kurt finished, "You then came down to Sarasota after your mother died and mentored under the Great Christopher, the Greatest Salesman in the World."

"That he was."

With that, Kurt and I went out to some local haunts to eat and drink a while. Our favorite place was Clancy's, a very upscale lounge and eatery which some would call a meat market. Kurt was on the prowl, as usual. Me, I just wanted a Guinness and some fish and chips.

The way Clancy's was laid out, those who were eating were perched higher above the bar to encourage food sales. It worked, since those eating had a great view of those coming in the bar.

Both of us were starting to relax and unwind, I was sipping and enjoying my Guinness and Kurt was downing his third rum and Coke. It was then that he brought up my message again. "Sounds like you are going to be getting a job in Vegas. That is great, so what was so confusing about the message?"

I grabbed my Guinness and sat back in my chair.

"Well, here is the strange part. Phil referred to Tim as 'our good friend.'

"So? Is it some kind of Mafia thing," he said, almost laughing.

I pinched my eyes with my thumb and middle finger. The bad thing about Clancy's was the smoke.

" A bit more than that. When I knew Phil, he hired Tim only at the beginning. Tim quit after about a year and started working for the government. The last time I heard from him was he was in Quantico. I don't know what he was doing there, no idea. But here is the mystery, Kurt. I don't know of any time that Phil and Tim had any interaction after that. Phil was in his world in Vegas and Tim, he was working for the CIA or somebody like that. Now Tim is OUR friend?"

This actually seemed to sink in to Kurt, but only for a moment. He caught the eye of a lovely young thing and he was off. I picked up the tab and walked to my Volvo, alone as usual. I looped around the Sarasota Square Mall on to Beneva Road and north to home.

TAMPA, FLORIDA
Monday, Noon. EST, April 20, 1987

Silas was relaxing watching Oprah just after the noon news when the knock came. Silas watched the bottom of the door as the plain brown envelop was slowly passed through. Silas waited, emptied his drink, and slowly walked to the door to retrieve the envelop.

Silas being a smoker was not bothered by getting assignments in a smoking room. All assignments were given in "smoking" rooms, since the contents of the envelop must be burned and the ashes flushed down the toilet. He sat the envelop on the desk and opened it. The stamp at the top agitated him. RUSH! Silas sort of chuckled; a rubber stamp for ordering someone's death, just as you would a gift from a department store.

Silas hated RUSH assignments. He became even more upset at the brevity of the packet. Usually he has pages to read about the target's background, history, work, habits, but this was the shortest dossier he had ever encountered.

Name: Clifford A. Zavitch
Occupation: Insurance Sales
Address: 20301 Ingram Ave, Sarasota, Florida
DOB: 9/6/51
Siblings: None
Parents: None

Comments: Zavitch is scheduled to fly from Tampa to Las Vegas Tuesday Morning at 11:45 A.M.—Delta Flight 733. Subject cannot make this flight.

There were two pictures of the subject, along with another pager number to call to accept the contract, and another to call if there were any complications. This number was standard in such contract, but Silas had never needed to use such a number.

Silas did not like the contract—too much of a rush, no information on the subject, but the contract price of $100,000 was very tempting. Usually a job like this—killing a nobody—paid his minimum of $25,000. This guy must have pissed someone off, but Silas could not care less. It was a job and this insurance sales guy was as good as dead. He placed the call to the pager to "seal the contract."

After a few moments of study, all was burned in the bathroom sink and the ashes flushed.

Silas looked at his watch and picked up the phone book to look for an "escort" to visit his room. From his experience, Tampa had the best looking "escorts." They were prompt and they had very bad memories.

Unbeknownst to Cliff, someone was watching every move he made since early this afternoon—watched him from the bar at Clancy's and followed him to his home on a sleepy street in Sarasota.

It was about 9:30 when I left Clancy's. Sure enough, Kurt had picked up a couple of young ladies and Kurt is not one to share.

I almost forgot the events of the day, as extraordinary as they were, and I was dog-tired when I turned off Weber onto Sweetland, which merged into Ingram and then turned into my driveway. After I parked my brown Volvo, I grabbed my briefcase from the back seat and proceeded to the front door.

When I entered, I heard the TV on—and froze. The only person who has a key to my house was Kurt, and he was preoccupied. Perhaps I had left the TV on. Who would break in and watch TV? I was suddenly very tense as I walked slowly through the living room, past the kitchen and into the converted Florida room, where I had the TV.

Relaxing on the Lazy Boy was a well-known figure who I had not seen for several years—Tim Floyd—and lying comfortable on my couch was a person of unknown identity.

I instantly relaxed. "Jesus, you guys seem comfy."

Tim laughed. "Oh, yeah, thanks for the beer and chips."

"No problem," I replied.

Both Tim and the unknown intruder stood.

I almost had to laugh. Tim was very tall, slim and trim. It was apparent that he was still running several miles a day and hitting the weights. His associate, on the other hand, looked almost like me, short and pudgy. In high school, when Tim and I used to walk the halls together, some joked about us being Oliver and Hardy, and it looks like Tim and his new sidekick still filled that bill.

I shook hands with Tim and gave him a semi bear hug.

"Cliff, this is 'Agent Parker'—Andrew Parker. He is on loan from the Tampa FBI office for this assignment," indicating that Tim usually worked alone, which is what I would expect of Tim.

So I was right Tim was with the FBI. I shook Andrew's hand and asked if anyone wanted anything, as I really had to go to the bathroom.

"Grab your tooth brush while you are there"—indicating I was taking a trip, now!

"Are you serious?"

"Oh, yeah," Tim said emphatically.

I stopped, turned and looked at Tim. "Jesus, you sound so serious."

"Maybe because I am, Cliff."

At this point things got dead serious, and for a moment I decided to forgo my trip to the bathroom and sat down at my dining room table.

"OK, let's talk."

Tim started. "Did you talk to Phil?"

"No, I only got a message on my machine, said he wanted me to come out today and you were going to provide transportation. That is it. Thought I won a vacation," I said with a chuckle.

"Not hardly Cliff. There is big trouble and Phil needs you out there now."

"Needs me?" I said scrunching my face with sarcasm. I went on, "Why would he need ME?"

"Cliff, it is complicated. All will be told to you as we go. Phil needs to explain most of it to you."

"When do we leave?"

"NOW," Tim replied emphatically, then when on, "Technically, here are your tickets. You are to fly out at 11:00 A.M. tomorrow morning. But, Cliff, we leave now."

"Like right now?"

"Go take a shit, grab your toothbrush if you want, and we are out of here."

"Clothes?"

"As soon as we land, we will have a wardrobe for you."

"Just like that?"

"Pretty much..."

"Phil is supposed to call me at midnight."

"We will call him en route. Cliff, get what you want. We have to go now!"

I started to look around the room; Agent Parker had not said a word. Then I noticed that the back door of the house from the converted Florida room lock was broken.

Agent Parker finally spoke. "Cheap lock. I'll fix that tonight when you guys leave."

I was really confused, "You're not going with us?"

"No, I'm you right now—and will be."

I responded almost angrily. "Tim, why the cloak and dagger shit?"

"We think someone is trying to kill you," Tim interjected matter-of-factly.

"Cliff, we think you are being followed and that there may be an attempt on your life, because of the stuff in Las Vegas."

"I haven't been in Vegas since the grand opening of the Kastle Kasino almost five years ago?"

"Like I said, Cliff, this is rather complicated."

"OK, this morning I am more or less suspended from my job. I get a phone message from one of my best friends ever in the world asking me to come to Vegas, escorted by another one of my best and longest friends in the world, and all of a sudden someone wants to kill me."

Tim cut in. "Cliff, and the key word in all this is the word friend, OK. "We have no reason to hurt you. Things just happened; then we found you are in danger. Andy resembles you enough to make them think he is you, at least till we get to Vegas."

Andy surprisingly spoke again. "I need the keys to your car, a list of who may be contacting you, and what time you go to work."

"You guys don't know? I got suspended today and that wasn't you guys?"

Andy shook his head. "We know of the problems down there, but we had nothing to do with that."

"A lucky coincidence," Tim said enthusiastically.

"Lucky?" I replied. "Things are moving just too fast here."

"Cliff, we really have to go," said Tim.

"OK, I'm ready. I really don't have anything here. But where is the tie-in? How are you, Tim, Mr. FBI, and Phil Irish, a great guy, but one of so many questionable ties and connections."

"That is just one piece to the puzzle, Steve Lambert."

"Captain Steve?"

"Yep, Captain Steve! We got to go. Andy, turn out all the lights while we go out the back... Wait."

Tim took a second to scan my wearing apparel.

"You better change," Tim said. "We are going to do some hiking. Go hurry."

I hurried to my room and donned a pair of jeans, shirt, jacket and rough-out boots, and reported back to Tim and Andrew in the back room. Tim looked at Andrew. He nodded his head and went to the bedroom and turned off the lights I had left on.

When Andrew got back, he requested the keys. "OK, car and house keys, list of friends who may call."

"Kurt, maybe."

"That's it? Any girlfriends?"

"I doubt it."

Tim, impatiently, said, "Let's go. Andy, kill all the lights."

I shook Andy's hand and followed Tim through the back portal of my house as Andy closed it behind us. It was a perfect night for a covert activity—less than a quarter moon and pitch black. Ingram Avenue runs parallel to the old railroad tracks, not abandoned but lately only used to move the circus train from Sarasota to Venice. Rarely was there any other type of movement on that track. We moved through my backyard and had to go over some really high brush to get to the railroad tracks that were well maintained. We headed north, walking along the tracks. I followed Tim, as he seemed to know exactly where he was going. Obviously I had a million questions, but we did not talk.

After about a mile, the tracks intersected Bahia Vista, a pretty busy street. When traffic cleared, we crossed the street and followed the track to the back of a new strip center with a trendy 1950s nightclub and diner. Tim entered through the back door, which it appeared had been preset to open for us. I followed him past the rest rooms, past the diner and into the nightclub area, to a table set for three. Waiting for us was an absolutely knockout blonde. We sat down in front of beers that looked like they were just poured. We just sat—no introductions, nothing.

The blonde then said, "Right on time, guys. Just got you fresh drafts."

Just as I was about to take a sip, Tim said, "No time. We got to go."

Why did I know he was going to say that? Tim looked at the check, pulled about $30 from a money clip, and stood to leave as I followed. The blonde, however, to my surprise and delight, grabbed my arm, kissed me on the cheek, and escorted me from the lounge. Tim took the lead and I followed, enjoying the company, to a waiting car. It was a typical rental car most Florida tourists use to transverse the state. Tim sat in the driver's seat, and my voluptuous sidekick and I were in the back.

For a moment, nothing was said. Then Tim broke the silence. "Cliff, meet Agent Toni Cardona."

"Truly my pleasure, Toni," I said as I tried to reattach myself to her arm. She gently shook her arm free and smiled

"So you work with Tim?"

"No, you met my partner, Andy Parker. We work together out of the Tampa office, but I have known Tim for several years. We all work, directly or indirectly, for the person you know as Steve Lambert."

I had known that Tim has worked alone I was just tiring to piece together the relationships. Tim made a right, then another right on Beneva, then a right on Fruitville Road heading to I-75.

"OK, now I am going to get what is going on here?"

Tim responded, "Some."

Toni continued. "Way back when the Midway Casino opened, Steve Lambert was placed in it by the Justice department in deep cover, to watch over and find out how the Kansas City and Chicago mobs were skimming."

Tim took over. "Steve was perfect—educated, well groomed."

I interjected, "and looked like Robert Redford."

"Still does," Toni added.

"So he was like that Donnie Brasco guy?"

Toni: "Not hardly. Brasco was bad news. Steve was working with accountants and financial folks and bankers—dangerous, yes, but nothing like Brasco."

Tim continued, "A captain in the Air Force, or I should say former captain, Steve had been working for the Justice Department for a year when he got the assignment."

"So he wasn't going to Nellis every afternoon?" I added.

"No, he was only going to be debriefed every day." Tim now seemed a little aggravated by my intrusions. "Each day they would go over conversation, make charts of who was who, followed the money and became statistical experts on gaming and how the money should flow in the casino. Steve recruited me right out of school, although I only worked for the Midway a short time. Steve rehired me and I was working both sides." A short pause..."Remember Danny Smith?"

"Sure," I replied, "not the sharpest crayon..."

I was cut off by Toni's chuckle.

Tim: "Well, Steve recruited him and then I recruited Beth." Tim stopped

"My Beth," I questioned.

"Well, I would not say "YOUR" Beth, but Beth Downs, now Beth Green who you dated a few times. Yeah, her."

"Married?" I asked

"Not right now" Tim replied

Embarrassed, I asked, "Oh God, will I have to face her?"

"Oh yeah she is semi on the team. She will be at the Midway when we get there. She really works downtown, but I got her an OK to meet us."

"Gee, thanks, Tim"

Toni: "Sounds like a story I want to hear."

"No," I shouted.

Tim, now laughing, said, "Toni, Beth loved this guy, would do anything for him. One night, after about a week, she gets him in bed naked, mounts him—and he refused her."

"Oh, shit, she told you."

"Oh, yeah, me and many others."

Toni laughed, "Yeah, that is enough to kill a relationship"

"She must still hate me," I said.

"No" Tim replied. She might think you are queer, but I don't think she hates you.

"I have prayed to have that moment back. I would do anything "

No one said anything. Me, I was totally embarrassed as we headed north and took the 275 split to St. Petersburg, then over the Howard Franklin Bridge. I finally broke the silence:

"OK, wait a minute, Steve recruits you, and a few other of my best friends, but I don't get recruited?"

Tim quickly answered, "We thought you were already recruited, but not by us. You, my boy, were one of the few persons to get close to Phil Irish. I don't know if you knew this, but four years before we met him, his wife and son were killed on the widow-maker highway coming from

Carson City to Vegas. Cliff, you were the same age, same build. Hell, we thought he was going to adopt you. How many times were you in the counting room?

"A few."

"Sixteen times," Tim corrected.

"OK, I didn't know anyone was counting."

Tim questioned, "Did you know any of us besides Steve to go in the counting room?"

"I never gave it much thought," I replied.

"Ever watch them weigh the coins?"

"Yeah."

"And what did you observe? Cliff, the weight of the coins, what did you observe? Cliff, I really want to know!"

"Shit." I gulped. I knew what Tim was getting at and all was coming clear. " Tim, shit, do I need a lawyer? Are we off the record."

"Absolutely, we are. Right, Toni?"

"You bet we are. I am lost—what did you see, Cliff?"

My stomach was starting to turn now and things were starting to fall into place. So I began to tell the story. "The weights were off, for the quarters only. Not the nickels, dimes, half-dollars or dollars, and they were always off 96 ounces per hundred pounds."

Tim, now all excited, pounded the steering wheel. "You knew, you fucking knew, all these years, you bastard, you fucking knew about one of the biggest skimming scams in the fucking world and said nothing. Phil trusted you and you said fucking nothing. That is why you were not recruited—we thought you were working inside and you were part of the game. Shit, actually you were. You know you almost broke Phil's heart when you moved. Then when you turned down their job offer, we got worried because Steve knew you knew, and we thought they were going to whack you just like they did the brothers. From what we knew, the only reason you are not fertilizing some farm is because Phil Irish loved you like the son he lost.... I can't believe it. You did know. Steve said you did. I really was not sure."

At this time, we arrived at the far east side of the Tampa International Airport. It was the

Rathon private airport and we had just pulled right up to a white jet with the logo of the Midway Casino on its tail. The three of us go on board and got buckled in. I sat facing the cockpit, and Toni was strapped in facing me. Now I almost felt like their prisoner. Tim went forward

This was my first time in a private jet. It almost has a new car smell, but only for a jet. Quite comfy, and the seats were definitely first class. My seat actually fit in the seat.

Once in, Toni leaned over and said, "OK guys, you are going to have to explain the weight of the quarters."

I glanced at my watch. It was a few minutes before midnight and I was beat. I was not really a party animal. I was usually gone after the eleven o'clock news. At midnight, I was supposed to talk to Phil. Tim was just one step ahead of me. He was coming down the aisle with a phone. He sat next to Toni, reached across from them, and plugged it in.

Tim held the phone to his ear and waited.

Nothing was said. Only the roar of the engines as they were getting ready was in the background.

Then, "Phil. Hey, it's Tim"...pause, "We got him. He is OK"....pause, "OK."

At that, Tim handed me the phone. I pointed and worded, "Phil?" Tim shook his head in the affirmative.

"Hey, Phil, it has been quite a day."

"Look, Tiger, I'm sorry for all this. It is not exactly how I would have done things, but circumstances have dictated this course of action. Things really have gotten out of hand here, but you should be safe now. We have an army of lawyers working on things right now and, unfortunately, they know everything. I will see you in a few hours. Bye, Tiger."

The phone went dead and I handed it back to Tim. Tim got up to return the phone to the front, leaving me with Toni, which was not a terrible thing. She caught me staring. Toni was not a beauty queen but she was very cute. I usually like women with dark hair, but I was willing to make an exception. Maybe it was the combination of the blonde hair and the dark penetrating eyes. With all that was going on, I felt safe with her, not in a romantic sense, but I think part of her job now was to protect me, and I felt confident she could.

I did a full body stretch and gave a yawn.

Toni broke the ice that was forming between us. I actually had some trepidations about talking any more. I could be in legal peril. Tim used to be my best friend but, hey, it is his job.

"Understand you are a pretty smart guy."

" Na. No, not me. If I were smart I would not be here right now, not knowing what was going to happen to me next. I would be some corporate attorney in bed right now, sleeping and dreaming of my next vacation."

Toni looking directly in my eyes. "From what I hear, you just don't know how to pull the trigger to actually initiate."

At first I had no idea what she was talking about. Then I realized she, too, probably had a dossier on me. And she was right—I had all this technical knowledge in many things but I do not have the confidence to actually put things in action. Then she could have been talking about Tim's story about Beth and me, or maybe both. Was she "coming on" to me? No, ridiculous. She is trying to be nice so I will blabber some more—more shit. What more can I tell her?

I made a conscious decision not to say any more. I would try to sleep when Tim got back in his seat. I became really quite and just stared north out from the window of this luxury jet toward the "Old Sombrero," the home of the Tampa Bay Bucs. Then I glanced at my watch. Where did Monday go; it was 1:45 A.M.

Finally, the plane roared down the runway heading west.

On Ingram Avenue, there was more than one non-Mennonite guest in the neighborhood—Andy Parker, now trying to take the identity of Cliff Zavitch, and just a block away, in a nondescript vehicle that shouted "rental," Silas was stalking the home.

The neighborhood was so quiet it bothered him—not a light, not a movement in this lonely, quiet area of one of the largest cities in Florida. Silas needed to make his move to complete this hastily-contrived contract. Silas did indeed think it strange to kill such a nobody, but his agent made the contract with the clients, and the money was good, so soon Cliff Zavitch would be dead. And Silas did not even know why, not that he really cared.

Silas knew Cliff had a morning flight to Vegas. Maybe he should just go in and kill him in his sleep; that seemed to be the most efficient way to do it. But, again, this contract was put together too fast. No time to research. Hell, the house could have security, a dog; he could even have a gun. There had just not been enough time to study. Silas hated sloppy kills.

Besides, Silas has a reputation. His specialty was accidents. The subject would be D E A D, but most everything would point to an accident. If Silas would have had more time, he could have gotten into the house and rigged an accident—maybe a simple fall in the bathtub. Silas loved those. His agent loved it, and so did his clients. The subjects would just die. He was not one of these guys who killed to send a message to others; he just killed in the most efficient and least assuming way. The more he could kill without suspicion, the more he liked it. With about seventy kills, he took delight in knowing more than fifty were not questioned, just ruled as accidents.

Silas pulled out a Nat Sherman Cigarettello, non-filter, of course, and lit up. After enjoying his smoke, he had made his decision. Silas would follow the target in the morning, and when the time looked good, just pull up alongside and shoot him in the head. It would just look like a case of road rage or robbery.

Silas crept up the driveway unnoticed. Now all he needed was a few hours sleep. He would be back at his post at about seven o'clock.

At the Midway Casino in Las Vegas, the swing shift, three to eleven, was just coming to an end, and the graveyard folks were already in place for a Monday night—Tuesday morning run. It was traditionally a bit slow, and usually the execs took Monday off. Not Phil Irish. It was imperative that he was consistent in his actions, not to show his hand. Too much was riding on this, not only for him but for his longtime partners and the life of a dear friend who just got pulled into all of this.

Irish was a workaholic—undisputed! So it was natural for him to be working even when the other execs would take off. Of course there was a reason. In a casino, there are three counts, one after each shift. And because of some sensitive accounting practices, either he or his long time friend Mark Karl would supervise the count. Do the math: if there are 24 hours in a day, three counts, and only two to supervise, then days off were impossible. And the two had kept this schedule for years. Vacations were nonexistent and no one was ever sick. There was a prevailing joke that the reason the Midway built a hotel was to accommodate sleeping facilities for Phil and Mark.

Now this would soon come to an end and Phil was glad. Finally, time to relax and sleep and not worry.

...well, not worry just having other things to worry about. Things seemed to be all set. Phil and Mark had yet another partner, one who did not live in Las Vegas but who really had set the deal up several years back. He was Tommy O'Sullivan, or just Tommy O. In just a few days Phil, Mark, and Tommy will be all together and that in itself was a rare occasion.

Phil glanced at his watch: 11:30. The Graveyard folks were all in place; no real problems, so it was almost time for his next meeting. However one of his subordinates, Steve Lambert, in reality was running everything now, including the next meeting.

Phil walked into his elaborate office, full of TV monitors and every electronic gadget known to man. For casino security, no expenses were spared. If it was new and there was a chance it could help, it was purchased—hardware systems, software, face recognition system—three actually. The Midway was indeed SECURE.

Within the office, there was another office, one that had been recently installed. This is where Steve Lambert had been meeting with Mark Karl, and Phil to plan the events of this coming week. Steve was already in the bubble, as it was nicknamed.

Phil closed the door of the bubble and, as they sat down, they started the security procedure, to make sure nothing said would be leaked. Both played with a few buttons on the panels in front of them, and then Steve spoke.

"I think we are OK; no leaks" (no evidence of someone listening or a device planted.)

"OK, just talked to 'Z' (not a code word; everyone in Las Vegas who knew Cliff called him "Z"). He is on the plane and should be here in a few hours."

Steve stared at Phil for a moment and then gave a wry smile. "No, he should be here about"... looking at his watch as he had the timetable on his wrist..."Noon or one, our time."

"I thought I would save the taxpayers some money. I mean why should the 'People of the United States' pay for a plane ticket when I have a perfectly fine jet aircraft available?"

Steve thought to himself, he did have a point, but he was in charge here. "Phil, I understand, but I am running this show and I would fucking appreciate it that you at least consult with me before you start changing the fucking game plan."

Phil did not bat an eyelash; it was almost as if he expected the reaction. "O-Fucking-K. Shit, we have put this guy in the box. He is one of my few remaining friends in the fucking world and I wanted him to be comfortable, so I sent my fucking plane, OK."

"Well, first, Phil, it is NOT your fucking plane. As a matter of fact, technically all the assets of this casino belong to the 'People of the United States.'

"Not quite yet," said Phil, pounding the table.

"What? Jesus Christ, Phil, that is the agreement."

Phil put his hands up, palms out, as to surrender. "OK, that is the deal. I'm fucking sorry, alright."

Steve shook his head. "I should have Tim Floyd's ass, anyway."

"No, no, stay off his ass. Tim is a good guy. Besides, I told Tim you approved it and he thought it was a good idea."

"Phil, how long do you need with him?"

"I would like a week."

"That will not happen, Phil."

"Then, shit, Steve, you tell me!"

"Time is not on our side here, Phil. I want to have this all done and everyone safe not later than Friday afternoon, so you have about seventy-two hours with him."

"Seventy-two hours to teach him what I have learned in thirty-five years?"

"Cut the crap, Phil. You were grooming this guy for five years, and if it was not for his Dad dying and mother getting sick, hell, he would be going away, too."

"I don't know. That is why I want him. I think he is one of the few incorruptibles."

"We have watched him. He does seem pretty straight, and when he worked for us, his nickname was arrow. It doesn't seem he changed." Steve paused. "What do you have in store for him?"

"First, Tim says he left with only his toothbrush, so he will need some clothes. We need to get him looking the part. After we get him fitted, we bring him here to the bubble and tell him everything."

"Phil what if he doesn't buy it? What if he says no?"

Phil sat back in the custom-made executive chairs that furnished the bubble, " He wouldn't refuse; he can't. We need to tell him everything. After all, he is in danger. I will convince him, or try to, without scaring the hell out of him. He just does the deal or he could be dead."

Steve, looking extremely concerned, flipped through some files in his portfolio. After a moment, he pulled out a confidential fax and slid it across the bubble's $20,000 conference table. Phil, half concerned and half curious, reviewed the document without picking it up.

"I'm not surprised, Steve. We have a leak somewhere. How else did they know to put a hit on 'Z'?"

Steve cradled his head. "I know, Phil, and the leak is close. The fax was from surveillance just this morning, and from what I read, this contract was put together quickly."

"Will he be safe?"

"Should be as long as he stays close to the Midway. Before we got this fax, I had Cliff on a regular flight tomorrow, but this does complicate things even more. What time did they leave Tampa?"

"About one-thirty. I expect he will arrive about two, our time."

On the plane Tim and Toni sat facing me, and Toni wanted more information about the quarters.

Toni, in a really sexy voice, asked, "Would you please tell me more about the quarters?"

I responded: "Actually I'd rather not, but hey, Tim, I think you got all the math on it. Explain it."

Tim happily obliged. "Toni, a quarter weighs about 5.670 grams 1 pound = 453.592 grams so 1 ounce = 28.349 grams; 1 pound = 16 ounce; 4.999 quarters per oz. 79.9 or 80 quarters make a pound so every 100 lbs 7999.9 or 8,000 quarters or $2,000." The scales were 6% off or $120 per 100 pounds. On a average day they would weigh 2.5 tons or 5600 pounds of quarters or a skim of $6,720 heck let's round up to $7,000. So over a day's time, the skim from the quarters would be about $7,000, times 365 days—366 every fourth year—for about 30 years. Not bad."

I had never been able to sleep while traveling and although it was going on a full 24 hours, I thought I'd be able to dose off in these oversized chairs, but nope. Just as I'd doze off, a phone would ring or we would hit turbulence or something. Then, in what seemed to be a short time, Toni told me that we were landing in Vegas. And in just a few moments, we were on the ground.

Things started to spin now, and everything was zipping by. Immediately after we landed, the door popped open and I was escorted down the stairs into a Midway limo, which was waiting for just me. The luxury was wasted on me because I was so tired. Toni stayed with the jet and Tim and I were whisked to the Midway.

We were directed to the VIP entrance in the back, and a awning covered our arrival like I was Michael Jackson or Robert Redford. A man who appeared to be a casino host greeted me, and then saw Tim's crew, obviously FBI or Justice, Treasury, or all of the above, and they looked serious. They half ran to an elevator that was open and waiting for me.

"Twenty-fifth floor," the casino host barked to one of Tim's colleagues, who became elevator operator. There must have been fifteen in the elevator and the casino host passed over a pass card that had to be inserted into the elevator control panel before it could move. Once in, we were expressed to the Twenty-fifth floor.

"The entire last 40 some hours were surreal, but this topped it all—fifteen persons kissing my ass, and I was the new occupant of a "Whale Room"—that is, a room exclusively held for high rollers, which was not me. I looked at Tim and asked, "I'm staying here?" He nodded yes.

I did not have a moment to savor the view of Sunrise Mountain. I was rushed into the bedroom where a tailor and a lady with a number of shirt samples were waiting. I was immediately overwhelmed as the tailor took my measurements and fussed around my sizable frame.

The lady from the clothing store then started to ask me a million questions: Which do you prefer? What color? Then a voice from behind me took charge. "We want browns and oranges." It was Beth. She took charge of selecting the colors and the styles of my new wardrobe. This entire fiasco took only about twenty minutes and we all were rushed out of the room.

Soon I was left with only Beth and Tim.

SARASOTA, FLORIDA
Monday, 5:50 A.M. EST, April 21, 1987

It was about six in the morning in Sarasota. Most of the inhabitants of Ingram Avenue had been up for one or two hours now, but Andrew Parker was just looking for the coffee to make. To his dismay, Zavitch was out of coffee. He had some decaf, but that would not do.

Parker felt strange being in someone else's house, so he packed Zavitch's bag and carried it out to put in the brown-colored Volvo. Silas, watching took note. He is leaving earlier than he thought. Great, this job will be a piece of cake. Get it done and maybe have some time for golf.

Parker checked the house to make sure it was secure, then went out the front door and got into the Volvo. He headed north, up Ingram, with Silas close behind. Parker turned right on Bahia Vista but missed the McIntosh turn because of construction. Silas just followed behind. Parker kept heading east and realized he was lost. Civilization ended quickly. He made a couple of turns and got on a road that he knew could not be right. He was lost and needed coffee. He pulled into a lone gas and convenience store. As he pulled in, Silas followed right behind him. This could not be more perfect, lost in a questionable neighborhood, no one around. Silas pulled right up beside him with the passenger window down, raised his revolver with his silencer extension, and shot two rounds in the head of the driver.

With no one around, he would go and rob the body. This was perfect. Silas exited his car and saw no one. He opened the Volvo's door, and with his surgical-gloved hand, pushed the body over to the passenger side, grabbed his wallet and went through the glove compartment. All this took less than one minute. He slid back into his rental and tossed the wallet onto the passenger seat. It was then he spotted the ID. He opened it in horror—FBI, Agent Andrew Lewis Parker. Uncharacteristically, Silas began to panic as he saw two sheriffs' cars pull in to get coffee. They had not spotted anything, but suddenly the corner was getting busy. Silas pulled out, and from across the street, took aim at the gas tank of the Volvo. Pop, he hit it, and gas started to pour from the tank., One more shot and the car was ablaze. Silas made a hasty exit.

LAS VEGAS, NEVADA ,MIDWAY
Casino, April 21, 1987

Whale suites, as they are called, have anything that can be imagined. It's used when a casino is able to land a Whale—that is, someone who can drop a million dollars or more and really not worry about it. Landing a Whale was difficult, to say the least, but once you had one, the games began. The competition to keep the whale in your house becomes extremely difficult and time consuming. Some are like spoiled kids; the demands they make range from having certain candy in the room to kinky sex, which was handled extremely delicately to protect the casino hosts and the execs.

The Whale suites at the Midway were no different. The suite occupied by the "nobody" insurance salesman was one of the finest. It actually was a three-story atrium with a three-story picture window framing the magnificent strip and a breathtaking view of Sunrise Mountain.

More than 6,000 square feet of wasted decadence: Italian marble, a grand piano on the second floor, on kind of an island that stuck out from the second floor so all could see if anyone played. It was rumored that, as a favor to Phil Irish, the great Liberace had put on a fifteen-minute concert with that piano to impress a Whale who was being tempted to take his play to another casino. And it worked.

The suite was equipped with a full kitchen. Why? Who knows? It appeared that the stove, oven, and other equipment was never used. There were six—count them, six—bedrooms, That way a rock star could accommodate himself, his entourage, and their ladies.

Electronics were everywhere. Games, toys, you name it the room had it. In addition each suite was assigned a staff of at least four, maybe more, as needed. These folks would be at the beck and call of any inhabitants of any of the suites.

Overwhelmed was an understatement; I had known about Whales, even had been tutored by Phil about the care and feeding of Whales and how important they were. It was said that the masses pay the bill but the Whales are where the profit is. The Midway initially had a lot of problems attracting the mythical high rollers because of its Carnival atmosphere. The real players could not concentrate, and a lot took their play elsewhere. Finally, after two years, the first "Tower" of rooms started, and the Midway was no longer a casino but a hotel and casino. This really made the change. The new hotel and the separation of the casino from the Carnival games made the Whales more comfortable to gamble high stakes. There was now a section where the moms and the pops hung out close to where their rug-rats were being taught to gamble by playing the Carnival games, and then as you walked north through the casino the atmosphere changed. No longer did the landscape sport nickel or quarter slots but dollar, five-dollar and up to $100 per-pull slots.

Suddenly under the same roof you were in a different world, the complete genius of Phil Irish. Phil understood that slots and mechanical games were the future. Fewer dealers, fewer absences, less labor, less labor headache. Within just 5 years after the opening, the Midway was a success and, because of the mechanical play, became the most profitable casino on the face of the earth.

Steve Lambert, leaving his home in Red Rock, received a call on his unsecured radio.

A cryptic message came from the box: "Steve, Queen's bishop has taken King's rook."

He had an agent down who he did not know, or how. He responded, "In the bubble in fifteen minutes" and he was there in twelve.

Agent Daniel Smith was waiting for Steve in the bubble. "Who?" Steve questioned.

"Andy Parker."

Steve just processed and sat back. "We have a problem. Who knows?"

"Only 'Control 3' (Steve's supervisor) and our folks in Tampa."

Steve looked at Dan Smith and ordered, "Get me Control 3 and leave me alone." Steve was bewildered. How did Control 3 know of Andy's death first?

Dan tapped on the bubble's window and pointed to the conference phone. Steve pushed the appropriate button and began to speak.

Steve :"Hello Bob, heard we have lost an agent."

Control 3:"Not one assigned to you but I understand he was doing some work for our group."

Steve wanted to yell out it wasn't his fault; it was a moron subordinate, But he could not. Someone in his position knew that everything is his fault. "One of my agents made a decision to sub agent Parker for our subject Zavitch. I guess it turned out to be a good idea."

Control 3 : "Funny how those things work. Here is what we have done here. First, we got our Tampa folks and made sure Andy's identity does not get out get with the locals. We need seventy-two hours. They need to put a lid on it to protect our operation. I will call you back in thirty minutes. I want to talk to the agents involved in the operation."

Steve was dying to ask how he knew first, but he was control. He was supposed to know everything.

Steve then paged Dan Smith. "I need to see Tim and Toni here—now."

Smith nodded and made a quick departure.

Tim and Beth were babysitting me and had let me get some sleep in one of the six spacious bedrooms when Tim got the call. He was summoned to see Steve Lambert immediately.

"I think he is asleep now. I think I will be back in an hour."

"I can watch him," Beth replied.

With that, Tim left the spacious quarters.

Beth was bored and wanted to have some fun. She quietly entered my room, stripped down to her bra and panties, which of course was totally against regulations, sat near my head and started to nibble on my ear. Soon I was aroused and was in a full face-lock with my longtime flame.

Beth took the lead. In just a few moments, she had me naked and was stroking my member with a deep kiss. At the height of passion, Beth removed the rest of her clothing, knelt in bed and asked, "Z, do you want me?"

I tried to grab at her. "Yes, Beth, I want you."

At that, she jumped off the bed and said "Na!!!" gathered her clothes and left the room.

I was devastated. Payback is truly hell.

It was time for a cold shower. When I got on some shorts and entered the main living room, Beth was watching CNN on the big-screen TV and I was not a bit amused.

Beth smiled at me coyly. I said nothing, walked over to the coffee bar and poured myself a cup. Well, it wasn't Kona but it would have to do.

Beth had not realized what I had gone through the last forty-eight hours. She was not really one of the players in the operation. Tim just let her in so she could see me again. At that point, she got only stony silence from me, which was uncharacteristic. I did not look at her. I just sat what seemed like a football field away from her and drank my coffee.

At the top of the news, CNN reported that a 1985 Volvo in Sarasota, Florida, was destroyed by what was reported as a car bomb. One unidentified person was killed. No other information was given.

"Shit, that is my car!"

Suddenly the magnitude of what was going on hit Beth, and she suddenly felt bad for the prank.

I was irritated, pointed to Beth and in a demanding voice said, "Get the fuck out of here and get me Phil Irish fucking now!"

Beth got to her feet. " Z, I..."

"Now! " I bellowed.

In the bubble, Tim Floyd and Toni Cardona had been summoned by Steve Lambert. Phil still had control of the security force and anything else in the casino, decided to wander into his office and into the security bubble to try to see what was going on. He was barred entry. The only two in the bubble were Toni and Tim, and Steve was gaining entry just as Phil was approaching.

"Keep him out of here." Gauging a degree of anger, there is no doubt he was as pissed off as he had ever been. He kept pointing at Phil and said again, "Keep him out of here."

Phil retreated, but not totally out of the security center. He found a friendly face at a desk and started to chat. Phil wanted to know what was being said in that room. The beauty of the bubble is that the glass, at the command of the occupants, could change color and become opaque.

Steve entered and the clear glass became milk.

Steve, visibly shaken, started the meeting. "Toni, no other way to put this. Your partner is dead."

Toni sat back on her chair. She wanted to cry but knew she could not. Agents did not show emotion.

Tim had a completely different reaction. He sat forward in his chair, put his hands together as if to pray, and placed his chin on the point his hands made, obviously wanting more information.

"Control 3 is going to conference in ten minutes. I will be right back "

Toni, puzzled, looked at Tim. "What is Control?"

Tim solemnly explained: "During the early '80s, there was friction between the law enforcement agencies. The FBI could not share information with the CIA or Justice or the Treasury. In order to manage situations where there would be joint operations, all the agencies agreed to have one person "umpire" the flow and control of information when two separate agencies had or were working the same operation. Technically, by law, agencies can't share information. The 'Control' would be completely in charge during the operation. He or she was on call 24/7 and had the final word, since he or she was the only one with access to all the information. There would be an agent in charge, Steve, who handles the on-site operation but the 'control' runs the show."

"I never heard of that."

"Yeah, it is a problem and the plan is not working. The program is being phased out. Rumor is that if things go good in this operation, Steve Lambert may be the next deputy director. There is a lot of pressure on him right now."

Steve entered the bubble again. Because the glass was opaque, neither had any idea what had gone on. Tim's best guess was he was trying to get Phil out of security.

Steve, still very agitated, asked, "Tim, what were your orders?"

"Specifically, Steve, you told me to get Cliff Zavitch to Las Vegas. You made no mention as to how; just to get him there. We had booked tickets on a commercial airliner. Then Phil offered the corporate jet, and I said, why not?"

Steve shook his head. "That is bullshit, Tim. Why do we get the Tampa office involved?"

"Well, Phil was worried. He thought someone would make a move on Zavitch, so I called Tampa and arranged a double to fill in for Zavitch and get him out., Steve, it worked. Zavitch is here."

"OK, let me get this straight." Steve recaps, "One of the most powerful mob figures in the USA, maybe the world is worried about a principal subject in *our* investigation, and supplies an aircraft because he was worried? What gives? What's a better way to take him out? He could have blown up..."

Just at that moment, the box went off. It was Control 3.

Again, Steve Lambert depressed the correct combination of buttons, and there on secure conference was Control 3, or just "Bob."

"Yeah, Steve. Who is there?"

"Agent Tim Floyd from Vegas and Toni Cardona from Tampa, Agent Parker's partner."

There was a long pause, either from the encryption, or "Bob" was taking copious notes.

"Agent Cardona, I am sorry for your loss. How long were you partnered with Agent Parker?"

"Not long, sir."

The condolences were dropped.

"Agent Floyd, why the abrupt change in plans?"

"Phil Irish was interested in when Zavitch was arriving. I had told him that he would be flying a commercial airline and he got concerned."

"For Zavitch's life?" Control 3 asked.

"Yes, he really thought that the security precautions were extremely lax and suspected that if he were on the other side, he would take Zavitch out."

"Who made the initial arrangements?"

"I did, sir" Tim Floyd responded.

Again a long pause.

" OK, then the Tampa office and you three were the only agency people who knew of the plan?"

"Agent Daniel Smith, also," Steve Lambert confessed. "But so did Phil Irish. That means any number of people could have known."

Lambert was staring intently at the conference squawk box with his penetrating blue eyes, while he tapped his pen in his left hand, fully aware that Control 3 was not happy with how things were being handled.

"OK, this is how we are going to handle this. Tampa is going to keep the fact that Agent Parker is dead quiet. The reporters are only going to be told the identity of the vehicle and that it was registered to Zavitch, but the authorities will not confirm or deny that the body found was Zavitch's. That way it will keep everyone guessing. Gang, we have less than seventy-two hours to get everyone in place and safe. Steve, you may have a leak. Find it."

The line went dead. Lambert was rather upset the way Control 3 had talked to him—upset, but he understood. He looked at Tim and Toni "We need to get this done. Meet me back here at 8 o'clock and I will give you information on our final plans."

Phil Irish had been exiled from his own security office. He sat outside talking with one of his longtime security officers, talking about old times and the way things used to be, when he spotted a young brunette pushing herself through the mass of people playing on the floor of the casino.

"Mr. Irish, I am Beth Green, You probably don't remember me but I worked with you for a few months with Zavitch. I was Beth Downs then."

"Yes, I know, and now you are with the FBI. Jesus, everyone is with the fucking FBI. Don't I have any employees here?"

"Z" wants to talk to you. Something about his car getting blown up in Sarasota."

Phil was not surprised. As he suspected, if Zavitch was killed and out of the picture, he would be more reluctant to go through with the deal. There was definitely a leak in the organization. Or could it be some kind of listening device? Phil could accept that, but to have a traitor knowing the plans? "Z" needed some explanations and it was time someone filled him in. After all, there were people out there wanting him dead. It was time he found out why.

"OK, let's go," and Phil Irish took the lead, with a security contingent of three trusted Midway security guards and Agent Beth Green close behind.

In just a few moments, they arrived at the "Whale suites," the section of the hotel off-limits to the general public. Only those who were important dared enter this section of the hotel casino. The guard at the bottom elevator instantly recognized Phil and called for an elevator. In just a few seconds, the spacious, lush, dark oak, gold, and red conveyance opened to welcome its guests. Once Phil swiped his VIP card, it proceeded to the twenty-fifth floor and deposited the riders in front of huge white and gold doors, with a Midway security guard standing in front of the entrance. The guards were Phil's idea, not the FBI's, which made Phil angrier. They knew who they were dealing with, but took no precautions. This was the only set of doors on the floor and this guard also recognized Phil and let them pass. Phil did not knock; he used his VIP swipe to gain entry.

Once in, he spotted me, shoes off, watching CNN news.

"Hey, Tiger."

I responded by standing and giving an unenthusiastic wave. Phil approached and I shook his right hand and gave him a bear hug with the left arm.

"We need to talk," Phil said, like a man who has to confess and pay penance.

"I would say so."

"Let's take a walk. Our conversations will be safe in the casino," said Phil, knowing exactly how the place was wired. Hell, he had it done.

I got up, put my shoes on and followed Phil. Following right behind them was Agent Beth Green. Simultaneously, Phil and I turned and gave her a very condescending "where are you going, little girl?" look. Then I said, "Beth, please stay here and wait for Tim."

She did, grudgingly.

In the elevator again, the door closed without the cab moving. Phil did this deliberately.

"Cliff, these are three of my most trusted security guards. They have each been with me for years and I have trusted them with my life before many times, as they well know!" Phil then introduced, from left to right, "Troy Dixon, Mike Houston, and Troy's father, Mat. Troy and Mike are going to be assigned to you; one of them will be at your side 24/7."

"Bodyguards?" I asked.

Phil shook his head. "I'll put it all together once we are in the casino."

Phil was puzzled and even agitated about the lack of seriousness the FBI was taking concerning my safety. Was it the FBI's zealousness, the idea that we are invincible, stupidity, or worse? And Phil hated to think about that, since he was intentionally going to turn his life over to them in a few hours.

There was silence in the elevator until we reached the lowest level. Then with the three security guards inconspicuously forming a circle around us we moved to the perimeter of the casino.

Phil started off, "Walk on the outside of the pit, don't walk to the right of Mike," as he pointed, knowing of all the listing devices employed. " Gotten any sleep?"

I laughed. "About four hours in forty-eight."

Phil nodding in approval. "Good. You will do well in this business."

"I am going to work with you again?'

"No," Phil said abruptly, "not exactly. What do you know?"

I stopped walking and looked at Phil. "About what? The earth is round; it rotates around the sun; there are 365 days in a year. What, Phil, what do I know? The weight of the quarters?"

Phil shook his head. And continued to walk.

I kept up with him. "So what? There was a skim. Phil, this is no big secret, so it really did not take a rocket scientist to understand the play. Besides, it was your associates who were getting the money."

"Not exactly." Phil paused and kept walking. "Years ago, Mark, Tommy O, and I agreed to skim about 3 to 6 percent of the skim."

"Oh shit," I blurted.

Phil went on, still keeping up a casual stroll. "We were grooming you. Remember the day Mark and I took you to lunch and wanted you to become a management trainee?"

I nodded.

"We all liked you, even Tommy O."

"I don't think I ever met him."

"Yeah, you did, several times. You used to take his kids around the Midway. He was the guy who always wanted to tip you fifty dollars, and you did not take it until I told you to. That was Tommy O. Tommy was our connection to our…" Phil stopped, looked at me, and then continued, "…investors in KC and Chicago. He is the one we sent the skim to, minus our skim."

Phil stopped. "You still like those fruit shakes?"

I gave my thumbs up and Phil strolled over to the juice bar for a liquid snack.

I ordered an orange banana shake and Phil ordered a pineapple one. We acted just like ordinary patrons until Phil signed for the drinks. With the drinks, he proceeded in the preplanned path.

"Mark and I were killing ourselves and we needed help. Both thought you would be an asset and someone who we could trust. But when you turned us down, we were faced with a dilemma. When you declined, we still needed help. We made two bad choices; we promoted Steve Lambert and hired Mike Roma."

"Why didn't you ask Steve first?"

"Well we felt Steve would be more…" Phil was a loss for the right word here.

"Greedy?"

"Yes, and you were more…"

"Naïve." Again I filled in the blank

"OK, greedy, naïve. We thought we also could control you better than Steve. We were forced to hire Mike Roma because of a friendship he had with a friend of Tommy's. Steve was great. He asked for nothing more that what we paid him. We should have known anyone who knew what we were doing and didn't shake us down had to be the LAW, but we just thought he was a great guy. Mike Roma was the problem. We tried to keep him out of the counting room, but he eventually found out what was happening, and then shook us down. First we had to hire his brother, Ed. Gave him a do-nothing job for about 100k a year. Then Mike got greedy."

Phil stopped near a nondescript door and said something to Troy, who unlocked the door. We proceeded through the door and climbed a steep ramp. We then came to two sets of stairs. Phil headed up the left stairs and I followed, with our security contingent of two. Troy stood at the door.

The Midway Casino was built before the modern electronics became a necessity, and this was a catwalk for the old eye in the sky, the old way the security folks could spy on cheaters. We both took a perch, and we were able to view the entire casino.

"We can talk freely here."

Phil continued.

" Mike was working us and wanted two points for himself and his brother. This cut into the skim to the investors. We went along with him for more than a year. Then business got bad and it was either our skim, or cut out the skim to the investors. So we called their bluff, stopped paying him. It seems that he was hired to watch us, and instead of watching us and reporting what he found, he cut himself in. Once we refused, he said he was going tell all. We haven't seen him or his brother in weeks."

"You think they fled the country?"

Phil smiled at my naiveté. Then he looked at me real hard, and I got the message.

Phil went on: "Suddenly, Tommy O had to leave KC and is hiding out in the Midwest. Word on the street is there is a hit out on the four of us."

"US?"

Phil nodded again. "Me, Mark, Tommy, and you."

"Me? What the fuck do I know that obviously the FBI doesn't?"

"It is not what you know; it is the deal."

Nothing else was said, Phil motioned me to follow him, back down the steps, down the hall, and out across the center of the casino to the security office. Janet Mendelson was a long time employee of the Midway Casino, and after she received her degree from UNLV, she became the director of Human Resources; Janet vaguely remembered me and was able to retrieve my paper file from the archives, which was unusual. But since I was a friend of Phil's, the paper file miraculously was spared from the shredder. Janet did not question the credentials: "full access"—that meant the casino, hotel, front of the house, back of the house, and, yes, even the hallowed counting rooms. Nothing was off limits for this pass.

She had been waiting at security for sometime now, but she was loyal to Phil. If he said wait, she waited; no questions asked. She did realize that credentials of this magnitude meant that I would have as much clout as Phil and Steve Lambert, who recently got cleared for all areas.

Phil approached Janet and gave her a professional hug with a firm handshake. Then Janet gave Phil the envelop. He quickly strolled over to the Keno parlor and sat with Janet and me. Phil first reviewed and studied all the documents in the envelop, one by one. Mendelson was very thorough; she had everything a new hire would need, including an employee manual. Once all the paper work met his approval, Phil handed me the contents of the envelop, except the security pass.

Phil stood up from the comfortable Keno chair, specifically designed to keep the players in their seat, thanked Janet, and signaled for me to follow.

As we approached the security at the great gate of the casino security room, Phil presented me my master code key—Security Pass.

"How about giving this a test run?"

I took the pass and swiped it. The door opened., Phil, not breaching procedure, swiped his card also. One of the major rules of security: Do not go through an open door without swiping your card.

Once in the security inner sanctum, I was amazed how things have changed; there were monitors everywhere. I followed Phil to the next room, which required the right thumbprint. Phil gave me a short instructional and I, bewildered, put my right thumb on a plastic flat surface protruding out from the side of the door like a funny doorbell.

After I removed my thumb, the door opened and a voice said:

"Access granted to Mr. Zavitch."

Phil made his thumb imprint and the voice granted access to him also.

"Access granted to Mr. Irish."

"OK, I give up," I said, raising my right thumb in the air. "How did you get my thumb print?"

Phil smiled, "Your sheriff's card from when you were 15. Fingerprints don't change, Cliff."

In the '50s and '60s, anyone who worked in any casino had to file their fingerprints with the Clark County sheriff—the sheriff's card. This was gold to any minor working, since Las Vegas had always had a curfew. If you were caught out after curfew, you could use your sheriff's card as an explanation. Your current employer had to stamp your card and it was a must that you had to return it to your employer when you were terminated.

Once in, I saw more monitors. This is where the real heavy work was done. It was Phil's office, his domain; very few people had ever been within its glass walls. The first thing Phil did was go over to the custom coffee service and fix himself a cup of coffee. While methodically preparing his cup, he asked, "Cliff, you didn't drink coffee. Do you now?" Phil was referring to the many Sunday mornings he and I would read the Sunday paper on an empty crap table. Even while in college, Phil always remembered me drinking juice, not coffee.

"Yep, do now."

"How do you take it?"

"I think I will need it black and strong,"

"Yeah, I guess you will."

In the middle of the office was "The Bubble." Phil ushered me in, closed the door and pointed to a comfortable chair for me to sit in. Once we both were comfortable, Phil activated the bubble and finished the story.

"On Friday evening during the height of the swing shift, both state and federal law enforcement officers are going to "raid' the casino and cease it."

"That has never been done before. They cannot do that," I blurted.

"Cliff, if there is one thing I have come to understand it is that the government can do anything they want to satisfy a few cocksuckers who are sucking the tit of the American taxpayer. The feds put enormous pressure on the state, and the state folded like a cheap suit. But it is why they folded. The Feds are going to let the state 'reorganize' the casino with their own people running it and selling the license to a person the feds want."

"But how? With no judge or jury?"

"The state of Nevada cannot have a casino this large closed. Jesus, we have 4800 employees. After the Feds seize us, they will open the books and find we are insolvent and do what they would do to, say, an insurance company. They call it 'rehabilitation.'"

"Rehabilitation?"

"Right. The feds will give the state the right to do what ever they want, employ who they want, and give ownership to who they want."

"Who knows this?"

"Cliff, it is hard to tell anymore. I think our investors know. I don't know how. No more than ten of us in the casino even had an idea of the situation."

"Where do I come in?"

Phil sat back in his chair and took a long draw on his coffee. "You are going to be assistant GM."

I smiled a crooked smile and said, "Nah, no, what?"

Phil smiled back and put his coffee down. "OK, there is more. The feds don't want Mark, Tommy, or me; they want the guys who are trying to kill us. Once we realized that we were out in the cold, and that hits were put out on us, we needed to tell Steve Lambert. Turns out for the last twenty years, he has been in deep cover for the FBI, and immediately cut us a deal. The three of us turn state witnesses for the feds, name names, give records, and we go into the witness protection program. But we want six points in the 'New and State-Improved Midway Hotel and Casino.' None of us will be in any position to watch over our interests. None of our families will be able to, either. All of us want something, so we elected you more or less to be our representative, to make sure our interests are served, and make sure that our families are taken care of."

"Wow," I said, taking a prolonged sip of java.

Phil continued, "Things always work out, Cliff. If you would have taken the position we offered you years ago, you would not be in a position to help us today. And let's face it, Cliff, at this time you have no life; this will be a great opportunity for you. You are a homegrown boy, from Sunrise Acres elementary school to UNLV. Cliff, some folks don't even know you left here, and most still think you still work here. You know, I kept your time card open for four years; then I made Janet Mendelson the head of Personnel.

He laughed. "I mean, Human Resources. She came to me and insisted we deactivate your card and badge, which I did."

Phil paused and sipped his coffee. "Cliff, I would prefer this would have never happened, but it did."

"Can I say no?" I asked.

"You can, but it would greatly complicate things. Obviously, someone is now trying to kill you, and that is not a good thing. I don't know if it was arrogance or what, but the FBI has taken a very laid-back attitude about your...our...protection. Cliff, I know the people we are dealing with. I have known them for years. I know their children; I have been Godfather to some of them; I have been to their homes; they have been to mine. But, Cliff, when it comes to protecting their business interests, I guarantee they would kill me, you, or Steve Lambert—it doesn't matter. "

Phil drained his coffee. "More coffee?"

"Sure."

Phil took my cup. He deactivated the security and opened the portal to freshen up the java. This gave me some time to process. Really, what did I have to lose" Things were so immediate, but, really, what did I have to go back to? I made my decision. Phil returned with two fresh cups.

I started with my questions. " How much? What is my salary?"

"Cliff, I make $375,000 per year, with a bonus last year of $200,000. It is yours. You will be doing what I am doing. You will contact and keep my clients happy; my clients will be your clients. I have already arranged it; I can make this so!"

I went numb. Jesus, the most I had ever made was $50,000, and here I was walking into a half-million-dollar-a-year job.

Phil interrupted the dreaming. "Cliff, you will be well taken care of, but I am going to need your pledge that you put aside about 80K for something."

"You?"

"No, not me, but that is a detail. I will get back to that."

I began to think this was very much a new league I was in when 80K was a detail

"I guess I start now!"

"RIGHT NOW."

"What about my house in Sarasota?"

"We can have an appraisal done and pay you. The casino will purchase it for the appraised value. Fair?"

I shook my head affirmatively, and Phil listed it into a journal of things he had to do.

"Can I go back?"

"We prefer you don't, Cliff. We will have a group of our folks box up everything and bring it here. Do you have much?"

I shook my head no. "I really don't care about much—pictures, mementoes. Hell, I have a new wardrobe."

"You will not have to worry about furniture since you will be living here."

"Here?"

"Yeah, not where you are staying now," Phil laughed. "You don't want to occupy that room. You want one of your whales in there, although it is at your disposal at anytime. Cliff, you get paid well because, for the most part, you will be here 24/7."

"Jesus sounds like I will be in prison."

"Some have called the "Midway" my prison. I have a great home, but I rarely am there. I live in the apartment that you will be occupying. I have cleared it out and it is being painted. I will show it to you later. The important thing is that you be safe. Soon after we are taken into custody, the safest place on earth will be right here. After a couple of years, things will be OK."

There was silence.

I shook my head. "OK, Phil, I am in."

"What about girlfriends?"

"None, my love life sucks."

"Good. I am glad to hear that."

"Gee, thanks."

"At first it will be overwhelming. There will be no time for romance, especially for the first two years, Cliff. People will be trying to kill you, I don't recommend dating. If you have the urge, get security to drive you 69 miles north—clean, legal, and efficient. If you do start dating, have the person checked out. Know everything about them. Be careful of any woman who comes on to you. Come on, Cliff, you and I are not Mr. Universe; if they are too aggressive, they are probably setting you up. Remember what I have always told you..."

I finished, "If you are betrayed, it was the woman."

Phil laughed, "You do remember."

"Phil, that is probably why my love life has been so fucked up. I remembered."

"Yeah, Cliff but you are still alive." We both laughed.

I held my coffee cup up as to toast. Phil followed.

Phil than took a last long draw on the coffee and said, "OK, a lot to do. You have about $15,000 now in clothes. Get into a suit and meet me back here in half an hour." Phil paused and closed the journal he had been taking notes in, and then grabbed my wrist, as he was inspecting my hand and fingernails. "This will not do." He dropped the wrist and dialed four numbers.

"Marge, Phil Irish here. I need a girl to go up to room 2511 and do a Cliff Zavitch's nails. Clear lacquer, and I need it now."

Marge, on the other end of the phone, was floored. She had never gotten a call from Phil before. She had talked to him when he came in to get his nails done, but never did she get a call from him. His assistant would make his appointments. She assured him she would have Ling her best girl take care of Mr. Zavitch.

"Troy, Mike, and Mat, they are paid very well. Keep them paid well. Mat, Troy's father, and I go way back. He owes me, more than just money. I believe I can trust any of the three."

"What about Mike?"

"Mike was a friend of my son's before..." Phil paused.

"...When my son and my wife were killed. His mother was raising Mike by herself. She works in the cage. Again, they owe me. That brings up one more thing." Phil stopped abruptly. "But let's talk about that a bit later. Get out of here. See you back outside the bubble. We have a lot to go over, and bring Tim Floyd. Hurry."

I now had three shadows, mine, Mike and Troy. Mat kept watch on Phil. Mike and Troy had no idea who I was. They knew something was coming down, but what? They had no clue. Their orders were 'watch Cliff!' That was it.

We walked quickly from the elevator to suite 2511, and entered on the second floor of the suite. When I walked in, I heard Tim and Beth chatting on the floor below, in the atrium area. I quickly moved to my room and found that the fruits of my first labors had arrived—custom-made clothes, a closet full. I counted four suits, five sports jackets, one tux, twenty ties of assorted colors, ten pairs of slacks, ten heavy-starched white shirts, and fifteen more of assorted colors, four pairs of shoes, accessories, and watches. They even duplicated my eyeglass prescription and had four new eyeglasses made. It is amazing what you can do when money is no object, I thought to myself. The dresser was filled with casual clothes, Polo shirts, socks, and underwear. Expensive underwear—Bay Harbor. I knew the brand: $12 for each pair. I usually got four pair for that price.

I had no idea where to start. I had always loved clothes; I just could never afford them. I decided that since Phil was wearing a white shirt, I would, too. But I sported a more colorful tie with a conservative navy suit. Just as I was walking down the spiral staircase to the first level of the suite, carrying my shoes, both Beth and Tim spotted me. Beth whistled and made some comment I really didn't hear. I was too preoccupied and didn't even crack a smile.

Ling was already set up in the corner of the living room, ready to do my nails. Tim and Beth met me at the bottom of the stairs.

"You look great," Beth gushed.

"Thank you," I replied in a very disinterested tone. Then I turned to Tim. "Phil wants us both in the bubble in about twenty minutes. Beth, we will be seeing you," as if to say, you are dismissed; go away. Beth went to hug me, but I put my hands up to stop her and took her hand to shake it. She realized she was indeed dismissed.

After a few moments in the chair, Cliff's hands looked great. Right on schedule, Tim and Cliff left with their security entourage close in tow.

SARASOTA, FLORIDA
Tuesday, April 21, 1987. Noon.

Silas traveled north on I—75 and took the I-275 split to St. Petersburg. He had been there only once before. He took the 38th Avenue north exit and headed east to 4th Street, then headed north looking for a nondescript convenience store—not a 7-11, not a large one; a small dingy one, the kind usually run by Mohamed. Soon he spotted an off-brand gas station with a store and pulled in. He pumped about ten gallons and went inside to pay. Inside was a pleasant, round, dark lady with a thick accent from where Silas did not know or care.

He paid for the gas and purchased two 100-minute phone cards.

When you dial with a phone card, you dial into a switch. Then you dial directly from that switch, not impossible but very difficult to trace. Of course cash was used in the transaction, and Silas was back heading north when he spotted an abandoned gas station with a pay phone outside. Perfect. It was imperative he report his failure. And for the first time in his life, he would have to remember the "second" phone number to report problems. He moved slowly and deliberately. He was just a guy wanting to make a phone call, that's all. He rolled into the once busy lot and got out of the car. The weather was beautiful—warm but not too warm, with a slight breeze from the north to cool it off. Silas hoped the phone was working. It seemed in good repair and there was no overt evidence of it being out of order. It worked.

Silas dialed the 800 number and waited for instructions.

"Thank you for using World Tel Com prepaid phone service; for English press 1, for Span..."

Silas did not wait for the full menu. He pressed 1.

"Thank you"...pause.

"Please enter your 15 digit PIN Code."

Silas entered 388729570198346 and waited.

"Thank you"...and another pause.

"You have ninety-two minutes remaining on your card. Please dial the phone number you wish to connect to, starting with the area code. For international calling, please follow the instructions."

Silas started to key in the number, then stopped. He pondered for a moment why he only had ninety-two minutes on a 100-minute card. Then he realized that there was an 80-cent connect charge. He finished dialing. It seemed like it was forever before the phone began to ring.

Silas was surprised. It was answered by a very calm female voice.

"Yes?" was the only thing, said very slowly.

"Is this a secure line?"

"Most certainly," the voice said.

"There was a problem in Sarasota."

"Oh, we thought it went well. A little messy for you, but what is the nature of the problem."

"The subject was not eliminated."

"Oh" was all that was said, and Silas began getting a little irritated with the person on the other end of the phone.

"There was a switch. A law enforcement officer was eliminated."

Another disinterested 'Oh,' then a pause. "What kind of officer?"

"FBI."

"Oh my," she said.

Then there was silence. Silas knew he was still connected because there was a faint background noise, maybe a TV or a radio. Then the silence was broken with the same methodical voice and cadence. "Please proceed and return the rental car as we had planned. Then call this number back. I will contact our client to see how they want to proceed." The line went dead.

Just up the street was a large car wash next to a drug store. This was perfect. He removed the rental car key ring that IDed the vehicle as a rental and pulled the auto up, as instructed.

"Good afternoon sir. Full service?"

"Yes, please. I borrowed this car from a friend and I want it cleaned up for him."

"Do you want it Armor All?"

"Yes, wipe it down good. I need to go to the drug store."

"OK, sir. We will have it done by the time you get it back."

Hell, he could not remember what he touched and did not touch but there would be at least five other sets of prints on the car, and hopefully they would wipe off most of his. He walked over to the drug store and purchased a small box of surgical gloves. In St. Petersburg, those kinds of things were in high demand and were purchased mostly by folks Silas's age with elderly parents. Of course, the transaction was cash, and as he walked back to get the car, he opened the box and removed two gloves, powdered on the inside. Great—easy and quick to put on.

He went inside to pay for the car wash. The car was parked, and three scantily clad teens finished wiping it down. He was interested and wanted to observe more, but he did not look in their direction. Once everything was done, he walked to the car, where a male attendant took the receipt and shut the door for him as he entered the car. The attendant left, and Silas slipped on the plastic gloves, took out a cloth and wiped the key down. He inserted the key and was off to the airport—north on 4th street to the Howard Franklin Bridge and exit to Tampa International. Once on airport property, he followed the signs for rental car return. He pulled into the express drop-off, exited the car, popped the trunk with his gloved hand and went to retrieve his single carry-on. Then he remembered; before he left the car, he had to wipe down the gas cap. He walked to the right side of the car, removed his handkerchief, bent down to tie his shoe opened the outside gas door, and wiped down the gas cap. He stood and walked into the terminal, ditching the surgical gloves.

Using a payphone from the airport was too risky, so Silas walked through the airport from Blue—departing flights—to Red—arriving flights—and walked to ground transportation, where he hitched a ride on an "off site" auto rental company van. They are happy to drop you off at their rental establishment. When he arrived, he was herded in a line for cars, but excused himself to use the pay phone at the perimeter of the lot.

He used the second calling card.

"Thank you for using..."

Silas did not wait for the full menu. He pressed 1.

"Thank you..." Pause.

"Please enter your 15 digit PIN Code"

Silas entered 388729570199843 and waited.

"Thank you," and another pause.

"You have ninety-two minutes remaining on your card. Please dial..."

Silas keyed in the number, and waited while another eight minutes vanished on the connect charge. Again, it seemed like it was forever before the phone began to ring.

" Our client wants the contract fulfilled. Where are you?"

"Tampa, at Alamo car rental outside the airport."

"Alamo?" the voice repeated.

"Yes."

Again a long pause. Silas could hear typing in the background , then more typing. Then the silence was broken."

"Mr. McMillen is a VIP member of the Alamo Quick Silver Club. In twenty minutes, walk in and over to the line of cars. Get in the car reserved for C McMillen. The key will be in the car with your documents. When you drive out, there will be four booths. Drive through the booth on the far left. Just ask the attendant if he is Dave."

"Proceed to the Orlando International, leave the car in express drop-off, and catch United flight 413 to Vegas. Our subject is in the Midway Casino with a security guard. Things have gotten difficult." In the same soft voice she finished, "Complete the contract and don't fuck it up."

There was little left of the 1985 Volvo when inspector Sam Simpson arrived on the scene. Sam was a long—time member of the Sarasota Homicide unit. Maybe too long; retirement was literally right around the corner. In less than 45 days, he would have 35 years, and that was enough. Sam was jaded, to say the least—three failed marriages, two children who will not talk to him, and, worst of all, a job that had owned him. There was a time when Sam really cared, but in all honesty, it took him some time to remember when that was. Probably after his last disastrous marriage; alcohol, cigarettes, and, yeah, women. But he was now pushing 60 and few women who were interested in him would even give him a passing glance. The good news: Sarasota could be called a retirement community and, yes, there were some rich 70-year-olds who were still looking for a roll in the hay. But this did not interest Sam.

Sam actually was a hell of a cop at one time, but right now, homicide was too serious and morbid. He wanted something else. Less pressure, more fun, maybe check fraud.

He had been sober for almost three years. The key word is "had." He has been off the wagon for a year now. Strange, he has not had any problems; he went out had a beer, maybe two, but that was it. He actually was kind of proud of that.

One of the fireman on the scene noticed what appeared to be bullet holes in the victim's head, but because the body had been so completely burned by the fire, it appeared that the only way an accurate ID could be made would be by running dental records, and that could take some time.

Most of the physical evidence here was incinerated; even the auto tag was melted. You could make out the make and possibly color of the vehicle, and that was it.

Crime-scene tape protected the evidence from the mass of reporters who seemed to be first on the scene. Two sheriff's deputies were nearby, but were called to a reported rape. Inspector Simpson donned rubber gloves as his criminalist arrived.

"Good morning, inspector," Stacy Spots greeted Simpson.

"Good morning, Stacy. Working this alone?"

"Yeah, we just heard that there was a vic. It was called in as a simple car fire."

"I don't think there is anything simple about this at all. One of the fireman/paramedics thinks there is a bullet in the vic." He paused and, to gauge the reaction of Stacy, he raised an eyebrow. He then went on, "Stacy, any way to find the V I N (vehicle identification number)? The plate on the dash is toast and the doors are welded shut."

"Sam, no problem. Manufacturers put the VIN in several places. This is a Volvo. Hang on."

Stacy carefully stooped under the wheel well. After a quick look, she reached up with a pair of needle-nose pliers. Clip, she found another VIN plate. After she put it in an evidence bag, she walked back to Inspector Simpson.

"Piece of cake, Sam."

"Thanks, Stacy." He took the bag and deposited it in his pocket, to be logged later.

"I think I will start with pictures. I have some help coming soon, since there is a vic."

Stacy had just started taking pictures when, suddenly, four black Fords quickly pulled across the street from the scene and an army of Men in Black Suits walked deliberately across the street.

Sam yelled at Stacy, "Hey, Stacy, remember when I said there was nothing simple about this fire?" When she looked his way, he pointed with his chin to the descending hoard.

"*Feds?*" Stacy questioned.

"Looks that way."

Within a few seconds, it seemed as if on cue, all the Men in Black reached in their pockets and presented their credentials to Inspector Simpson.

One, the AIC (agent in charge), spoke. "Good morning, detective, Agent CP Willis, FBI. Our group will be handling this investigation," as he proudly displayed his ID.

Simpson preferred inspector. "Inspector Simpson," with the emphasis on inspector.

"What do you have here?"

"At first, this was reported as a simple car fire, but one of our firemen found a vic in the driver's side with possibly a bullet in his head."

"Road rage," Willis interjected.

"On a quiet back road? OK, if so, why are you here?" Simpson asked.

Inspector Willis did not respond. Instead, he began to deploy his staff.

Willis turned to Simpson, who had just been joined by Stacy. "We will handle this from here, and we have a specialist coming to extricate the body." Then he walked away.

Sam looked at Stacy and shrugged, "Looks like they have the varsity team in on this one. Better call off the rest of your unit. Thanks for the help, Stacy."

Inspector Simpson walked away, puzzled. He has heard of the feds coming in and taking over an operation, but why this one, a guy found dead in a car? Sam had a lot more pressing cases, so he returned to his car to head back to write his report.

LAS VEGAS
Tuesday, 1:00 PM, PST April 21, 1987.

With Steve Lambert off property, Phil Irish was still in charge. It would not be until Friday night that the feds and the Great State of Nevada take over his domain. Phil sat in what was referred to as the captain's chair, a large chair inside the main security office. The occupant of the chair was usually the chief of Security or designee. Of course, Phil or Mark, at any time, could request a turn in the captain's chair, but both usually were in their own offices inside the main center, or on the floor. Both, however, knew exactly what each button, monitor, computer, and software program can do.

Phil was perched in the captain's chair for probably the last time. He was going to miss it. In actuality, the job sucked. Sure, the money was good, but you were truly on call 24/7/365. Days off were rare, vacations were non-existent, and the pressure was intense. But he loved it, absolutely loved it, and would certainly miss it. Phil had sacrificed a great deal. Although he had lost his wife and one of his sons many years ago, he had tried to establish relationships, even got married again. What a joke—married for two weeks. The honeymoon: guess where? The penthouse of the Midway. She was sweet, but from the first, she knew it was a lost cause.

There had been several others. It is easy to court and impress women when you wield so much power. If he wanted a date, all he would have to do is select any lady he wished, and then find out which Strip shows were absolutely impossible to get into, make a phone call, secure the best seats, and then ask the lady out. No woman ever refused.

When you are the license holder of a Strip casino there is an unwritten law. If it is a personal favor, everyone accommodates everyone else. Many years ago I came to him for a favor. I wanted to take a young lady friend to see the final performance of Diana Ross and the Supremes. No problem; Phil wanted to do me a favor. He actually owed me a few. I was excited. I would have probably gotten laid that night, but at the last moment, I was needed at the Midway and my date ended up taking her sister while I worked. Good training for me, Phil remembered. Whether or not this was a test of loyalty and devotion to the casino would never be known. However, it was a fact that I had a very light work load that night. If it was a test, I passed.

Tim and I reported as requested, and it was time for me to start my "graduate studies in Casino Management—real life." Phil stood, and stepped down from the chair.

"Cliff, let me introduce you to Dave Morris. Dave is our IT guy. He makes all this work."

Phil looked at his watch; it was a bit after one. "Are you hungry?" Phil was really addressing Tim, and I was looking at the "captain's chair."

Tim turned and said, "Sure."

Phil responded, "Good. Cliff can concentrate more on an empty stomach. Let's go, Tim," and Phil and Tim left, leaving me with the head resident geek of the casino.

Dave directed me into the chair and started, "Cliff, you actually control everything from where you are now sitting. Entrances, exits, the cage. And with this button here..."—he pointed to a button with a red plastic cover with a key under it—"...shuts down everything. Here is your key; there are only six." The key was on a lariat and he hung it around my neck. "Phil has one, Mark, Steve Lambert, the chief of security, the person sitting in this chair—it is passed from shift to shift. And now you." Dave paused.

"Probably a good idea to avoid using it," Dave laughed. "By the way Cliff, who the hell are you? That key, opens every door in this casino and hotel. It is the mother of all "skeleton keys." It even overrides electronic locks. I don't ever ask questions, but we have never had more than five of these keys out—ever. I had to make this one myself."

I did not really know what to say or how to answer. "I'm a long term employee," was all I said.

Dave continued with the tour. "There are 64 main monitors that service 600 cameras placed everywhere in the casino except the bathrooms. Privacy issues, you know. If the State did not have laws, they would be there. We do have listening devices in the bathrooms, though along with 1000 other mikes in various locations. We can see and hear just about everything in our house."

I spent the next four hours with Dave, learning about cameras, software, facial recognition. I was given manuals to read and maps to study. Of course, any studying done had to be within the confines of the security office. Dave found a desk for me to make my home, to store the books and other info.

Nothing could be taken out of the security office. Dave started the quote, "It is not a matter of trust...

I finished without looking at Dave "...It is a matter of procedure."

Dave seemed surprised that I knew one of Phil's favorite sayings.

I recognized the surprise and said, "Dave, I told you I am a long-term employee, real long-term."

Dave seemed to be at an impasse, and the timing was perfect. It was going on five o'clock and the chief of security, Roger Mackey, had entered the room. The first thing he did was make his way to the coffee set-up. Roger introduced himself. It was his turn with me, and I ushered him into the bubble. For the next two hours, Roger explained policies and procedures. There was a procedure for everything—if someone dies at a table, there was a procedure; guns and other weapons, and there was a procedure. "We have a procedure for everything," Mackey said. "Everything except what will happen Friday night."

Mackey sat back in his chair to gauge my reaction.

I shook my head. "New to me, too."

"Here is what I understand will happen. Sometime Friday night, probably late, we will get a court order to cease and desist operation. But they will not just use a piece of paper—this is a political statement and they will probably storm the place with weapons drawn. Makes good press."

Mackey sat up and took a sip of his coffee.

"Here is my plan. Starting Thursday night and continuing into Friday morning, I will have a meeting of all my security staff. I will fill them in on what is going to happen. We, of course, will yield and cooperate with anyone who has a badge. I will temporarily take control of the casino and be with Phil. Phil then will turn his key and pass cards over to me." His emphasis was on ME.

"I then will turn the key and card over to their designate, only after they sign for them."

"Sounds good, Roger. It even sounds like you are asking my approval."

"I am, Cliff. I have known you for some time. You probably don't remember me, but when you first started here I was assigned to watch you. Folks liked you; you were home grown. You are still a known entity and you were hand-picked by one of the most beloved folks in this casino."

"I remember times when that wasn't so," I added.

"OK, that is right, and actually my point. When the Midway opened, the license owner was Mr. T, an asshole of the first degree. Phil had an uphill battle but won the war. Now he is out, and it is my understanding the general manager the feds are bringing in is a real prick."

"Why don't they let Steve Lambert run the show?"

"No one would trust him. Shit, I don't trust him. He worked with us for almost twenty years, and now it turns out he was a fed all this time. God knows what he has on all of us, and he would use it to get what he wants. Besides I think he wants to be the FBI director, and with this operation he will probably be an assistant director."

Mackey took another sip of coffee and turned around in the expensive and very comfortable chair of the bubble, facing a two-drawer file cabinet with what appeared to be a digital lock with a large display.

"OK, seven, press enter, then one-one, press enter, then two, enter, three, enter, and finally twelve, then enter twice. It opens."

An audible beep sounded and the file cabinet opened.

"Close the drawers, hit enter twice; it locks."

Mackey smiled, "Crap players have no problem remembering the combination."

In the game of craps, seven and eleven are the two winning rolls on the come out and two, three , and twelve are "craps."

Mackey took a blue file obviously segregated from all the other files, removed it from the drawer and slid it across the table in front of me.

"The newly-anointed GM, anointed by politicians from both the state and federal levels, will be Edward Michael Milton, a full-fledged member of the "Lucky Sperm Club.". MILTON BANKS," Mackey said, half questioning if I had heard of them? "Big money here, and it seems that Milton Banks are going to back the state's play for the Midway."

I thumbed through the file.

Mackey continued, "Study it later and keep the file in the bubble. I will give you the Reader's Digest version. Born into money; has had two scrapes with the law, drugs and arson; then he beat the living shit out of two of his girlfriends; those were handled by attorneys and payoffs; no court of law. Pictures are in one of the envelops in the file. Has a hot temper and just generally thinks his shit doesn't stink. Bottom line is this, Cliff—OK , what do you prefer to be called, Cliff, Z, Mr. Zavitch, what?

"I like Z."

"OK, Z, the bottom line is this. You are one of us. This asshole coming in, to most will be an unknown entity. We have already begun the mutiny. I am an old union man; as a matter of fact my son is union steward, and I will tell you right. Nothing is going to be done unless you,

Z, want it done. The asshole will have to come to you to get anything done. My understanding is you are the only one he will not be able to fire."

I pondered the heavy words. "Does this loyalty have a price?"

"Of course. Status Quo". Mackey not surprised by my question; he even expected it. "Milton is going to want to clean house, no doubt, but he can not fire 4,800 employees. If he is smart, he will start right here, security. But, I have things so tight it will take him at least six months to transition, even if they have a replacement today, which I doubt."

"A coup d'etat," I mumbled.

"OK."

"Of course I will need to talk to Phil."

"Of course, but talk about this only here in the Bubble, Z. This is the only safe place to talk. In the meantime, I've got your back." Mackey stood to leave.

"Thanks Roger."

As Roger left, I pondered the file on Mr. Milton. He was a bit scary—from money, spoiled, and an egoist. Egotists are bores but egoists are dangerous. Mackey was right. I returned the file and secured the cabinet. It was six-thirty and I was starved. It was time to eat.

Charles McMillen, or so his papers said, had little trouble getting into Las Vegas. He had four hours to contemplate how he was to complete his assignment. Vegas is like any town, really, and like any town, there was a seedy side where for cash you can get anything.

Silas knew Vegas well. He had done several assignments, and of course had partied there many times, so he knew his way around. He avoided the Strip, taking Eastern Avenue out of the airport through the construction. He drove on Eastern to Sahara and turned left, toward the Strip and downtown. At Las Vegas Boulevard (the start of the Strip), he turned right and then left past the needle. In just a few more blocks, he could find what he needed. First stop a pawn shop, where for cash he acquired a weapon, though he doubted he would use it. This time the demise of Cliff Zavitch would be a quiet one. For an extra $100, he got the name of a young lady who worked at the Las Vegas Free Clinic.

Silas met her and, for only $50, he got an entire doctors' prescription pad. All he needed was two sheets, but he now had an entire pad. From there, he drove to a nearby Albertson's, purchased a diabetic kit complete with syringe, and submitted two prescriptions to the pharmacist. He agreed to come back; after all, the store was open 24 hours and he had the time. It was time for him to check in somewhere and take a nap. He needed to relax and plan. He would check out the Midway later that night.

My day was far from being done. Walking out of security into the general population of visitors, players, and staff, Phil came in looking for me.

"Hey, Tiger!"

"I'm a bit starved."

Phil opened his arms wide "What is your desire, sir?"

"Fish and chips would be great. The Jesters Pub used to have the best in town. Do they still?"

"Of course." Phil turned and pointed to Troy. "Troy two fish and chips to my office, please."

Phil turned back to me. "Drink?"

"Coffee—better make it black and strong."

"Troy, got it? And get me a dark beer."

"OK, boss. Fifteen minutes."

Phil put his hand on my back and ushered me back into the Security Center. "The night is just getting started and we have a lot to do."

I wondered if I was on the clock, but for between 375 and 500 K a year, I thought I could put up with this. I followed Phil into his office, which was passkey protected.

"Cliff, try yours. It should work."

I exited the office, inserted my passkey and the door unlocked. I entered under Phil's approving eye. Phil's office was posh—overstuffed chairs, couch, big screen TV, and a giant desk. His executive chair must have cost at least $5,000; just the chair. It had imbedded controls a back massager and more.

I swiveled to face a file cabinet very similar to the one in the Bubble. "Remember these numbers four, enter, sixteen, enter, 1965, enter." The cabinet beeped and was unlocked. "My son's birthday."

April 16, 1965? Impossible. His son died in 1961 and was a teen? "Son? I thought..."

Phil put his hand up to say stop. "We'll talk about that later, but now I need you to get familiar, no, intimate, with our clientele. Each player has a code name. Memorize it, and refer to the code name only. Don't be bragging that you have this player and that player. If you do, you will not have them anymore. Use the code names and shut up. These files are my client file. Don't let them out of this office. Drawer 1—first half are whales, big-time players. You need to read the files, know what they like or dislike, what they play, and if they are ahead of us or we are ahead of them." Make contact with them at least once a month. Birthdays, holidays, it does not matter. Contact them and make sure marketing keeps our name in front of them. The number One Rule—get them back here."

"What if they owe us money?"

"The rule is the same; get them back here, and make sure they bring cash. They will. "If they are really in debt to us, I move them to the back of the first drawer and use them as a center of influence. Let's say they are in debt to us for five hundred grand. I will tell them to put together a group of friends. For every dollar they pre-deposit with us before they arrive, I will give him thirty cents off his debt."

"You said you moved them to the back of the first drawer?"

"Right."

I gave a shrug and a gesture to say, more information please.

"The front of the drawer, these guys don't care how much they lose, and they cover it with cash. Look through the files; they play at least a million. Some are movie stars and most stars fall. When they do, we move them from our whale file to centers of influence. Hell, we have a couple that work for us now organizing junkets. Study the files. I will go check on dinner."

I was astounded with the names of some of the whales. Many I did not recognize by name, but by position and company. Several congressmen, senators, a couple vice presidents, and even a past U.S. president, a rock star. It was a who's who. I did not realize Phil was so hip. The amounts of money they dropped were incredible. Some dollar amounts could even be the entire GNP of small countries. That was just the U.S. The Whales were broken down into countries—Japan, several Arab countries, a duke, and members of the English Parliament. The list went on.

Troy and Phil entered the office with a fish-and—chips feast. This was not just a couple of orders; there was a lot of food there. It could be an indication I was going to be there a while. It was. Each file was studied; each like and dislike was recorded. We moved into the center of influence file when I pulled one out. Using only her code name. Jesus, 'SuperCin,' spelled 'Cin.' God, I have a crush on her."

"Yeah, and I think she owes us some money."

I checked the file. "About $200,000."

"Oh yeah. She came in and offered me a blow job if I could make it go away."

"Oh, my God. It may be worth it."

Phil lowered the file and looked disapprovingly at his protégé ."Z ! I hope the hell you are kidding. Trust me, no blow job is worth 200 K!" But look, Cliff, once I am gone and you get settled, give her a call. Offer her 50 percent. If she brings her friends, you will knock off fifty cents on the dollar of her debt. That is, if she invites her girl friends—25 percent if she brings guys. I guarantee she will bring girls. Bet you get laid, maybe not by her, but by one of her friends."

Phil smiled like he knew this to be so from prior experience. My heart missed a beat.

It was going on to eleven o'clock when Phil asked me a very unusual question. "Cliff, do you carry in Florida?"

"Carry? Carry what?"

"A weapon."

"A gun?"

"Yeah, a gun."

"No."

Phil swung his chair back to the phone and pressed a button. "Troy, can you come in here?"

In just a few seconds Troy was inside Phil's office.

"What's up, Boss?"

"The range is open 24/7, right?"

"Oh, yeah."

"Cliff here needs a crash course in guns—tonight."

"Phil you are kidding. I have slept only five hours in the last 48."

"Auhhhhhhh" Phil said mockingly. "Get used to it. Troy, have him back in four hours, he can sleep in till nine tomorrow."

With that, Troy escorted me out of the office, through the back corridors and over to the 24-hour gun range—only in Las Vegas.

LAS VEGAS TUESDAY, 10:00 PM. APRIL 21, 1987

It was about ten-fifteen at night and Silas knew that the swing shift would end at eleven. He also knew that blackjack dealers rotated every 20—25 minutes. He found a five dollar table and sat down. He played recklessly. He really didn't care if he won or lost; he was fishing for information. Each time a dealer would come on, he would ask if they knew an old friend of his, Cliff Zavitch? None did, or at least they said they didn't.

Frustrated, Silas retired to the uppermost part of the casino so he could see the entire facility. For about an hour, he watched and observed; then he had an idea, a brilliant but simple one. Silas walked over to a white phone and asked to page Mr. Cliff Zavitch.

In just a few seconds...

"Paging Mr. Zavitch, Mr. Cliff Zavitch.

A moment went by and the voice bellowed again...

"Paging Mr. Zavitch, Mr. Cliff Zavitch.

Then about two moments later, the operator said, "Sorry, he does not answer."

Silas hung up. The page fell on deaf ears. He left the casino to come back in the morning. Now he would pick up his prescriptions.

LAS VEGAS, NEVADA—DOWNTOWN
Wednesday, 7:00 AM

Control 3 had arrived. At least that is the word Steve Lambert got from a colleague who said he had been summoned downtown to Vegas FBI headquarters. The facility was a few steps down from what Lambert has been used to at the Midway for almost 20 years, but they would have to do. No posh desk, no fancy monitors, no glamour, no perks, no beautiful women around you. Is this what he had to look forward to? Lambert had been in deep, deep cover, and his cover was third in the record book for length. One of the others, the agent was in deep cover for exactly 20 years. The other, an agent who had infiltrated a mob family in New York, was a boss himself and was still in deep cover. It appears Lambert would have to get used to fetching his own coffee.

Control 3 (Robert J. James—a/k/a Bob) looked nothing like he sounded on the phone. Lambert had talked to him many times over the years, but had never met him. He was a short man, about 150 pounds, and balding, but definitely in command. The conference room was set so each had briefing papers in front of their assigned seats. Of course, Control 3 was at the front of the conference table, and Steve Lambert was on his right.

On the other end of the table was the representative from the State of Nevada. Fred Mercer, the general counsel for the Nevada Gaming Control Board, and his group filed in and sat to his right. Feds on one side and state on the other.

After introductions, the meeting began. Fred Mercer started:

"Bob, the board is still concerned about the legality of what we are going to do, we cannot afford any embarrassment. After all, there is no denying we are a political entity."

Bob answered. "And who is not? We all suffer from external political forces." He then pointed to Samantha Terry from Justice. Samantha was not unattractive, but it was apparent her outward appearance was not the most important thing in her life; her work was.

"We expect an immediate court challenge, probably to be filed Tuesday morning at the earliest. We should catch them with their pants down. With the evidence our three witnesses can provide, we can invoke the RICO act." She paused, "Then after that, we can do just about anything. Even if they tie us up in court for years, the state of Nevada under a "state trust" will operate, under the federal government, the casino for the people of Nevada and the employees."

"How secure are the witnesses?" Nick Stewart from the state side asked.

Bob answered this one: "Secure."

Nick pressed, "Where are they?"

Bob again: "Secure."

Fred Mercer spoke up. "Mr. James, we don't want details, but our political lives are riding on the well—being of three not-so-reliable individuals."

Bob relaxed a bit. "Mark Karl, and Phil Irish will be taken into custody Friday Night and will be transported to an undisclosed location for debriefing. Tommy O'Sullivan, Tommy O, is hidden away in protective custody already, and will be moved Friday night to the secure location."

Bob, realizing that the one who asks the questions controls the meeting, turned the focus on the operation of the casino after the seizure. "Is your general manager in place?"

"Michael Milton is ready to go," Nick said confidently. "He has a lot of experience running the family banks. He will be able to assimilate quickly and nicely."

Steve Lambert mumbled almost unintelligibly, "Right," knowing the casino business would probably eat him up.

Bob again: "When will you install him?"

Fred Mercer: "The Idea is for the casino to be closed for the shortest time possible. We hope to have the cooperation of the security and other key employees and to be up and reopened Saturday afternoon."

Steve Lambert added, "Cliff Zavitch may be able to help with the transition."

There was silence from the state side. Mercer looked at Stewart, then spoke, "This guy Zavitch, he is nothing, just a pacifier for the three criminals that have turned state's evidence. We really do not want him to have any role in the transition at all. As a matter of fact, we want him out of the house until we reopen. Then he is going to get lost in the shuffle, no active role in management at all. He will just be there."

Surprisingly, Lambert said nothing.

From this point, the meeting became very detailed. The press was going to be right with the team going into the casino. Maximum exposure was desired. Both the feds and the state wanted to portray your government in action, protecting you from the 'old' Las Vegas."

LAS VEGAS, NEVADA—MIDWAY CASINO
Wednesday, 7:00 AM

I had finally gotten to sleep at 3:45, after my crash course on guns and weapons. I was dreaming about the care and cleaning of various handguns. I also signed up for a Nevada permit to carry, and Troy promised that Monday, when all the paperwork was done, we would go gun shopping. Although I had never really had any need for a gun, the prospect of owning a sidearm intrigued me. At the very least, it could be a hobby.

At Exactly 7:00 A.M., there was a sharp knock on the door. "Room service."

Paranoia set in. "Who ordered room service?" It was my day to sleep in.

A familiar voice shouted back, "Z, relax, it's Troy. Phil ordered it."

I knew Troy had a security pass key. "Then, hell, come on in."

The door opened and the waiter brought in a tray of coffee. I nodded. "Breakfast of Champions. What is on the agenda?"

"You need to meet Phil in the bubble in twenty minutes."

"Dress code?"

"PTR."

"PTR?"

"Play the Role—suit, the whole nine yards."

I poured a cup of coffee and hurried into the bathroom. In record time, I had showered, shaved, dressed, and met Troy, my newly acquired friend and bodyguard, in the foyer of the massive room. We made it to the security center with no time to spare.

Phil was poised in the Bubble already, reading printouts from yesterday's activities.

"Morning Phil. Saw you last night on the floor when I got in. Don't you sleep?"

"No, I don't. Today you are going to shadow me. Unless I ask you, don't say anything."

I nodded.

"OK, Cliff. Remember these reports?"

"Yeah, play, drop, and win reports. You had started to go over them with me just before dad passed."

"Good. You remember what you are looking for?"

"Absolutely. Deviations from the norm."

Phil smiled "Good, exactly. If the numbers fall within the norms, don't worry about them. You are looking for numbers that are whacked."

"I remember the cigarette numbers and how we caught the dealer for stealing them."

Phil was a bit surprised. "God, you remember that? That was years ago."

"Yep, we use to have cigarettes at the tables for the players."

"How times have changed," Phil interrupted.

"And you were concerned about the increase in the cost. So you had the computer guys track the cigarettes. You found that when three tables were running, 40 percent more cigarettes were being used. Then we tracked it to two dealers on a shift."

Phil nodded in approval.

"Every morning, starting at 6:00 A.M., I am here checking for deviations. When I find one, I mark it and save the data sheet. I then track the game and the staff, including the floor man and the pit boss. I don't get excited when I find one-deviation. Anomalies do occur. But if there's a pattern, you have a problem; then you must become a detective. I call for reports for all their folks from where that pattern occurred. Then I track each. After thirty days with no other deviations, I eliminate them. But I keep tracking anyone who has deviations occur. I may even put folks on different shifts. Whatever you do, while you are tracking, tell no one. Last year, I found a pit boss skimming."

How ironic, I thought.

Phil looked at his watch and said, "Let's go."

I followed. As we exited the security center, a woman whom I had not yet been introduced passed two folders to Phil. Phil signaled me to keep up and, as I walked abreast, handed me one of the folders. "We are heading to the shift meeting. We will have the managers from each department from both the incoming shift and the outgoing shift. These are the incident reports. Trips, falls, drunks, security call, any kind of problem is lodged and the info is passed shift to shift. You want to be brief; the outgoing folks are beat and the incoming folks want to get things rolling."

We entered Midway West, a midsize conference room.

Things seemed very unorganized. Phil was great, one on one, but he could not command a group. He sat in front of the assemblage on the stage and kind of mumbled into a microphone.

"Ah, OK, we have a couple incident reports here. Sam..." pointing to one of the floormen, "...How the fuck did some silly bitch climb on one of your crap tables?" Now, of course, there were women in the audience, but none took offense to anything that Phil said, or even how he said it.

"Phil, we had a high roller on table 6 and I was approving an over-limit."

Phil, not really buying it: "She takes off her clothes?"

"Well, some."

"Some? Really now." Phil, half smiling and shaking his head, said, "Tell me, Sam, have you checked the count on the table where the striptease occurred."

"Ha, well...er."

"Ha, well...er is not an answer. Yes or no. Jesus Christ, people, would you people start just answering yes or no." Sam was going to continue to defend himself but Phil cut him off. "Look, people, all of you. Nothing in this house just happens. We must be aware of everything. We must anticipate and we must be right on our hunches. When you hear something going on, call for help; ask for additional people, more eyes.

Phil twisted his head and looked right at me. "Make a fucking note. I want to see what the drop and win was on that table 6 last night. Bet we will be short a few grand." I, with pad always ready, took notes.

"Yeah, some of you old timers remember Cliff 'Z' Zavitch. He has been a member of our family on and off from the opening, and now he is back. Going to help me. Hell, he is going to run this meeting tomorrow."

A shock to me, but I did not bat an eyelash, and Phil watched me closely.

"OK. Sue, one of your waitresses was assaulted? What is this, Roger (Mackey)? Where the fuck was Security?"

Roger responded concisely as he opened his notebook, "Phil, we responded from the center. We saw it at 3:13 A.M. and we had men there at 3:16—three minutes, Phil."

"How is the girl?"

Sue spoke softly. "Probably out seven to ten days. Security was there fast, but he was a big guy and he did some quick damage."

"Roger, what about the asshole?"

"We called Metro and they took him into custody…" Roger's voice trailed off.

"AND!" Phil wanted more.

"He was out in two hours."

Phil pounded the table once, hard. I observed frustration on Phil's face. Back in the '50s and early '60s, Phil knew exactly how he would deal with this, but not today.

"OK, er, Roger, get with me. We have the asshole's address?"

"Yes, of course."

"Is he 86th?"

"Of course."

"OK. Cliff, make sure she has access to one of our attorneys. I want her to sue the son of a bitch."

Phil was visibly pissed off about this incident. He went through several more sheets—it is amazing how much happens in a hotel casino in just one shift. Someone scalded in "their shower," a drunk tripping out of the elevator, two fights, patrons stealing chips from patrons, pickpockets; you name it, it seems to happen.

Phil entered into some banter with a couple of other department heads and the risk manager. Phil was upset about some stupid lady tripping over her own feet, no rug, no wet floor, no nothing, getting paid $7,500. The risk manager explained it was go-away money, Phil understood, but did not like it a bit.

The natives were getting restless and wanted to go, Phil just tossed up his hands and told everyone to get out.

"Can you do this?" Phil asked me.

"Yeah, no problem. When do I get the incident reports?

"When do you want them?"

"Forty-five minutes before the meeting."

"Done. Your show tomorrow."

CHICAGO, ILLINOIS
Wednesday, 9:00 AM

The view was breathtaking from the Sears tower window of Bruggerman, Jancan, Frasier and Scott, not the largest but one of the most influential law firms in Chicago. The office was on the 77th floor and, like most private firms, you could have access to their lobby with a special access elevator card.

As soon as the elevator door opened, any occupant saw a magnificent Italian pink marble wall as the entranceway of their law firm. Once inside that portal, only the word opulent came to mind. The desks, even of the lowliest paralegal, secretary, or research assistant, were custom made. Since the firm took up the entire 77th floor, each partner had a corner office, smartly and individually appointed to meet the personality of the inhabitant.

Fresh flowers abound. Money was spent on I M A G E. But, strangely, only a few really understood whom they were trying to impress. Mr. Bruggerman had just become partner emeritus, making J. Jancan the senior partner.

J. Jancan was brilliant. He had twice successfully argued in front of the U.S. Supreme court, and was well versed in any kind of law, but had a love for criminal law, although most of the crimes he handles now were more tax and white collar issues. The clients of the firm were confidential, and each desk had a shedder. Security precautions were evident everywhere.

J. Jancan was in a negotiation conference and had left orders not to be disturbed. But his private assistant, June, sheepishly snuck in the room, tiptoed around the massive table, and quietly put a slip of paper in front of him with the Roman numeral 5 or "V" on it. J. Jancan immediately stood.

"Ladies and gentleman, please go on. I must be excused," and then quickly took his leave to his corner office.

J. Jancan closed his door and picked up the phone. "Yes, what is needed?"

"Friday, you will be needed in San Francisco."

"I will assemble the team and be there. Will the details follow?"

"This afternoon, by special courier." The phone went dead.

J. Jancan quickly called for his personal assistant. "June, I need Team 'V' in San Francisco Friday morning. Please make the arrangements."

"Very well, sir. I will reschedule your appointments starting..."

"This afternoon," Jancan finished for her.

"And reschedule for..."

J. Jancan hesitated, "Next week; next Wednesday."

"Oh, you do know Mr. Scott is on his honeymoon on St. Kitts."

"Not any more. Get his ass in San Francisco, June. It is his third honeymoon. Just tell him where to be. He will understand and I'm sure the new Mrs. will, too...". He paused "... eventually."

LAS VEGAS, NEVADA—MIDWAY CASINO
Wednesday, 11 A.M.

All morning, I had shadowed Phil. Day shift was 7 A.M. to 3 P.M.; Swing, 3 P.M. to 11 P.M.; and Graveyard was from 11 P.M. to 7 A.M. The counts for each of the shift usually started four hours after the last shift ended, and it was time for the count.

I followed Phil through the catacombs of the Midway Casino. Of course, the public did not know the location of the counting room. Very few knew the exact route and had access to the secluded room. Once there, a myriad of security checks were made to gain access.

I had been there before. Now my job was only to watch and take notes. Things certainly had changed. Now both Phil and I were only spectators; the FBI and IRS were the ones who ran the game now. The count was not yet over, but after about one hour, Phil started to lose interest.

Phil tapped me on the thigh and nodded. I took the hint and followed Phil out of the room.

"Phil, shouldn't we have waited?"

Phil shook his head. "No, not much to do anymore. Hell, in the old days it was only Karl or me who supervised. Now the entire U.S. Treasury Department is in the room. Hell, just make an appearance each day and read the report."

It was lunchtime, and none too soon. After all, six hours had elapsed since I had grabbed a quick coffee and roll.

Phil stopped, opened his arms wide, and shrugged, "Where do you want to go to lunch? you have nine restaurants to choose from."

"Really?"

"Name it."

"Jesters Pub, fish and chips."

"Can't you get enough of fish and chips?"

"Nope. I love it. What about a Guinness?"

Phil said, "Cliff, I would rather you didn't."

I knew that meant, NO WAY. OK, I thought, no booze while in the house. Nothing more was said.

Of course there was a line waiting for the Jesters Pub—after all, it had the best fish and chips on the West Coast. But no lines for Phil and me. Dressed in our Armani suits, I followed Phil to the front of the line. The greeter—you really can't call them a maitre d' at a pub—recognized Phil. The velvet rope was parted and both were ushered to a vacant table. I was impressed; folks watched us and wondered who those guys are. I could get used to this.

Immediately, a young woman came tableside.

"Hello, Mr. Irish."

"Hi, Betty." Phil had an uncanny ability to remember everyone's name.

Of course, very few of the execs did not wear nametags—Karl, Phil, Roger, the security manager, and now me. My ranking was now evident.

After ordering, Phil motioned for a phone, and one was produced in a flash. Phil picked up the receiver and dialed a few numbers.

"Kevin, Phil. We are in the Jester. Need the daily runs, please."

Phil hung up.

Halfway through the fish and chips, two gentlemen entered Jesters and delivered a greenbar computer run.

Phil pushed his dish away and started to review the greenbar. After a few moments, he pulled out his pen and started to make notes. After a few more moments, he passed the pages over to me for my review. This was the analysis of last night's Swing shift that ended at 11:00 P.M. This report had every table that had been opened, how long it was open, who the dealer or dealers were, what the drop was, and the win. Then there was a breakdown and comparison of each table with last year's, last week's. Then there was a report on how many people actually came through the door.

After that report, there was more analysis, using the "daily population" visitors to the casino, and then an analysis of the tables based on the increase in visitors.

Stats, stats, stats, but I kept up. After all, I was a numbers guy. Time flew and we were still in the Pub when the Pub manager brought Phil the phone.

"Phil Irish...Yeah, OK, be right there."

Phil hurriedly packed up the greenbar, stood, and walked out. I was right behind him and followed him to the Security Center.

LAS VEGAS, NEVADA—MIDWAY CASINO
Wednesday, Noon.

Silas entered the casino the same way thousands of others filed in, bringing both money and hope. The hope for Silas, however, was quite different. In hundreds of assignments, this was the first ever to go bad. He needed a second chance to complete his mission. Not only was it a matter of $100,000, but for Silas, it also was a matter of pride. He was, after all, one the very best in his field.

Silas casually walked through the casino, stopping occasionally to play a quarter slot. He made his way to the third floor of the casino. On third floor, cheap vending machines and arcade games circle the casino. Silas made his way around the vast casino perimeter. It was on the third floor that many parents dumped their children with a few dollars to amuse themselves, while they pursued games of chance on the lower level.

Finally, Silas spotted the perfect place. He hurried over to a hotdog vender and purchased a dog with green relish and onions, with a Pepsi ® on the side. Not that he was hungry; the place he wanted to occupy was a lone table perched above the casino where wary children may sit have something to eat while they watch their parents feed their inheritance or education to the ravenous machines.

This was perfect, he thought, as he spotted a white house phone to his left. Silas sat down; no one even noticed or even cared. He removed a small set of high-powered binoculars and surveyed the premises. When he was comfortable, he picked up the white courtesy phone and waited for the operator.

Again a raspy voice answered, "May I help you, please?"

"Cliff Zavitch, please."

In just two moments, a voice broke through the dull roar of the casino, "Paging Mr. Zavitch, Mr. Cliff Zavitch."

His timing was perfect. Phil and I had just left the Jesters Pub and were heading to the Security Center. Upon hearing the page, I stopped and smiled at Phil.

"Hey, I'm getting famous."

"Believe me," Phil responded, "It will get old."

We changed course, stepped down into "the pit" and walked over to a column that held two white courtesy phones. I turned and smiled at Phil as I picked up the phone.

"This is Cliff Zavitch" as I had done it hundreds of times during my prior tenure at the Midway.

"Thank you, Mr. Zavitch. I will connect you to your party."

I waited; then I was connected.

"Hello, this is Cliff Zavitch."

The phone was dead and Silas was on the move. If he only had a high-powered rifle he could have done this the old-fashioned but sloppy way—just take off his head. But there would be no way he could get such a weapon inside the casino's extremely tight security. Silas was moving fast now, almost running down the ramp just about fifty yards from his target. If he could get close, he could just bump into him and inject him with an air bubble.

I waited, and then hung up, smiling. "I guess they really weren't a fan."

Phil looked extremely concerned as he pointed to Troy and then to the Security Center door. "Troy, get him into the center." Troy and Mike escorted me into the center.

Phil started to scan the casino area as he picked up the white house phone. "Princess Fatima."

A second did not go by when a loud voice said, "Paging Princess Fatima."

"Paging Princess Fatima."

As he expected, Roger Mackey answered the security call. "Mackey."

"Roger, someone paged Zavitch. It was a ghost call; no one there."

"OK, I am on it, boss."

"In the center," Phil ended the call.

Phil stepped back from the column and again searched the casino for anything or anyone suspicious. Then he turned and quickly made his way to the security center.

Silas moved with the crowd and was able to observe the movements of his target. Now he would blend in and study his subject.

Inside the Security Center, I waited for Phil, still surrounded by my security entourage.

"What was that all about?" I queried.

"Instinct, gut feeling. OK, what do we have?"

Moe Miller was in the captain's chair. "One of our 86th cheats has slipped in." He stood and ceded the platform to Phil.

"Who?"

"Our Chicago friend, Vince Morgan."

"All right, let's see him."

In just a moment, there were at least twelve screens from all different angles.

"Sound, please," Phil commanded. "Get two floormen close, but hold."

I watched and learned. It seemed that Mr. Morgan used an elaborate disguise to get in the door, but it was the experimental face recognition software that flagged him. He was one of the worst kinds of cheats. He knew the machines and would use small electric drills and magnets to manipulate the outcome.

"Get a twelve o'clock view, please" requested Phil, now standing. In just seconds, a view of the perpetrator directly above him was on the main screen.

"Close in."

The camera zoomed in.

"OK hold. We are rolling tape"

"Oh, yeah!" responded Moe, who was one step down.

Phil folded his arms and watched. Then when the cheat felt comfortable, they had him. From the cuff of his right shirtsleeve came a small drill that penetrated the outer door of the slot casing.

"Got it, got it," Phil shouted.

"Yep."

"Ok, get him. Get a dupe of the tape, call Metro, and get him out of here."

Moe smiled. "Done boss."

Phil stepped off the podium and Moe took his place.

Phil then retrieved a cup of coffee, signaled to me, and entered the bubble.

When the bubble was secure, Phil looked at me, smiled and said, "God, I am going to miss this job. Then he started to laugh.

"Need anything?"

"Sleep."

"Naa, sleep is for our customers, not us. I have some more paperwork for you and then Troy is taking you to the range again."

I sighed and took a long swig of coffee.

"You are doing great, Cliff. You have not forgotten much."

I nodded.

"The way we have it set up, Cliff, you are going to make a lot of money. Your job is to make sure our families are also taken care of." Phil started to shake his head negatively. "I just don't fucking trust them, but, hell, I don't know what to do. We have had our lawyers do most of the work. Here is your employment contract, and we need to sign it now."

"Should I read it?"

"Absolutely. I think you will find that is takes pretty good care of you. Read it now. Back in half an hour."

Phil stood to take his leave and let me alone with the extensive contract.

Phil was correct. The contract was between Cliff Zavitch and a new entity called FECMAC, Inc., short for Federal Emergency Casino Management Corporation, the entity that would be set in place to manage the casino. The employment agreement was for seven years, with a guarantee of five years, with a salary of $385,000 per year for me, plus another possible bonus of up to $200,000 on a sliding scale depending on the performance of the casino. Obviously FECMAC would have to take over the operation for this all to work. Even if the casino were sold by FECMAC, I would be paid just under $8,000 per week for a minimum of five years after the sale, just under two million dollars.

At that point, I whispered, "Jesus."

My duties were mostly operational. Apparently I would have only staff authority, and would be an assistant to whoever would be brought in by the feds to operate the casino. My responsibilities would be to make sure three families received 6 percent of the total "profits." The way the "profits" were calculated was very specific, but because of my advanced finance background, I was able to follow the convoluted process. The families were guaranteed at least a million dollars per year as long as ownership was retained by FECMAC.

Again, if or when the new entity sold the casino, the families would each share in 6 percent of the net proceeds, with a guarantee of at least ten million dollars.

Other perks I would receive would be: I could elect to be a "resident" manager and live on property, have access to any of the casino's cars, have a meal allowance, and a clothing allowance. Phil was right. I was taken care of.

The government officials had already signed the execution page of the contracts; including persons representing the Justice Department and Treasury, and it was even signed by a federal judge.

I had to look at my watch, not for the time, really, but literally to remind me which day it was. Wednesday, 7 P.M. I slumped back into the bubble's luxury chair. Just a few days ago, my job was in jeopardy, and most everyone I worked with hated me. Now I was staring at a contract worth two million dollars.

I sat up and signed all five copies of the contract. As I finished, Phil returned to the bubble and sat across the table from me.

"Hey, tiger, we have a problem."

"What's that, Phil?"

Phil pulled out his Rolodex and turned it for me to see. Bud Slidale came in unexpectedly, one of 'your' whales, and we are short a luxury room.

I sat up, "Do we have any rooms?"

"Sure and nice ones."

I contemplated. "Have someone move my things into one of those rooms and give Mr. Slidale my room."

"OK. Good idea."

Silence overtook the bubble. I expected Phil to pick up the phone and give the order. Then I began to smile, then laugh, and shake my head. "You already moved me, didn't you?"

Phil laughed, reached into his pocket and produced a code key. He slid it across the table "You are on the 12th floor, Tower B, room 1224. Nice room. Sign the contract?"

"Oh yeah"

"Any questions?"

"Who is your family?"

Phil nodded, knowing that his old friend would ask the question.

He lit a cigarette, something I had not seen him do for years. "Sandy and Todd were killed, a few years before I met you. I threw myself into my work. I had no desire to fall in love again, but after a time I started to date and met a lady who I thought I could fall in love with. A year before I met you we had a child out of wedlock."

Phil paused and reached in his wallet.

"Do you recall the night you helped those kids with Downs at the Fascination game?"

"God, yeah, that loud Jewish bitch who almost started a riot."

"Remember what happened after?"

"Yeah, you called me to your office and I thought you were going to fire my ass."

"...And what did I say?"

I paused and pondered the past a moment.

"You told me I would have a job with you forever. I was somewhat confused, but I certainly was not going to argue."

Phil took a long drag on his cigarette, opened his wallet and removed four pictures which he passed over to me. I turned the pictures over to reveal four pictures of a person of various ages. The person obviously had Downs Syndrome.

"My son, my second son. His name is Josh. His mother's name is Cindy. She could not handle it; you knew that the kid wasn't right just by looking at him"

I listened intently and shook my head.

"She left us. Tried to find her, but stopped trying to find her after a while. I heard she became a religious nut."

Phil took another drag on the cigarette. "Me, I couldn't handle it either. I certainly could not take care of him. And I kept him probably one of the biggest secrets of my life. Only Roger and Mark Karl know; that is it. With their help, I shipped him up to an excellent home in Washington State. That night you were helping those kids; I had just sent him north. God, I felt worthless, but it was that night I realized that there truly was something special about you, something I did not possess. I pay about $70,000 a year for his care. When the FECMAC or what ever the fuck they call themselves take over, I expect you will be pretty much set, and I want you to make sure Josh gets taken care of." Phil took the last puff of the cigarette and snuffed it in an ashtray. "If...er...when I am dead, I have it set up that all will be taken care of for him, and while I have been working, it has been no problem. But this situation concerns me. If it looks like these cocksuckers are going to fuck us, call Judge Toliver. He is the one who signed your contract and is a good friend of mine. Will you do what you can to take care of Josh?"

I looked up and said, "Phil it shall be done. When will I get the information on him?" I handed the pictures back to Phil.

"I would guess in about a week. Karl and Tommy O will have information packets for you about the families and bank accounts. Josh's info will be there, but that is the least of your worries now. Starting tomorrow, you are the GM. Let's take a walk."

We left the bubble and made our way out of the security center. We walked around the pit very conspicuously, with the security entourage in tow. By doing this, Phil was passing his authority to me. As we moved through the pits and the change booths, Phil would make the introduction, "This is Cliff Zavitch our new assistant general manager."

We moved slowly, Phil explaining new sections of the casino to me. Then we wandered up the ramps to the second and third level, then through a locked door opened by a swipe, and up a ramp to a perch where Phil and I could see the entire premises.

"Great view, I can control the entire operation from here. I watch the bosses, and they know to watch me from here. Damn, I will miss this job. I want you to go get a bite, change, and go with Troy to the range again. You are running the meeting tomorrow. Tomorrow, I shadow you."

"The range, the guns? Are they necessary?"

Phil did not answer. He just gave one of his looks.

"OK, then I will get something to eat and Troy and I will go shoot guns."

I turned to a smiling Troy, shrugged, and said, "Let's go."

Roger Mackey passed Troy, Mike, and me. Roger walked forward and stood next to Phil, who was grasping the brass rail.

Phil, not even looking at Roger: "OK, what did you find?"

"We pulled the house phone and dusted the table. He is an assassin named Silas, works out of Chicago"

Phil, still not looking at Roger: "They are going to kill him. Shit I never should have called."

Roger responded confidently, "They are not going to kill him, Phil," with an emphasis on the NOT. He continued, "We have two of our best on him and there is FBI all over the place. Hell, they are here even as customers"

"And that is what bothers me, Roger." He finally turned and looked at Mackey. "Jesus, and where the hell is Lambert?"

Roger, who is charged with having to know everything, said, "He has been downtown with the FBI all day."

Phil said nothing and parted Roger's company.

CHICAGO. THURSDAY, 5:22 A.M.

Franklin Frasier sipped on his coffee in his travel mug, waiting for the firm's limo. He knew he would not have to wait long. At 5:30 A.M., as scheduled, the Bruggerman, Jancan, Frasier and Scott Limo approached and blinked its lights. Franklin activated the security in his posh 6000-square-foot home. He was currently between wives and had no hugs or goodbyes to convey. As the alarm counted down, he grabbed his suitcase and exited. The chauffeur had the door open in a matter of seconds and they were off to the airport. They were just ahead of the miserable Chicago traffic. At exactly 5:55 A.M., the limo delivered Frasier to the corporate jet. Upon his arrival, the door was closed and the jet taxied for takeoff.

At 7:00 A.M. Pacific Time, the jet touched down in San Francisco's Pacific Aviation private airport. Franklin appreciated the time change, since he only wasted one hour in time. Franklin exited the jet and immediately looked at his watch, which he had just adjusted for Pacific Time. Standing with his hands crossed in front of him, with his bag to his right side, he waited for the limo. Franklin did not move; in exactly five minutes, he checked his watch and repositioned his stance. A look of disgust masked his face. At 7:07, the limo arrived. The chauffeur nonchalantly exited and opened the passenger door for his passenger.

"You are late."

The driver knew it was best to say nothing except, "I apologize, sir."

Nothing else was said. The driver knew the destination, The Clift, at 495 Geary St. The Clift is one of the must luxurious hotels in San Francisco. Formerly the Clift was the private home of the late Frederick Clift, the hotel's original owner in 1913.

The Clift was expecting Mr. Franklin Frasier and, as he entered the hotel, a very proper concierge instantly met him.

"Good morning, Mr. Frasier. I am Martin."

"Good morning, Martin. Is our floor ready?"

"Yes, of course. We have had security seal off the entire ninth floor."

"Ninth? I thought we had ordered the eighth floor," Frasier replied with an irritated tone.

"Mr. Frasier, sir. I am sorry but logistics were just not on our side, sir."

Mr. Frasier raised his hand in surrender. "Martin, the ninth floor will be fine."

Martin sighed a long sigh of relief. The truth be known, a U.S. senator and his staff were occupying the eight floor, but he was not about to let "Mr. Frasier" think that there was someone in the hotel of greater importance than he.

"Martin, is our communications expert available?"

"Yes sir. Our phone people are on the floor now waiting, as well as a Mr. Fitzpatrick from United Workforce and Personnel.

"Very good, Martin."

Martin had an elevator waiting.

"How many floor cards do you wish me to order, Mr. Frasier?"

"Mr. Jancan will be here later this afternoon. I will advise him to notify you. I will need one for myself now."

"Of course, sir," and Martin handed over his elevator key card.

As the elevator door opened, it was evident the telephone folks were hard at work. A tall gentleman who could obviously be identified as Chuck Miller by his ID badge stopped and introduced himself to Mr. Franklin Frasier.

"Mr. Frasier, we have wired the entire floor based on your specs. I would recommend Tie communication phones. They are durable, work well, and are fairly inexpensive. All we need is a final sketch for the exact locations."

Frasier nodded, "When will you be ready after I give you the sketch?"

"We will work all night and you will be up by 7:00 A.M. tomorrow."

"Excellent. Thank you and carry on. I will provide you a sketch within the hour."

Frasier looked around for the United Workforce and Personnel representative. He saw a portly gentleman looking over the one of the telephone workers' shoulders.

Frasier signaled Martin to retrieve the United Workforce and Personnel individual. Martin, of course, complied.

The portly, gregarious man offered his card, "Pat Fitzpatrick with United Workforce and Personnel, sir," bowing slightly.

With his left hand, Frasier accepted his card, as he extended his right hand to shake hands.

"Franklin Frasier, Bruggerman, Jancan, Frasier and Scott," deliberately stressing Frasier.

"Happy to meet you, Frank," Mr. Fitzpatrick replied, smiling.

There was a very awkward silence.

"Mr. Fitzpatrick, please refrain from truncating my name."

A bit taken aback, Fitzpatrick replies, "Yes, of course. So sorry, Mr. Frasier." Then quickly changing the subject, "you will have fourteen of our top paralegals here by here by 3:00 P.M. today. Correct?"

"Yes, but we want to interview them. Please have forty-five candidates downstairs in the..." He looked to Martin.

Martin, looking quickly at his clipboard, "We will have the Ava meeting room available, sir."

"Mr. Fitzpatrick, a problem?"

"No sir, of course not. Forty-five paralegals here this afternoon. You will select fourteen."

"More, probably. Send your best."

Mr. Fitzpatrick shook his new client's hand and took his leave.

Martin watched as Fitzpatrick entered the elevator, and then turned to Franklin. "Sir, will there be anything else?"

"Mr. Jancan and Scott should be here this afternoon. Will they have access to your hotel computers?"

"Yes, of course. Shall I inform you of their arrival?"

"No, I am sure they will find me."

SARASOTA, FLORIDA
Thursday, 9:00 A.M.

Inspector Sam Simpson took a last draw on his cigarette while reading the memo that carried the edict that he soon would no longer be able to smoke inside the police station.

"Fuckin' bureaucrats," he mumbled as he crumbled the communication and tossed it into the appropriate file. A bit frustrated and contemplating retirement, Sam sat back in his chair to plan his day.

On his desk, he spotted the evidence bag with the VIN of the crispy Volvo. First a pang of panic stuck him for not registering the bag; then again, it was not his case and he was sure that the feds had IDed the owner of the vehicle, that is if they didn't already know whose it was.

Curiosity got the better of him and he fired up his computer. He hated computers, but he knew that they were an invaluable tool in solving crimes. Using his index fingers, he pecked the VIN into the database, hit enter, and sure enough got an error message.

"God damn it." He meant to say it under his breath, but it just came out too loud and his long-time desk neighbor, Harry Seed, looked over the top of the divider. "Bad day, Sam? Harry, too, was a veteran of Sarasota's finest. A large, graying black man who carried his years well.

"No, I just can't even get a simple VIN number from this piece of shit."

Harry laughed, "Hold on," as he came around his desk to Sam's aid. "What ya got, Sam?"

"This VIN plate—I know I typed correctly but I keep getting this error."

"OK, let me try." Sam stood and Harry took over the keyboard.

Harry, obviously a lot more proficient at typing than Sam, had no trouble inputting the data but had the result Sam had had. Again Harry inputted the data, but to no avail.

"No, I will find this. I am going to access the State DMV and access it right from the registration and insurance records." Harry took a moment redirecting the computer's efforts and confidently typed in data and code to redirect the machine to the state's computer, then the VIN…

Error.

He tried it again.

Error.

One more time, he thought.

Error.

"Where did you get this, Sam?"

"It's off the toasted Volvo the feds were so interested in."

"You know, Sam, these Volvos, got one myself, real safe car. Anyway they are a real pain in the ass as far as service. They have this "Soyn" light that comes on, and you got to take it to a dealership. What are you doing right now?"

Sam cracked his first smile of the day. "Going down the trail to the Volvo dealership. Want to come along?"

"Sure would, Sam, sure would."

Sam and Harry gathered their necessities and were out the door.

LAS VEGAS, NEVADA
Thursday 5:30 A.M.

The phone rang at exactly 5:30 A.M. as programmed, and a mechanical voice announced that it was time to wake up. I dropped the phone in the cradle and was hoping for a snooze button, but no luck. I literally rolled out of bed. I had only gotten four hours sleep since Phil had mandated I go to the shooting range with Troy. What a waste of time, I thought.

Room 1224 was not the plush suite of rooms I had started the week in, but it was quite comfy and the bell staff had done a wonderful job organizing my new wardrobe and accessories. God, I loved my new clothes. It took me longer to decide the color coordination than it did for me to dress. Out of the shower, I called Mike, my morning babysitter-bodyguard.

"Mike, how do I order breakfast to be delivered to the bubble?"

"You eat more than just coffee in the morning?"

"Yes, usually."

Mike laughed. "Just call room service, just tell them who you are. They know you now; you got 'juice' son, and have them deliver it to the security center. One of our guys will check it and bring it in."

"Great, I'll see you down there."

"No" Mike interrupted emphatically. "I will be outside your door in less than ten minutes. Wait for me."

"OK, OK. I'll see ya."

I did as instructed—ordered my poached egg and rye toast, and then finished dressing. As promised, Mike was at my door and we walked down to the security center. Then I went into the bubble to study the incident report for the AM managers' meeting that Phil had promised I would run.

It was almost 8:30 A.M., and time for the shift meeting. I had been preparing for about an hour. I wanted more time but this was the best I could do. I felt I was ready.

I had coordinated with the banquet manager. The staff was going to be surprised. There would be no place to sit, only high cocktail tables from the bar; no seats, except, of course, for Phil.

I was just finishing up when Phil came in. "OK, Tiger, this day is yours. Let's go."

"I'm ready."

Phil and I were not the first to the meeting, and the natives were not happy. One was sitting on the floor.

"Chairs? What is this, a budget cut?" Dean Stone said, sitting on the floor.

"No, new procedure."

I had employed the services of one of the cocktail waitresses to hand out summery packets. At 8:45, everyone filed in, expecting to sit. "Surprise no chairs," Dean yelled.

I took charge immediately. "OK, folks, you will each make sure you have a packet with the list of incidents and other problems from last night. Note the Goldenrod sheet. That has a list of announcements. Take note of items four and five—those have to be communicated to all your staff. A new rule on medical insurance, and on the back of the sheet is a list of times for orientation meetings. There is a stack of the Goldenrod sheets in the back; as you exit, please take one for each of your employees. Those who have more than fifteen, call HR for a packet."

"Questions on the goldenrod pages?"

No one said anything.

"OK, back to the first page. There are four departments with incidents we need to talk about. OK, those department heads; you guys need to stay, along with anyone who witnessed the incidents. The rest, get out of here. Those going, get some sleep; those coming have a great day."

Most stood there almost in shock. Then, almost as if someone had just been startled, they moved out quickly.

I wasted no time. I passed more pages to Hilda the cocktail volunteer. "OK, gang, Mr. Franco, would you come up here. A short, stout gentleman walked forward. "Folks, this is our risk manager. He is the one we funnel all these incident reports to. Here's what we are going to do. If there was an incident, you will stay just a few moments so Bob can quickly review the report. If need be, we will give you a phone number so you may make a recorded statement. It is something new, called voicemail; you can talk as long as you wish. Bob will review your statements and, if need be, will call you back for a face-to-face interview."

Bob quickly reviewed the incident reports. "Sandy, the coffee that was spilled? Hot?"

Sandy "No, no, it had been sitting there. I think we will pay some drycleaners."

"OK, good, but next time be a little more detailed."

Bob looked at me.

"OK, guys, questions?"

"Either go home or get to work."

Phil, impressed, looked at his watch. Eighteen minutes.

LAS VEGAS, NEVADA
Thursday, 10 A.M.

Silas had been able to observe his target so very close just a few hours ago, and he felt confident now he would be able to get to him. He had noticed that there were two kinds of executive types. About eight of them were wearing very expensive suits, and there were about a dozen who wore off-the-rack suits and seemed to do nothing.

Silas surmised that there was more going on here, and that the off-the-rack—Sears or J.C. Penney suits—were FBI or perhaps other government "fuzz." If this was so, and it certainly appeared so, something was about to come down, and his client wanted Mr. Zavitch dead just as soon as possible.

Silas had not forgotten that he still was in possession of Andy Parker's FBI ID. To avoid the outside wallet being recognized, a new leather casing now carried the ID, which read Andrew Lewis Parker. It just may be his passport to the land of information. It was time for him to get into an off-the-rack suit and blend in with the rest of the gang.

In less than an hour, Silas was back on the floor of the Midway casino, now sporting a dark blue suit with a blue cotton shirt with button-down collar, and looking as much like Andrew Parker as his kit of disguises would let him. He would not offer information here; he would just act as if he belonged and go with the flow, never volunteering who he was, but if challenged would show his ID indignantly. After all, his ID was legit.

Silas kept his distance from everyone but would follow the crowd. When Phil and "Z" appeared from the security "sanctuary" (since getting into the center to kill Cliff would be virtually impossible), a cadre of blue suits would loosely follow the entourage.

Only once was Silas challenged, and it was by a Midway security officer with four FBI and Treasury looking on. One large officer in full Midway casino security regalia had been watching Silas while on the podium outside the Security Center. Once he was relieved, he walked over and politely asked, "Sir, I don't recognize you. May I ask who you are?"

"I am Lewis Parker," he said, using Andrew's middle name as his given. Silas shrugged and looked at his "comrades" as he reached into his pocket to produce the standard FBI credentials.

The security guard then took the ID in both hands and scrutinized it. "Andrew Lewis?" the guard queried.

"Yes, there are a couple of Andrews; we get mixed up all the time," he said loudly. "I go by Lewis."

Like serendipity, the other agents filed in closer to 'Andrew Lewis,' almost to grant him support. The guard closed the wallet and handed it back to Silas.

"Thank you, sir." The guard withdrew.

"Jesus, and some people think we are tight asses. These casino guards don't trust anyone." The agent extended his right hand. "Frank Gallino."

Silas, relieved, shook the hand of Agent Gallino. "Lewis Parker." Silas knew not to volunteer any information and just listen. It appeared a miracle had happened now. 'Lewis Parker' was now one of the family of several different families. When he was introduced, he found that there were agents from Justice, Treasury, IRS—it was just one big, confused, happy family, and Lewis Parker was certainly glad to be part of it.

SARASOTA, FLORIDA
Thursday, 12 Noon.

Sam Simpson and Harry Seed made their way through the sunshine to the Volvo dealership on the South Trail. Soon after arriving, they made there way to the service department where, Harry, a lifelong Volvo owner, seemed to know everyone in the house.

"Mister Seed!" a young mechanic yelled across the garage.

"Hello, Steven. Is Teddy around?"

"Lunch."

"Where?"

"Management tends to get to sit down for lunch. I would guess the Salty Dog, across the way."

"Thanks."

Not in any hurry, both thought it would be a good idea to get some grub, and started across the street. As they entered, a loud, booming voice came from the back of the restaurant.

"Hey, Seed!"

Harry waved and smiled, and walked back to join his old friend.

"Harry, I just started. I am sure you can catch up."

"Teddy Patrick, magician of motors, I would like you to meet Sam Simpson, detective extraordinaire."

Teddy and Sam shook hands and they all sat down.

A young waitress came right by. "Can I help you guys?"

"Sure. Teddy, what's good?"

"All-you-can-eat boiled shrimp. They just keep bringing it." Teddy endorsed

Sam was a bit excited. "Certainly sounds good to me."

"I'm on for shrimp, too, and give him the bill for all three of us," pointing to Sam, "and sweet iced tea."

Sam: "Make that two."

"Damn, Sam that is nice of you," Teddy said to his brand new friend.

"Consider it a bribe," Sam responded.

"Cool. I take bribes. What do you need?"

"The owner of this VIN." Sam produced the plate.

Teddy picked it up. "Sure, no problem. If they ever had the car serviced in the Volvo system, we can find him. Do you want me to call it in, or can it wait until we get back?"

Just then, the iced tea arrived. Sam and Harry looked at each other as the waitress brought Teddy his first plate.

"We could be here for a while, but it can wait," Harry said.

"Yeah, it can wait."

LAS VEGAS, NEVADA MIDWAY CASINO
1:00 P.M. Thursday.

Silas was just hanging around with the other agents when word got around that there was going to be a meeting at the west conference room. No one was to enter until 5 P.M., since the room was being swept for bugs. Of course, the events of the last 48 hours of the Midway's life were a secret, and would be unveiled under seal.

In the meantime, Silas just blended in, making sure that he only talked about sports, gambling, and sex. If he tried to enter into a conversation, he could show his hand. It was amazing; most of the other agents thought he was brilliant, mainly because he did not say much.

Steve Lambert finally arrived after 36 hours sequestered at the FBI building, along with Tim Floyd and Toni Cardona. Toni was a rarity, an honest-to-God foxy agent. But of course no one spoke a word, although she did get a few long looks.

This was crunch time, the countdown; everything that had been done the last 20 or so years had come down to this. Everyone was in place now at the Midway, all except "Control 3." He would run the operation from an undisclosed location.

Steve Lambert led the entourage to the security center for a meeting with Roger Mackey. Steve used his active code key at the Security Center and entered with Tim Floyd and Toni Cardona in tow. I was in Phil's office, studying the numbers from the previous shift and taking notes of statistical anomalies.

Steve motioned to Tim and Toni to huddle with him. "You guys go fill in Cliff..." He paused, "...keep it to generalities right now. Our plans are still fluid and dynamic, so let him know that nothing is in stone right now."

"OK, just general info now," Toni responded.

Tim did not answer, and drew a long stare from Lambert.

"OK, mushroom time. We feed him shit and keep him in the dark."

Lambert said nothing for a long moment, then responded with a short pointed "thank you," and walked off toward the bubble and his meeting with Mackey.

Roger waited alone. Lambert entered and activated the anti-bugging software. Roger started the conversation: "Tomorrow still D-Day?"

Lambert sat and opened his brief case without making eye contact. Then, with a snap of his wrist, he laid down three files in front of him, then sat back in the custom made-chair of the bubble. "8 P.M. tomorrow night."

"I thought it would be earlier. It would make sense."

"8 P.M. in Vegas, 11 P.M. on the East Coast, ready for the 11:00 o'clock news."

Mackey smiled in disgust. "Are you going to meet here?"

Lambert sat up in his chair, elbows now on the table. "No. Throughout the day, we will have agents filter in and position themselves at various positions around the property."

"Will I have knowledge of them?"

"Of course. You will be key in the whole operation."

"Then?" Roger asked. "You and your guys will come in and take over the security center, cage, and counting rooms?"

Lambert, now very uncomfortable, adjusted his position in his chair and drummed the desk with his open palms."

"Roger, we are really going to need you on this; your folks are going to...," he corrected, "...need to contain themselves and stand down."

"Jesus, you guys are going to storm the place."

"Not my idea. It is the new GM and the State. They want a spectacle."

"A spectacle. Christ, it may be a blood bath."

"No, No, Roger. It is your job to keep everything cool."

"Steve, you know this is bullshit. It is fucking ridiculous. Just come in here with warrants and I will give you the fucking keys to the kingdom, and no one has to know."

"Roger, that is the point. They want a spectacle. That is why it is going to be news at 11. OK, here is how it is coming down. You and I will be here to run the show. At 7:00 P.M."

Steve rolled out a diagram of the property and continued. "At 7:45 P.M., we will seal the doors. No one will be able to enter. Anyone wanting out will be allowed to leave. Then, at 7:55, twenty-five fully armed agents will enter here." Steve points to the map "Main entrance, twenty-five agents at the rear, and ten at each of the side entrances."

Roger shook his head. "Press?"

"Oh yeah. Following the armed agents will be four groups of agents who will systematically close down all the table games, and you will have to shut down the electricity to all the slots. This next group will seal everything. Total lockdown."

"You guys are fucking nuts, Steve. You got enough guys here right now. Hell, I will shut everything down now and give you the place. Someone may get hurt."

"Roger, no one is going to get hurt. Do your job and all will be fine."

"I need to debrief my folks."

"Tomorrow at 3:00. We are debriefing out agents here at 5 P.M. today."

"I heard."

"Phil and Mark?"

"I will tell them, I owe them at least that," sounding guilty for his betrayal.

"They were both fucked, one way or the other," Roger said in a consoling manner.

Steve nodded.

"What happens next?"

"We round up all the execs and put them in the main ballroom."

"Arrest them?"

"No, we just want them out of the way."

"Phil and Mark?"

"Phil, Mark, and Cliff will be separated, and each will have an agent assigned to them. It will take us about six to eight hours to secure the casino. At 6 A.M., we will take them out to the

Searchlight Air strip and then Phil and Mark will be off to witness protection. Cliff will have a vacation until Monday, and we will get him back here for work."

"Wooo. Zavitch was NOT to leave the property."

"Things change. The new GM does not want any old 'apparent' authority. We want to have the property up and running Monday morning, and he will just get in the way."

Roger did not like what he was hearing, but had very limited options.

Things were more upbeat inside Phil's old office.

I was up to my elbows in paper and greenbar computer printouts when Toni and Tim walked in.

I sat back behind my former boss's desk and tossed the pen down.

"Gee, guys. I thought you guys were gone. I am glad to see you back. Understand things are happening and the new management will be taking over tomorrow?" What is happening? Big meeting at the conference center for you guys. Should I be there?"

Almost simultaneously, both Tim and Toni said, "No!"

"Well are you guys going to fill me in? How about over lunch? I'll buy; you know I can do that." I laughed.

"Yep, I understand you can do pretty much want you want here now" Tim responded.

"Cliff," Toni cut in on Tim's last word, "our situation is fluid right now and we will let you know just when and where you need to be."

I leaned back. "Jesus, that sounded good," looking to his old friend. "They are going to leave me in the dark. Does Phil know what is happening?"

Both again, "No." Then they looked at each other and both laughed.

I again suggested lunch.

"Hey, I need to watch over shift change in less than two hours. Let's go."

"No fish and chips," Tim said emphatically.

"What? I live on fish and chips."

"I know. I want steak."

I turned to Toni, trying to get some support for the Jesters Pub.

"I vote for steak, Cliff."

"You guys are ganging up on me. OK, it's the Ringmasters Steak House."

We left the security center. I knew that I would have to be back by 2:45 to supervise the shift change, then two hours later make an appearance at the count. I had not stopped working for days.

SARASOTA, FLORIDA
Thursday, 1:00 P.M.

The Volvo supercomputers churned out the address, phone number, and when Cliff Zavitch had last had his oil changed.

Harry and Sam gave their thanks and headed for the address over on Ingram Avenue. While Sam drove, Harry called in the Zavitch information and, as they arrived at the Ingram House, Harry had the complete boring information on Zavitch

Both exited the car and started to look around the quiet house in the very quite neighborhood. Harry followed Sam as Sam peeked in every window and tried each door.

"OK, what is the deal with him? Did he become a crispy critter because of a drug deal or something?"

"No, this guy sounds like a real honest-to-goodness Boy Scout. Nothing, and there is a missing persons report filed yesterday."

Sam kept listening to Harry as he stood in the carport where the burnt Volvo once was.

"Who filed the report?" Sam asked.

Harry looked at his notes. "A Mrs. Bear on Lemonwood."

Sam suddenly was interested. "Mrs. Lisa Bear?"

"Yeah."

"And Cliff Zavitch worked for Great International Global Life and Casualty."

"OK, are we becoming psychic?"

"No, her husband Chris was my insurance agent, and I think this Zavitch guy took over his account when Chris died."

"Did you know this guy well?"

"Who, Bear or Zavitch?"

"Bear."

"Well, Chris Bear was big-time in Sarasota. Everyone knew him. He was everyone's insurance guy when Sarasota was small. Great guy active in the community. Hell, I helped him build a couple houses for Habitat for Humanity. We are going to Lemonwood; it is only a few blocks away."

Lisa Bear was everyone's grandmother. She and Christopher Bear had four grown kids of their own and two grandchildren. You could never find better, more hospitable folks than the Bears. Sam took the lead as he walked to the door.

"Oh my, Sam Simpson. God bless you, I am so happy to see you." She was truly excited to see him

"Lisa, it is great to see you. This is Detective Harry Seed," as he gave her a hug.

"Hello Harry. Please, please come in."

Once in Lisa, turned and pointed. "Please sit. What can I get you to drink?"

Harry declined, "No, thank you."

Sam: "Are you still brewing real Southern iced tea?"

"Absolutely."

Both were still standing when Sam suggested they move to the kitchen, and get some tea and chat.

"Sam, are you here about Cliff?"

"Yes, as a matter of fact we are."

Lisa Bear passed a large tumbler of her special brew to Sam. "I know something has happened to him. I just know it. He always comes over here on Tuesday afternoon for lunch. You know both of them, Cliff and Chris, would be here to eat Tuesday's. Sam, he missed. He did not call. I drove by his house." She started to talk slower.

"And I heard about that car. It was the same kind Cliff drove that burned. Sam, is he dead?"

Sam was not going to lie to his old friend's widow. "Lisa, we cannot tell you much, but there is something very strange here. The FBI took over the investigation on the burned car. It appears it was Cliff's, but we do not know where Cliff is."

Harry questioned: "Mrs. Bear, can you tell us when was the last time you saw or talked to him."

"Last Tuesday."

"Anybody else know about him—friends, parents, others?

"No, maybe the Elwood boy. He works with Cliff."

Sam and Harry took notes, and then decided it was time to visit Great International Global Life and Casualty. They arrived at the Pender building at about 4:00 P.M. There was only a handful of agents left; most were getting ready for their after-dinner prime time presentations. No one said anything to them when they saw a sign that read Tony Lopez, Managing Agent. There seemed to be no one around and the door was a bit ajar. Sam tapped on the door and proceeded inside.

Tony was relaxed, lying back, and was startled.

"Who the hell are you guys?" he screamed in a panic.

Then there was a thump as if someone had hit his or her head on the bottom of his desktop.

Harry and Cliff produced their shields, looked at each other, smiled, and then looked back at Mr. Lopez.

"Mr. Lopez, excuse us. The door was open. "I am Inspector Simpson, this is Detective Seed, and we are here about business. We need to talk."

"Certainly. I must fix this computer," he said as he disappeared under the desk.

Sam and Harry looked at each other, but were not amused.

In a moment, two bodies emerged—Tony and a very beautiful young lady, who wiped her mouth and quickly exited the office without introduction.

Sam started without any hesitation. "Mr. Lopez, do you know a Mr. Clifford Zavitch?"

"Zavitch, yes. Are you investigating the fraud case with the SEC?"

Sam and Harry looked at each other, puzzled.

"SEC fraud?"

"Yes, officers. Mr. Zavitch had been implicated in a huge fraud case. As a matter of fact, Mr. Zavitch has been suspended from this office."

At this point, Alexandria returned, very composed.

"Mr. Lopez, is the computer fixed?" She tried to deflect her past compromising position. Normally, she would not have come back, but curiosity got the best of her.

"These officers are investigating Mr. Zavitch."

"Oh, about the fraud case?"

Again Sam and Harry looked at each other, more puzzled than ever. Sam cut in:

"No, Mr. Zavitch has disappeared."

"That does not surprise me" Lopez said confidently.

"Really, why is that?" Harry asked as he opened his notebook

"Trouble," Alexandria butted in.

"We found his car burned Monday" Sam mentioned.

"Doesn't surprise me at all" Alexandria said.

"Why is that?"

"Sounds to me that it was a drug thing. You know, I always thought he was a drug pusher," Alexandria firmly stated.

Maybe too firmly. Sam and Harry started to smell a pile of bullshit.

Sam thanked both of them for their information, and then asked if they knew a Mr. Elwood?

"Yes, Mr. Elwood works with us," Lopez said.

"Could we get his phone number and address?"

"Yes, of course. Alexandria will be happy to get you that information."

Alexandria opened Tony's Rolodex, found Elwood's information, and wrote it on a card.

Harry tapped his notebook on his knuckle. "Thank you so much."

Sam said nothing.

In the elevator, Sam spoke:

"I thought they were going to accuse Zavitch of killing Kennedy."

"You buy any of it?" Harry asked.

"Nope, not a bit."

Harry looked at the card given to him by Alexandria. "This guy Elwood lives just across the way at the Watergate."

Sam shook his head. "OK, let's go."

It just took a few moments to make it over to the high rise across the street. The condo was a very high-end building. They met the doorman, who offered to announce them to Mr. Elwood.

Kurt did not invite the officers up to his condo; instead, he made his way down from his digs to the lobby.

In the interim, Harry took in the opulence. "This guy must sell a shitload of insurance."

Sam shrugged.

As Kurt made his way off the elevator, they looked around.

Sam loudly asked, "Are you Kurt Elwood?"

"Yes, I am," Kurt said politely. "How might I help you?"

"Do you know a Mr. Cliff Zavitch?"

"Yes, very well."

"Do you know where he is?"

"Yeah, he is in Vegas."

"Vegas? Are you serious?"

"Yeah. It is his hometown. It was strange; his old boss from one of the casinos called and asked him to come out. One of his old classmates was to pick him up and escort him out?"

Sam and Harry were now more bewildered than when they spoke to Lopez.

Harry asked, "Are you sure?"

Kurt shrugged. "Yeah, I last saw him at dinner at Clancy's Monday night. He left to meet his friend."

"Remember his name?"

"What is this about?" Kurt asked.

"We found Cliff's car burned Monday."

"Shit, yeah." He paused…"I think it was either Jim or Tim Floyd.

"What about the casino?"

"That is easy, it was the Midway, and his boss, his old boss, the one who called, was Phil Irish. Cliff always talked about him."

"We talked to a Mr. Lopez. He thought he could have been mixed up in some drug deal," Harry told Kurt.

Kurt laughed. "No, not Cliff. The management hates his guts. He is a good guy and will not play their games. They are out to get him. If anything, hell, I would think they would kill him."

"Who?"

"Lopez and the insurance company." He paused. " I have the keys to his house. Do you need them?"

"No, not yet, but we will note that."

"Thank you, Mr. Elwood."

They walked out, making notes. Once in the car, Sam asked Harry to call in and find out what they could find out about Tim Floyd and Phil Irish."

LAS VEGAS
Thursday, 3:00 P.M.

I excused myself from dinner and headed over to the catacombs beneath the casino. It was time for the count. Phil was not with me, so it was becoming apparent that I was in charge. I was walking confidently and followed Phil's routine as if I had been doing it for years.

I entered the counting room, was given a clipboard, and took my seat to quasi-supervise the count. Although I looked like I was intensely reading the report, I was studying notes I had made about the last shift discrepancies. After about 45 minutes, I had enough. I got up and signed off, and handed the clipboard to one of the Treasury guys.

It was now going on 5:00 P.M. and I wanted to catch up with Phil to compare notes regarding tomorrow's festivities. I walked directly through the pit, confidently stopping and talking with floor persons, all wishing me well, and a few welcoming me back after so many years.

At 5:35, I arrived at the Security Center, but Phil was nowhere to be found. I sat in Phil's office and picked up the phone to have him paged. Just as I hung up, Kevin tapped on the door. I motioned for him to enter, and he walked in with what looked like a ton of greenbar.

"Cliff, here are the daily runs. Where do you want them?

"Right here." I pointed right in front of me. "Any rumors floating about tomorrow?

"All kinds. Can't tell what is even partially true; there is a bunch of bullshit out there."

"What is your best guess?"

"Don't really know, Cliff. Do you need anything else?"

"No, thanks."

Kevin withdrew and I went on studying. It was about 7:00 when Phil entered the office.

"Need any help?"

"No, I think I am getting the hang of it. Have your heard anything about tomorrow?"

Phil extinguished his cigarette in the ashtray that occupied "his" desk. He turned and looked to the Bubble, then stood and exited the office. I followed. Once we were both comfortable in the bubble, Phil shook his head, "Cliff, they are supposed to keep me and Karl in the dark. I had to go off property to find out what the fuck is going on."

"And…?"

"It is not fucking good. Those cocksuckers from Carson City and D.C. are going to make a spectacle of the takeover. It's going to happen about 8 :00 tomorrow night. I want you to stay put stay with Troy and follow his lead."

"Do you want me to handle the takeover?"

"NO!" Phil said loudly, using his left hand in a striking motion.

"Absolutely not. I don't want your picture or name in the paper associated with anything negative. My understanding is once the takeover is complete, that you will be announced as part of the new régime. The general manager will be someone named Michael Milton. He is very politically connected and is, I understand, a first class prick."

"That is going to be my boss?"

"Yep."

"Shit. Any other good news."

"Yeah, one more thing. He hates you."

"Hates me? Hell, I don't even know him."

"I think he anticipates what is going to be happening. Cliff, the staff and all the management is going to look to you. He can't fire everyone, and if you play your cards right you could pull an all-time coup and get rid of the cocksucker."

"So what happens tomorrow?"

"Hang loose and stay close to Troy. But tonight you are in charge. Better go and check things out."

With that, both left the bubble, and Phil went off property to relax with friends and say some good-byes at other casinos.

I certainly had my plate full. I attended a staff meeting for the day shift, received some requests from some departments heads, and everyone was asking what was going to happen tomorrow. Rumors flew, and were of various opinions, from a quiet transition to an extreme takeover. I was taking pages for Phil, which I had done several years ago. Then I only had to take a message; now I had to act on whatever the situation called for. At 6:15, I got a call from Sid Goldstein, one of the hotel's hosts. It seemed that one of his whales was unhappy with the accommodations and requested an upgrade.

"Sid, what has his play been?"

"Light."

"Family here? Wife?"

"No."

"No friend?"

"Girlfriend?"

"Ooh, yeah."

"OK, here is what I want you to do. Tell him we are working on the upgrade, but tell him we have arranged for a makeover and spa time for his friend. See if that improves his play. If so, make arrangements for an upgrade; if not give him a comp for the late show."

"Spa? What if she doesn't go for it?"

"Sid, try it. Let me know."

"OK boss."

I put down the phone, then realized I had just been called "boss." In Vegas, that is huge. I continued to take care of putting out fires, approving markers, and rejecting a few. Then I heard my page.

"Mr. Zavitch, Mr. Clifford Zavitch."

I looked at Troy. "You are getting popular, boss. Better take it" Troy smiled, but at the same time he keyed the radio to check on the page.

"This is Zavitch."

"One moment, Mr. Zavitch."

"Hello." A familiar female voice seemed to be shouting into the phone. The caller was obviously calling from the casino; the background noise was extremely annoying.

"Yes, this is Zavitch."

" Z, it is Beth. Do you have time to talk."

"Hello Beth. Ah, sure." I was both scoping out the casino, trying to find a suitable meeting place and seeing where she was. "Marry Go Round Lounge—five minutes." I said.

"OK, five minutes."

I filled Troy in as we walked over to the lounge. Silas was watching intently, now completely accepted as an FBI Agent.

I had to take two more calls to put out a couple of fires, and was delayed by about twenty minutes. Beth was already sitting and had ordered and paid for her drink, something I would have been able to do with a stroke of a pen.

As soon as I arrived into the lounge, with Troy a few steps behind, everyone seemed to jump into attention. A host ran up to me. "Mr. Zavitch, can I help you?" Just then, I spotted Beth sitting alone in the corner. Upon my arrival, Beth stood and gave me a hug that I abruptly rejected. In less than a second, a waitress came tableside.

"Mr. Zavitch, what may I get you?"

"Coffee, black in a glass."

With nothing else said, she walked away.

"So, you are with the FBI also. Jesus, am I the only one not working for the government?"

"It just seems that way."

" OK, can you tell me what is going on and what will happen tomorrow?"

"No, I don't have a clue. I am not an agent, Cliff. Tim just invited me to the room Monday to see you. By the way, I am so sorry about what happened. Can I make it up to you?" She paused. "Dinner, my place?"

I sat back and was paged again. I signaled for the phone, which was promptly fetched.

"Zavitch."

"Cliff, it's Moe Miller. We got another hit on that face recognition software. I think we have a card cheat visiting us tonight."

"Playing yet?"

"No, just walking around."

"Page me when he's found a table."

"Done."

I hung the phone up just as my coffee arrived—as I requested, in a cocktail glass with a napkin around it, held on with a rubber band.

"So, Beth, what have you been doing the last eighteen years?" I smiled.

"Well I went to Nevada-Reno, graduated top in my class, and then fell in love with a man who wanted to be a doctor. Worked my ass off putting him through med school, and then he dumped me."

I said nothing and let her continue.

"OK, let me see. That is about 1978. Fell in love yet again, to a real freak. My skin crawls; what did I ever see in him?"

She drained her glass and I signaled for another drink for her. Here was the love of my life baring her soul to me, and I was just overwhelmed and could not say anything. She took a moment and her drink arrived; she took a sip.

"I only stayed with him eighteen months. I..." She started to stammer.

"Did he hurt you?"

She did not answer.

I quickly changed the subject. "How did you get with the FBI?"

"Well, my degree was in psychology and I saw an ad, interviewed, and I am with the FBI."

"What do you know about this, me, my situation?

"Cliff I don't know anything. What about you? How did you get here?"

"I live…er…lived in Sarasota, Florida. Phil called, and Tim picked me up, and I am here running a casino."

"Just like that?"

"Pretty much."

"And your car?"

"Oh, yeah, and I have someone or a group who is trying to kill me."

"That is a small detail."

'Yeah, something I could do without."

"Your mom?" Beth asked with concern.

"Dead."

"Married?"

"No."

"Girlfriends?"

I laughed. "Nothing to talk about."

"If I ask you a question, would you tell me the truth?"

"About the casino?"

"No."

"Sure, ask."

"Did you love me?"

I answered without hesitation. "Yes, always have, and still do. And you about me?"

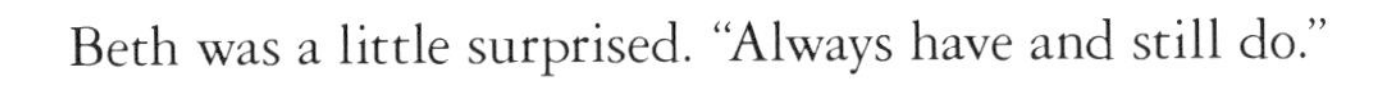

Beth was a little surprised. "Always have and still do."

Then I was paged yet again. This time the phone was at my side."

"Zavitch."

"Cliff, he found a table."

"OK Moe. I'll be right there."

I hung up and looked at Beth.

"OK, Cliff, what do we do now?"

"I don't know Beth. This is my life now it is a lot less glamorous than folks think. I know I would be married to the Midway, I doubt I will have time for a life."

"Tomorrow?" Beth asked hopefully.

"Morning?" I asked

"I work, Cliff. Call me." I then met my escort and proceeded to the security center.

SARASOTA, FLORIDA
Thursday, 6:00 PM

Sam and Harry finished giving their presentation to Captain Larson. Captain Larson was a cop's cop. He had started with Sam years ago and they were friends, but Lawson had progressed and furthered his career. He liked Sam but he knew Sam could press the envelop.

Larson summarized: "OK, we have a missing person, a charred Volvo that belonged to the missing person, witnesses who say he was involved with high level white-collar crimes as well as drug trafficking. Other witnesses say he was a boy scout. Then others say he is vacationing in Las Vegas."

Captain Larson adjusted his posture and sat upright at his desk. "I think our boy is relaxing in Vegas having a good old time."

"What about the FBI?" Harry asked.

Larson again sat back in his chair. "Now that is strange. I can't find out anything about the car, where it is, where it went, nothing. Nor can I find anything out about the body that was in it." He paused and looked at Sam, "OK, what do you want to do?"

"Go to Vegas, of course. Need to follow these leads. A Sarasota citizen could be in trouble" Sam said, only half believing that Clifford Zavitch was in any peril but wanting to boondoggle a trip to the Magic City in the desert.

"Are you nuts? For a missing person?"

Harry cut in, "Captain missing person, one dead body, one totaled Volvo, and FBI intervention."

"OK, have you guys tried to contact the FBI?"

"They will not tell us a thing, total stonewall," Sam said.

"Anyone call Vegas?"

"The Midway has him checking in one day and now he is gone, and they are not answering any questions about him? We checked the airlines; nothing. He could be kidnapped."

"Vegas police?"

"Nothing."

"Captain, there are some problems here. This guy could be either a victim or a perp. Maybe he could have killed whoever was in the car and torched the car," Harry Seed speculated.

"This looks like an FBI problem," Larson said.

"Captain, really, we have a missing person, a missing persons report. We have pictures of a burnt car and a body here right here in our city, and you think it is a federal problem?"

"Oh shit, I think I am going to fucking regret this., OK, you guys. Call in every day, check in with Las Vegas Metro, and if there are no leads there you guys are back. No parties, no gambling, no women, is this understood?"

"OK Captain. We can leave tonight at 2 A.M."

"Get the fuck out of here." The captain paused "And have a good time," half knowing that this was a bullshit assignments and a free adventure for two veteran cops.

Harry and Sam hurried out of the office. Once out of earshot:

"Sam, that went well," Harry laughed.

"I honestly didn't think we could pull it off."

"Sam, do you think this guy is in trouble?"

"No, we will probably find him with some honey. This will be a stress-free vacation."

"How do I explain this to the wife?"

"Police business. Thank God, I don't have that problem," "Sam chided. "Don't you want to go?"

"Of course, my daughter is at the house with four of her girlfriends for semester break. I think it is best for me to get out of here anyway." Harry shrugged. "Pick you up at 11:30."

"Sounds good. I'll go downstairs to make arrangements. Got any cash?"

"A few bucks."

"Can I borrow a C-note?

"Shit, things never change. See ya at your house at 11:30."

CHICAGO, ILLINOIS
Thursday, 4:00 P.M.

The sleek black jet of Bruggerman, Jancan, Frasier and Scott made its way back to Chicago for a quick turnaround back to San Francisco. Although this was not the most economical arrangement, the firm could not care less, since their client had deep pockets and would not squabble about a few thousand here or there.

Mr. Jancan was alone in the large conference room. Like all the offices, it had a spectacular view of the great city of Chicago.

The entrance of Mr. Grant Scott, the fourth partner of Bruggerman, Jancan, Frasier and Scott, disturbed the serene atmosphere.

"Jesus fucking Christ, J. What is so God damn important to get me away from my fucking honeymoon?"

J did not flinch or even look up. "Grant, it is not like it was your first one. Besides..." Mr. Jancan turned to look at Grant, then continued, "...Besides, we need the best constitutional lawyer in the U.S. for this," and he pointed to the stack of files on the desk.

Scott put his suitcase on one of the huge leather conference room chairs, sat down in front of a pile of files and started to read. "J, they can't do this, no way."

"I agree, but it will happen."

"And how do we know this will happen?"

The now senior partner merely raised his head above the files he was reading and lowered his reading glasses as an answer.

The subject was dropped.

"San Francisco?"

"Frasier is already there and has us set up."

"When do we leave?"

"Now" He packed up his files and called for the limo. They were off.

LAS VEGAS, NEVADA MIDWAY CASINO
5:00 P.M. Thursday

The feds were migrating to the north conference room, including. Silas, a/k/a Andrew Lewis Parker, and his new best friend, Agent Frank Gallino. While drinking coffee, the agents slowly made their way to get the rundown on what will happen the next day, and what their individual assignments were going to be.

Steve Lambert would run the meeting, with Tim Floyd and Toni Cardona absent since they had already been briefed. Roger Mackey was there only for show; he would be introduced but would say little. There was only one person at the door checking for valid IDs, but there was no roll call to check off the attendees.

Steve Lambert looked at his watch and signaled to have the door sealed.

"OK, folks, this is the culmination of almost twenty years of work. I know most of you know the situation, but here are our final plans. First, let me introduce the Midway's chief of security, Roger Mackey."

Mackey, who stood behind Lambert stone-faced, raised his right hand and took a half step forward and then back. There was no applause of acknowledgment, and he expected none.

Lambert began: "It goes without saying that nothing, I mean nothing, leaves this room. Complete surprise is the key to our success. Now, at 8:00 P.M. tomorrow, the United States government will seize the Midway Hotel and Casino. With eighty armed agents, we will secure the premises. Mr. Mackey will order his security force to "stand down" and aid us in the takeover.

"Warrants and subpoenas will be given to Mr. Phil Irish and Mr. Mark Karl. Mr. Irish and Mr. Karl will be taken into protective, again protective, custody. They will aid us in gaining control of sensitive areas. In some of the areas, such as the counting room, we have agents there 24/7. We will need to get access to accounting and several other locations. After we have secured all departments, all executive personnel will be removed to this conference room and held until they can be processed."

"Will they be under arrest?" one agent questioned.

"No, detained."

"What processing?"

Lambert shook his head, half smiling and half irritated. "I am getting there."

"We want everyone treated with respect. First, check their credentials. Make sure they are on our employee rosters. New hires may not be listed. Those folks will need to be processed with Mr. Mackey and his staff. Next, if they are a 'department head', they will need to be detained and moved to another location. Right now, they will be escorted to the main ballroom."

Lambert continued: "Those working on time cards, non-department heads, non-exempt employees, are to be told to call 702-555-1212 for reporting instructions. They will need to explain what they do, their job function, who they report to, and their shift or hours. Then they can sign out and will be free to leave.

"What about the hotel guests?"

"Only the casino and the restaurants will be closed. We will encourage guests to leave, and we will not check in any guests until Monday, but we will keep a small group of hotel personnel to maintain service—minimal service."

"When will the casino open?"

"We wanted it to open Saturday, but expect the hotel and casino to open Monday afternoon, swing shift—a new entity, partly operated by the state of Nevada and the federal government. The new entity will be known as "FECMAC, Inc., short for Federal Emergency Casino Management Corporation."

"What do we tell the employees about pay?"

"They will be paid if they were to be scheduled during the time the casino is closed; time off with pay. About the execs and the department heads, they will be detained until we can interview each of them. It may take some time. If the interviewer, our attorneys, finds that they will not be witnesses for our case, they will be free to leave and given the number to call to return back to work. Those who we think can be a witness will be subpoenaed and ordered not to leave Vegas."

"How many of those do you think we will find?"

"Not many. We already have most of our witnesses already sewn up. We are just making sure no one is falling through the cracks."

"Will all of the execs be rehired?"

"Most. Our goal is to get this property up and running, without the least amount of interruption. A Mr. Michael Milton will be taking over for the state as general manager and a Mr. Clifford Zavitch, a former employee, very well liked and not involved with the problems, will be the assistant GM."

Silas sat forward in his seat and took note. Things now were making sense. Clifford Zavitch was not to become assistant GM. Frank Gallino then asked the question he was dying to ask, "What about Irish and Karl?"

"As soon as we have interviewed all execs, we will transport them to Searchlight and hand them off to the witness protection group."

"When will Milton and Zavitch be brought in?"

"Both are here. Milton is staying downtown and Zavitch is here now. I don't want them around. I will have Zavitch stay in his room or I will get him off property. We don't want him around until they are ready to take over."

Lambert paused.

"OK, security gets briefed tomorrow at 3:00 P.M. I want all of you back here at 4:00 P.M. tomorrow for final instructions.

LAS VEGAS, NEVADA MIDWAY CASINO
6:30 P.M. Thursday

I had entered the security center and Moe Miller was in the captain's chair. Moe stood to cede his place to me, but I motioned for him to stay. "I'm going to be a spectator this time."

"OK, boss, I'll drive. Right now, he has been straight up, and actually losing. His M.O. is to use a partner to feed him cards. So far, nothing." Miller just watched, then gave an order, "Give me a wide shot of the table" Instantly the large screen in the middle of the control room showed a wide shot of the table and the two tables on either side.

"OK, pan left." The screen moved. "OK, right."

I asked, "What is his play?"

Dom Stimus, who was sitting at a smaller console, answered "$100 per hand and losing."

"Keep him playing."

All laughed. "Boss, something will happen. Trust me; these guys don't change."

Things were starting to get boring until a busty attractive blonde took a seat next to him.

Moe ordered, "Run a face on the blonde, please."

"Running," a voice replied.

After a moment, "Nothing on the blonde; may be new talent or just a player."

Just when it was getting good, I was interrupted. "Cliff, Phil is on the line. Wants you to take it in the bubble."

I entered the bubble and activated the security.

"Hello Phil. Where are you?"

"Just making the rounds and saying some good-byes and looking for some information. How is it going with you?"

"Pretty good. One of Sid Goldstein's players has a girl friend who was distracting him from play, so I got her a Spa package."

"Spa?"

"Yeah, Spa—facial, hair, massage, the whole deal."

"Good idea. Let me know how it turned out. Look, got some info. It is from one of our folks who passed it on outside so it would get to me. Looks like the shit is going to hit the fan at 8:00 P.M. Those cocksuckers are going to come in and make a big deal out of taking over—about 100 agents, guns and everything. Tomorrow morning, get with Troy. I want you to meet me at the Dunes Buffet for breakfast. The place is huge, and we can blend in. Nine-fifteen."

"OK, 9:15 at the Dunes."

"Look, you are in charge tonight. Concentrate and watch everything. Use all your senses. Watch, smell, listen, feel, and even taste. You must become aware of everything, and don't play hero. Keep Troy with you at all times."

"OK, Boss, I'll be careful."

The phone went dead.

It was almost 8:00 P.M. and the floor was getting busy. I walked out of the bubble and found Troy.

"Let's take a walk."

"Right behind you."

Once out, I took the outside perimeter of the floor, remembering that was the safest place to talk. Once in a safe area, I motioned to Troy. "Tomorrow morning."

Troy interrupted, "9:15, Dunes."

I wondered why I was surprised. We continued to walk and cut through the floor, stopping occasionally to watch the play. I spotted Sid Goldstein and walked next to him.

Sid turned to me. "What a brilliant idea—the Spa! She is in seventh heaven and he is up to his old play. Good thinking, Boss."

We exchanged smiles and parted. Troy and I positioned us on the first level and got a good inconspicuous view of the blackjack pit with the known cheat. Whatever he was doing, he was not doing it right. He was losing, a little strange, but good for the house. It was 10:37 P.M. It was another 15 hour day, but I would get used to those. I made my way up to the third level, to a lookout with a velvet rope barring entry to most. With Troy a few feet behind, I removed the rope and gave myself access, then closed the rope behind me. Troy turned to guard the entrance.

It was almost time for the shift change and I, the one who had gone to school and studied how to run a casino, was now in my element. I stretched my arms wide, leaned on the rail, and watched the smooth shift change. Sarasota, Tony, Alexandria, sweet Alexandria, if she could only see me now, in a $700 Armani suit with my personal bodyguard, running an entire casino. The humiliation I had endured at their hands was now behind me. I was home.

SAN FRANCISCO, CALIFORNIA
Thursday, 8:30 P.M.

J. Jancan had been to The Clift several times, but he was always impressed. Franklin Frasier was there to meet J and Grant, and immediately gave them a tour of their temporary office. It was impressive; the entire ninth floor was made into an efficient office.

"I selected twelve researchers and paralegals. They are sharp and competent and will be here at 7:00 A.M.

Of all the partners, Frasier was the least spectacular of practicing lawyers, but Frasier was an organizer and Jancan knew it. He was detailed and meticulous. Frasier was the front man and he had outdone himself. In less than 24 hours, he managed to clone their Chicago office on the ninth floor of a swank hotel 1,500 miles away. Frasier had taken pictures of Jancan and Scott's offices and desks, and had made duplicate offices so the partners would be comfortable and able to function.

"Frasier, you did a hell of a job."

Jancan instructed, " OK, as soon as our staff is in we start them doing research. We know we are going to be hit, but not exactly sure how. I have an idea but I want to cover every possible contingency. The faster we can get our job done, the better for our client and the more money we can make. We will have to move fast, Grant, what was the fastest you ever got in front of a federal judge?"

"Eight hours."

"Emergency interpleader?

Grant nodded his head.

"We need to be there in no more than five hours; it certainly has to be less than eight hours. We must have this resolved in our favor in less than eight hours. Time will not be our friend.

Grant scratched his left temple with his index figure. "OK, at 7:00 A.M., I will take a walk to the court—it is just a few blocks away on Seventh Street—to make new friends and see if I have any old acquaintances who can help.

Frasier interrupted. "Grant, I have hired two cars to be at our disposal at all times. If you wish, they will drive you there."

Scott answered, "Thanks Frasier. It will depend on traffic; it may be faster to walk."

"What do we do now?" Frasier asked, looking at his Rolex."

Scott replied, "How about we eat?"

"Fishermen's Grotto 9, Fisherman's wharf" suggested Jancan.

Frasier summoned a limo and they made their way to the Grotto.

LAS VEGAS, NEVADA
Friday Morning 5:30 AM

Unfortunately, there were no direct flights from Sarasota to Las Vegas. It was difficult to get any rest since they had to change planes twice. The last leg of the journey was truly an experience. The flight was filled with "Nick the Greek" wannabes all ready to try their luck at any game of chance that they feel suits them best. It was a total of six-and-a-half hours of travel. In Sarasota, it was 8:30 A.M., but in Vegas it was 5:30.

Sam and Harry rented a car and drove directly downtown to Metro to check in and to notify them that they would be carrying while in Las Vegas. After some brief introductions, they made their way to the Western HO on the Strip. The officers dragged themselves into the Western HO about 9:00 A.M., only to find that they could not check in until noon. But the front desk manager said he would do his best to get them in earlier.

There is something about Las Vegas: you can be dog-tired but when you get into the casino you feel invigorated. Sam and Harry were no different. The lack of sleep while traveling was no longer an issue. They were given coupons for $1.99 steak-and-eggs breakfast, which they promptly redeemed.

Although the breakfast was $1.99, each dropped at least $10 waiting for a table. Once they had eaten their fill, they checked with the front desk and their room was ready. A bellman had taken their bags to room 3012, a standard sleeping room with two double beds. Nothing fancy but sufficiently comfortable. Harry wanted to take a two—or three-hour nap, so Sam agreed to let him have the room while he went downstairs to get directions to the Midway casino.

Sam soon learned how easy it was to get a cash advance on his Visa. He now had $500 to invest. The good news is that he spent a couple of hours learning to play craps and learned strategies of blackjack. Now he felt like an expert and would let his partner get another hour or two sleep before they made their way down the street to the Midway.

LAS VEGAS , NEVADA MIDWAY CASINO
Friday, 7:15 A.M.

I didn't get much sleep. I was in and out most of the time. Finally, my phone rang, signaling the end of my slumber.

I rolled out of bed and started the one pot coffee percolator in the bathroom. Just a few days ago, I had the luxury of a full kitchen. But this would do at least until breakfast. In just a few moments I had taken care of the Three S's of the morning.

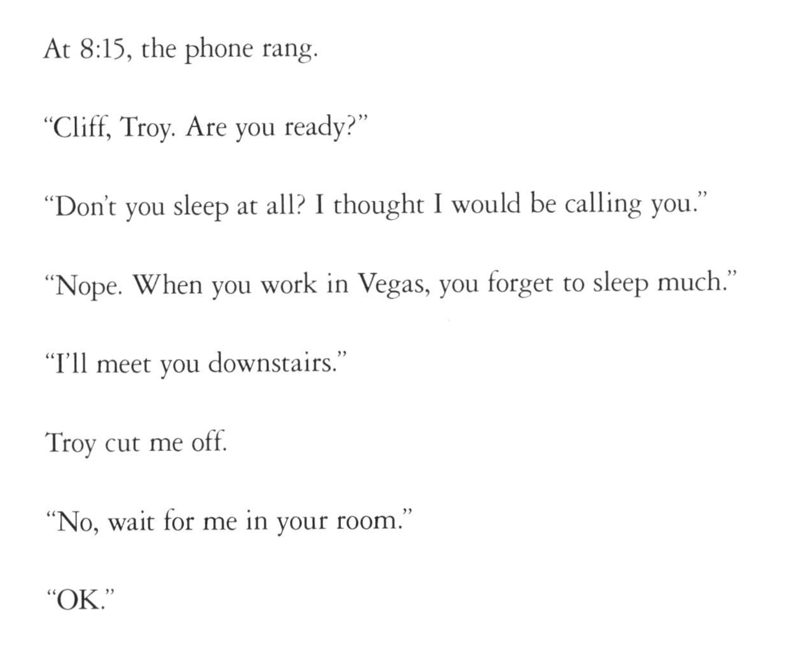

At 8:15, the phone rang.

"Cliff, Troy. Are you ready?"

"Don't you sleep at all? I thought I would be calling you."

"Nope. When you work in Vegas, you forget to sleep much."

"I'll meet you downstairs."

Troy cut me off.

"No, wait for me in your room."

"OK."

At 8:30, there was a tap at the door. I used the peephole to verify it was Troy. It was.

I opened the door and was surprised that Troy was in civilian clothes. "Ready for breakfast?"

I put down my coffee. "Oh yeah, let's go."

Although Troy was in his street clothes, we went out the front door of the hotel to the waiting limo with the Nevada License Midway 1. I sat in the passenger seat and buckled my seatbelt; Troy took the driver's side. He drove south to the Dunes.

As we pulled into the Dunes, Troy was greeted by a Dunes security guard who took possession of the Midway limo.

Troy and I entered the Dunes. Troy led the way around the casino and left to the back of the building, then up an escalator. At the top landing, Troy turned right into a huge open dining room. There was a line of about thirty people waiting to be fed.

As soon as the rope keeper saw Troy, she removed the rope and let Troy and me through, past the waiting patrons. We were led back to a large round table that was set off to the back of the huge hall. There was Phil sitting by himself.

"Hi guys, let's eat," Phil said, smiling.

With that, he led the way to the enormous buffet line. After our plates were full, we headed back to our table. We got through most of the eggs, ham, and sausage before Troy spoke.

"Phil, do you want me to leave"

"No, hell no. You need to know what is happening, also."

I wiped my mouth with the cloth napkin, set it atop my plate, moved it away, and slid over my cup of coffee.

"OK, Phil, I'm ready."

"At eight o'clock tonight, about eighty storm troopers of the FBI, Justice, and Treasury Departments, armed to the teeth, will block all the entrances to the Midway and shut us down." Phil sipped his coffee.

"Armed?"

"Armed—automatic weapons and hand guns."

I rubbed my eyes. "What the fuck are they thinking?"

"They want a production. It is a wonder they don't have Steven fucking Spielberg directing this thing. Remember, as I understand it, 8:00 o'clock here is news at 11 in New York and D.C. This is a show, a big fucking show." Phil explained

"What about us?" Troy asked.

"You guys are standing down and keeping the peace."

"They are then going to herd all the employees into the various different rooms to be processed."

"What about me?" I asked.

"You are off for the rest of the day. You need to keep in your room or stay off property. Troy, you stay with him. Then the feds will find you; you are supposed to take over on Monday."

"What about you?" I cut in.

"Me? They will be taking Mark Karl and me out to the Searchlight air strip and whisk us away to who the hell knows where."

Of all that had happened this week, the realization just hit me like the proverbial ton of bricks. This would be the last time I would ever see my old friend—the man who almost adopted me; the one who became my surrogate father; the person who helped me when I was in trouble years ago with union thugs. I now realized this would be the last time I would ever see him. I felt myself tearing up, only to be snapped out of it with Phil loudly saying "Z!"

Phil rarely called me Z.

"We both knew this day would come."

Phil rose and extended his hand. "God bless you, Cliff Zavitch. Thank you for your loyalty and friendship."

I shook his right hand and gave him a huge bear hug with the left arm. We each patted the other's back. Troy could see both were emotional but stood his ground.

Phil broke the embrace and looked at Troy. "Troy, take care of him."

With that, Phil took a few steps away from the table, turned and disappeared.

"Z, let's go."

I followed my bodyguard to the limo. Troy asked, "Where do you want to go?"

"Well, I don't want to stay in a fucking hotel room, that is for damn sure. Take me for a tour of Vegas. I want to see what is new."

"What about seeing Beth Downs?"

"Jesus, you guys know it all. Do you have the address of her office?"

"No, but we can get it.".

"OK, just drive, Troy."

LAS VEGAS—MIDWAY CASINO
Friday Noon

Mark Karl had taken over the duties while both Phil and I were away. It was nothing new since he and Phil shared days off. Mark Karl was in the security center when Phil arrived. Once in the center, he signaled for Mark Karl to meet him in the bubble. When the security safeguards were activated, Phil asked:

"Did you get the info?"

"Yes. I met Brian Kramer from the Riviera about midnight last night. One of Vegas's worst kept secrets."

Both laughed.

"Are you ready?" Phil asked his lifelong partner.

"No, but I feel better knowing we will have some control with Cliff around."

"Yeah, he is a good guy."

"It would have been great if he'd have taken the job we offered him years ago."

"Yeah, but if he had, he wouldn't have been able to help us now."

"Ironic."

They were interrupted by a knock on the bubble, something that was a sacrilege. No one knocked while the bubble's top was milk-white. Phil pushed a couple of buttons and the bubble top became clear. It was Steve Lambert, their savior / prosecutor.

When the door was opened, Steve walked in.

"Is it time, Agent Lambert?" Phil asked.

Steve nodded.

"Yeah, we are going to take over the Security Center an..."

"And you want us the fuck out of the way," Phil finished.

"OK yeah. Here are Agents Brooks and Stiles. I have personally picked them to take care of your safety from now on."

Brooks and Stiles introduced themselves and all shook hands. Lambert cut short the niceties. "OK Phil, Mark, we will take it from here. Just stay close.

"Well Mr. Karl, I think we still have signing privileges for a while. How about a nice juicy steak and let's get a bottle of DOM."

"Phil, I am right behind you."

"Then let's go." With that, Phil stood, took a last look at what was his domain for many years, turned and left.

DOWNTOWN LAS VEGAS—FBI HEADQUARTERS
Friday 1:30 PM

Control 3, Robert J. James (Bob), was at the Las Vegas office of the FBI, setting up shop for the final phase of this mammoth operation. Robert J. James was really a political animal, a truth that was mostly swept under the carpet. The success of this operation meant everything to him.

This was the final meeting until the big event. In attendance were Tim Floyd, Toni Cardona, and seven others who had been instrumental in bringing down the biggest mob figures in the U.S. On the secured line by the squawk box was Steve Lambert, who put everything in motion.

Bob opened the meeting.

"OK, Tommy O status, please."

Fredrick Vogel from the Kansas City Bureau spoke up. "I will be flying to Kansas. He will surrender to us tonight at 10:00 P.M. Kansas City time, about 8:00 our time. Everything seems to be going smooth. We have had our best agents on this from the beginning. We are ready. At 8:00AM tomorrow morning he will be transported from his home in Kansas City to Forbes Field Airport in Topeka, and then delivered into protective custody. U.S. marshals will then transport him to a location that only the pilots know."

"Good."

"Steve," Bob said, almost yelling at the box in the middle of the table. "Irish and Karl?"

"So far, so good. They are pounding down a few in the lounge. Karl will have his family come visit him one last time before he leaves."

"Have they reconsidered going into the program."

"No Bob. He and his wife are cold to each other, and the kids are too old and too detached. Most of these guys kept their families separated from most of the business."

"What is your timetable? We may need Irish and Karl to help keep things cool. We expect them to be ready to travel early AM. Four, maybe five."

"The sooner the better, Steve," Bob said.

"We are taking them in separate cars and will be going to the old Searchlight airstrip."

"All secure?"

"Except for some warehouses, no one goes out there anymore."

"Warehouses checked?"

"Oh yeah. The biggest stores paper and ink for several newspapers in the area."

"No problems?"

"None. We are ready."

"How about this guy Zavitch?"

"Like you wanted, he will be kept in his room till we need him Monday."

"Good. Thanks Steve, good job."

Bob turned from the phone to his legal staff across the table. "Legal, how does it look?"

Lead attorney for the government was Samantha Terry from Justice, with her assistant, David Lee. "Sir, we are ready to go. What we are doing is unprecedented, but I am certain with the testimony we have developed from Tommy O, Karl, and Irish, we will have no problem. Besides, I don't expect them to challenge us until at best Tuesday of next week. I actually think it may be Thursday. By then, the State of Nevada will be in full control."

Dave Lee interrupted. "Tora Tora Tora," referring to his ethnicity and the code for complete surprise from Pearl Harbor.

"I hope you are right," Bob responded. He then turned to Tim. "Tim, I want you with me. You are going to be utility, just in case; we have a chopper ready. Let's hope you and I have a nice quite and uneventful night." He then turned to Toni, "OK, our latecomer in the operation. I want you over at the Midway, baby-sit Zavitch. Please keep him out of sight and safe."

"OK, group. Keep on our scramble frequency and keep in touch. There are a bunch of bad guys out there who have nothing to lose."

LAS VEGAS—WESTWARD HO
Friday 4:30PM

Sam entered the room and fell on the vacant double bed.

"What time is it?" Harry asked.

"About 4:30—7:30 Sarasota time."

"Thanks for the sleep, but we need to get to work," Harry said

Sam said nothing.

"Hey Sam, how much did you lose?

"Did you know you can take cash advances on your Visa?"

"Certainly."

"OK, then about $500."

"Serves you right. It is the evils of gaming, a sin against society and family," Harry Seed preached in his most evangelical voice. He paused, then said, "What did you play?"

"Roulette. The dealer was really cute."

"Worst game in the house, Sam. Let's find this guy and do what ever the hell we are suppose to do with him, and I will show you how to play 21 and Craps." He sat up. "We better get over to the Midway and find our boy."

"I am sure he is fine," Sam said, with his face in his pillow.

"I'm taking a shower."

Sam did not respond. He was exhausted.

Harry let Sam sleep for about an hour, then woke him up when he was through with the facilities.

Sam rolled out of bed, removed his holstered weapon, and then went in to wake himself up. After forty minutes, he emerged a new man, ready to hunt for the evil, or perhaps not so evil, Clifford Zavitch.

As soon as Sam was ready, Harry asked him a very important question. "Did you find any place good to eat?"

"Right here. All you have to do is show your out of state driver's license and they give you this huge pastrami sandwich for only forty-nine cents."

"No shit? Forty-nine cents?"

"No shit. Had two, could do with another."

"Sounds to me that's our first stop, before we go out and either save or arrest Zavitch. Still really don't know which."

"Follow me, partner; follow me."

With that, they were off to be fed and make contact with Clifford Zavitch.

DOWNTOWN LAS VEGAS FBI HEADQUARTERS
Friday 4:30 PM

I knew I owed Beth a visit and, through Troy's connections, found the federal office she was working. On Troy's advice, they stopped by a flower vendor to pick up a dozen roses. They walked into the new high-rise federal building and walked into the lobby.

"Flowers can't hurt, Z, can't hurt," Troy said.

"No, I guess not. Hey, you look pretty good in civilian clothes."

"Oh yeah. Are you my permanent assignment?"

"Being my babysitter?"

"I prefer bodyguard."

"Don't know, Troy. It's OK by me, but I understand I'll be having a boss."

"Michael Milton. Hear he is a real prick."

"Me, too."

"He is going to have a tough time. Most are going to look to you; after all, you are kind of part of the family. Most all of us, managers and supervisors, were here at the beginning, like you."

Since Troy was packing, he opted not to go through security and explain himself. Besides, we were in a secured federal building. What could happen to me in a federal building?

I passed the security check and proceeded to the fourth floor. I walked down a long hall of nondescript doors, most with numbers, only a few with names. At the end of the hall was a glassed-in area, very open and almost friendly. I entered carrying my bouquet, and instantly made friends with every woman I came in contact with.

One tall black woman remarked, "Gorgeous flowers. Are those for me?"

"No, this is a very overdue gift for a friend."

"Can I help?"

"I'm looking for Elizabeth Downs."

"Beth? Sure. I hope you are Cliff."

"I am," I almost shouted.

With that, I suddenly felt all would be well.

"Follow me."

I followed her through a maze of offices. Then she stopped. The yet unidentified woman knocked on the door."

"Oh, Beth, there is a flower delivery for you."

I heard, "ME? I haven't got flowers in years." I hear the voice getting closer and surmised correctly that she had run hurriedly from behind her desk. She walked through the portal, saw me, and stopped cold, wanting to hug me but not to breach protocol.

"Hello, Cliff. This is my boss, Wanda Phillips."

I turned and, with my free hand, awkwardly shook her hand, as I had not given Beth the flowers. "How do you do."

Wanda laughed. "Hell, Beth, if you don't give him a hug, I will," and she turned to leave. Beth then grabbed the roses as she pulled me into the privacy of her office, and then gave me a huge hug and a big wet kiss. Beth was not wearing shoes and was about a foot shorter than I.

I had been on many dates and, contrary to popular belief, had been laid a few times, but this hug, the hug I was now receiving from my old flame, was powerful and different. I could feel the warmth and the electricity. I did not say it but this was my soul mate.

"Flowers, WOW! It has been forever."

"I'm glad you like them."

Beth quickly looked around the room for a makeshift vase. She selected an old award, shaped like a vessel, and temporarily stored the flowers. When she was done she looked at me and a quiet awkwardness filled the room.

I finally broke the ice. "Would you like to go downstairs to get some coffee?"

"I don't drink coffee."

"Well, a..."

"Tea. I would love a cup of tea," as she scooted to slip on her shoes.

Both of us were acting like we were in high school again.

"Let's go," she said excitedly.

Once her shoes were in place, she took the lead down the hall to the elevators. Nothing was said until we arrived at the lobby level of the office complex.

"Cliff, I am really glad you came by. I was hoping you would at least call me, but the flowers. I was having a bad day. Seeing you has really helped. Thank you."

"Absolutely!"

"What is happening at the Casino? They let you out."

"I was told to take the day off." Cliff looked around and saw Troy watching him, but Troy was staying out of earshot, just keeping his charge safe. "I can't say much. Your folks are going to have some big party, I understand. I'm not supposed to say much more."

"Then don't, Cliff. Look we have a new coffee shop called Starbucks in the building, and they have something called Chai Tea. Do you have Starbucks in Florida yet?"

"No, this is the first one I've seen."

"I was going to invest in it, but my broker talked me out of it."

"Can't help you there. I am lousy when it comes to picking stocks, and the irony of it is that I am in financial services."

"Do you like it?"

"I did. I had a great mentor. He just recently died."

"I am sorry."

"Yeah, he kept me balanced I would be working and out of the blue, he would make me leave the office to shoot basketballs at the rec center. He was really cool. I miss him a lot."

They arrived at the counter to order and Beth spoke as if she was speaking another language.

"I'll have a hot Chai tea with light…"

I did a double take. "I'll have a large coffee."

The person behind the counter smiled and corrected me, "A ventie, sir."

I responded, "no sir, coffee," then started laughing as I saw the display of cups illustrating the cup sizes. "Yeah, venti, please," I said, laughing.

In just minutes, the drinks were served and we found a faraway table.

"Sorry about your Mom." Beth said.

"It has been a rough last couple of years, but that should all change now. Starting Monday, I will be working at the Midway in an executive capacity, and the money is awesome."

"Yeah, but Cliff, the hours—it is almost 24/7 non-stop. I dated a pit boss for about three months. I think we were able to get away only once. Who knows if you will have any time as assistant GM?"

I half shut one eye and cocked my head to the left. "I didn't say anything about assistant GM."

Beth smiled. "I know enough to worry about you, know someone is trying to kill you. And I know about tonight and I also know that starting Monday you will be making a bucket load of money."

"Great, do you want to start dating again?" I said, wide-eyed, smiling, and extending my arms as if to give a big hug. Beth did not move or crack a smile. She just looked at her tea. I then collapsed my arms.

"I love you, Cliff, always have. But I need stability. Let's just play it by ear. If things start to become normal, where I can see you for eight hours straight or have weekends together or, hell, Cliff, one weekend a month. Yeah, I would love to start seeing you."

"I understand. I'll accept a definite maybe." I smiled and extended my hand across the table and she did the same.

After about a two-minute gaze at each other, Beth excused herself to go back to work. We walked to the elevator and shared one last embrace.

I watched the elevator take my love away, and Troy had found his way and was standing behind me.

Troy spoke first. "Food, I am starved."

"Anywhere but the Midway."

"How about a famous shrimp cocktail at the Golden Gate? I'll buy," Troy said.

"Big spender. Aren't they still ninety-nine cents?"

"OK, I'll buy you two and a soda."

"I guess Fremont Street, here we come."

MIDWAY CASINO—SECURITY CENTER
7:00 P.M. Friday

Steve Lambert was in the captain's chair, since it was the best vantage point.

"Mr. Miller, please round up Irish and Karl."

"OK, chief, will do."

Moe Miller left to find his old bosses and bring them back to the security control center one last time. The mood in the casino was, to say the least, "edgy." It seemed everyone knew something was going to happen, and they were all waiting for the next shoe to drop.

Miller found his old bosses in the Ringmaster Lounge. Irish was still maintaining some semblance of sobriety, but Mark Karl was gone. With Miller's help, all made it back to the confines of the security center.

Steve checked his watch as Irish and Karl stumbled in. He then stood and stepped down from the captain's chair, as Moe Miller took his place.

"Well, it looks like you two have been having a good time."

"Eat, drink, and make Mary," Mark Karl shouted.

Phil laughed, "Easy, Mark."

"Shall we adjourn to your office?"

Phil corrected, "My old office."

As they entered, Lambert looked over his shoulder and requested a large pot of coffee.

Meanwhile, the action outside the casino was starting to escalate. Unfortunately, as usual, the cooperation and the communication between the FBI, Justice and the state and local entities were not going smoothly.

Although Midway security was tipped off, the local police were not yet told of the massive attack on a major casino. Several of the vans that carried the federal officers were stopped and/or detained. The 8:00 P.M. deadline was now in peril. Outside, in the parking lot, it was starting to look like a real circus. Families with children were parking their vehicles while troopers with automatic weapons ran past them trying to get organized. Some patrons got cameras and videos and started to roll tape; others could not get back in their cars and leave fast enough.

Federal vans were parked all over the place. No one had set aside a place to park, nor did they plan a staging area. All thought that they would pull up to the entrances, disembark the vans, and stroll into the casino.

It was now 8:00 P.M. and the press was arriving and starting to roll tape, nationwide tape that revealed the circus at the Midway casino.

Steve Lambert was back in the captain's chair, and most of the monitors were showing the confusion outside. "God damn it, who the fuck is running the show out there? Why is there no staging area?" Lambert was now standing in front of the massive control chair. Phil was amused at the contrast between his bright blond hair and his face, now getting beet red.

Lambert could not stand it anymore "Would someone find Mackey and get him the fuck in here?"

In just a few moments, Roger Mackey was looking up at Steve Lambert, who did not even wait for him to say hello. "Who the fuck is running the show outside? Why isn't there a parking area for the vans? Didn't you make arrangements?"

"Steve, in all due FUCKING respect, yesterday my staff offered logistical support and your people told us that they would be handling it. I believe it was Mr., or Agent, Gal-an-o," he said, trying to pronounce the name correctly.

Lambert stepped off the captain' chair and moved a step away from everyone to compose himself. Steve then turned to Roger, his open hands flat against his face. "Cold water, please." He paused again. "Roger, I am sorry, would you, and could you, please take control of that abortion outside and see our wayward agents in."

"Of course, sir. Please notify your people."

"Done," Lambert then picked up a radio. "This is roundup leader. The Midway security force will be assisting the operation. Please follow their directions."

The radio squawked, "Roger that, roundup leader. We welcome the assist."

Roger took his force and, like a well-organized machine, set out barriers and made way for the vans and the troopers to enter the entrances. Because of Mackey's effort, the network cameras picked up minimal confusion. All was starting to fall into place. At 9:30 P.M., the feds started to move in and take charge of the various departments. The patrons inside the casino could not understand what was happening. Some thought it was a movie being made; some thought it was an act; no one realized that it was the real deal and that the federal government was taking over the Midway Casino.

Once all the confusion outside was subsiding, Roger Mackey made his way back to the Security Center to close the floor down. Although things were now running about two hours behind schedule, they were still moving forward. Once Roger entered the room, Steve Lambert looked and him and ordered, "Roger shut it down"

Roger glanced around the room to see Phil, and then said, "Mr. Irish, may I have your assistance." Calling his old friend Mr. Irish was a sign of respect he wished to give. Phil stood up and made his way to the console with Mackey. "Steve, do you want to make an announcement now?"

"NO. Shut it down," he responded emphatically.

To shut down the power to the slot machines and other electric games required two key cards. One had to be from Roger Mackey, chief of security, or Moe Miller, his second. The other card must be from Mark Karl, Phil Irish, or, Cliff Zavitch.

Mackey swiped his card first, triggering a synthesized female voice.

"Mr. Roger Mackey, please enter your ID code."

Roger entered what seemed to be a ten-digit code.

"Thank you, Mr. Mackey. Please enter command."

Roger then entered another multi-digit code.

"You have requested the shutdown of all electronically-powered gambling devices. Was this your intent? Press 1 for yes, 2 for no."

Roger pressed "1."

"This request requires an additional command from another level 1 manager. A correct card must be swiped in thirty seconds or the order will be terminated."

Phil laughed. "Jesus, she sounds sexy. I wonder if she gives good head?

Lambert, losing patience: "Phil, please."

"OK , OK." He swiped his card.

"Mr. Philip Irish, please enter your ID code."

Phil also entered what seemed to be a ten-digit code.

"Mr. Irish, a request has been made to shut down all electronically-powered gambling devices. Is this your intent? Press 1 for yes or 2 for no."

Phil pressed 1. Instantly, all games were disabled.

You could immediately hear the shouts of protest. They all watched as one man wound up and threw a glass at the slot he had been feeding. Glass shards sprayed everywhere, and it appeared that a nearby patron was injured.

"Oh, shit," Mackey yelled, then barked into his radio: "Sector 3, sector 3, please send a medical team to machine..." he squinted at the screen and paused "...machine 244." He then turned to Lambert. "An announcement, please, Mr. Lambert," he shouted with a certain amount of I told you so.

Lambert then grabbed the mike. "Am I queued up?"

Moe Miller: "You are. Just push the button."

"Ladies and gentleman...",He paused and looked at Miller. "Please turn up the volume."

Miller made an adjustment. "It is cranked all the way up now."

"Ladies and gentlemen..." Steve's voice boomed so loudly that almost everyone immediately stopped and looked up as if it was God himself talking.

"This is Steve Lambert, federal agent. The Midway Casino has been seized by the United States Department of Treasury and the State of Nevada. Please vacate the building immediately."

Steve looked at Moe. "I'm going to say this again. Please tape it and run it every two minutes."

"Good idea."

"Ladies and gentlemen. Ladies and gentlemen. May I have your attention, please? This is Steve Lambert, federal agent. The Midway Casino has been seized by the United States Department of Treasury and the State of Nevada. Please vacate the building immediately."

Moe pushed a few buttons and said, "Got it. Listen."

"Ladies and gentlemen. Ladies and gentlemen. May I have your attention, please? This is Steve Lambert, federal agent. The Midway Casino has been seized by the United States Department of Treasury and the State of Nevada. Please vacate the building immediately."

"Good, great. Thanks."

LAS VEGAS OUTSIDE THE MIDWAY CASINO
Friday 8:30 PM

Inspector Sam Simpson and Harry Seed walked leisurely down the Strip after they had been sufficiently fed. It was easier to walk than fight the traffic on the Las Vegas Strip. The Midway was in sight but still a good walk away.

They arrived at the outer edge of the mammoth parking lot and saw what seemed to be a cross between the Keystone Kops and a riot at a British soccer game. At the front entrance, just a few moments after the feds had taken over the casino, Sam and Harry were barred from entrance. They found a person who tended the door with some apparent authority and identified themselves.

"Sorry guys. We are in the process of getting everyone out. I can't let you in."

"What happened here?"

"Sir, I am a metro cop here on a temp gig. I was called in at the last minute. I honestly don't have a clue. Something that has to do with the feds. Hell, they are all over."

"Look, officer." Sam looked for some ID, only to see a nametag with his first name. "Joe, we need some help here. Could you just call with your radio and see if you could get someone to answer a few questions?"

Joe looked around and saw that all seemed somewhat under control. People were filing out of the casino a bit confused, but they were moving well. "OK, hang on."

Joe took one step back, turned slightly, and spoke through the radio, although they had no idea what he was saying. In a minute he took a step forward. "OK, guys. I got one of the feds coming down. It will be a while." Joe shrugged, "Hell, most of us don't even know why we are here."

Suddenly they heard the announcement.

"Ladies and gentlemen. "Ladies and gentlemen. May I have your attention, please? This is Steve Lambert, federal agent. The Midway Casino has been seized by the United States Department of Treasury and the State of Nevada. Please vacate the building immediately."

Joe looked and them and said, "OK, now we know why we are here."

Both thanked him and stepped back to let him do his job.

Sam took out a cigarette and lit up. "Hey Sam, I'll take one of those," said Harry.

"I thought you quit years ago."

"Hey, it is Vegas, baby."

Sam passed a fag over to his partner and laughed.

"Harry, do you think this has anything to do with our guy Zavitch?"

"Sam, it would be a stretch."

"No, not really Harry. Follow this. First the guy…"

Sam clicked his fingers.

"Elwood," Harry added.

"Yeah, Elwood said Cliff's old boss asked him to come to Vegas. We know he is not dead; he was checked in here. His car is destroyed and we know that there was a dead body in the car. The FBI covers up the car, the ID of the dead body, and makes the VIN disappear from the Department of Motor Vehicles in Tallahassee. Now we are here and the feds take over a casino, stressing 'a casino'."

Harry took a long drag on his cigarette. "Damn, that is good. How about this: maybe Zavitch is dead; maybe it was him in the car, and the person who checked in and then disappeared is an imposter. Bring his picture?"

Sam nodded. "Several copies."

"Maybe he was being followed by someone, and Zavitch killed him and burned him up in the car?"

"But why would the FBI cover it up?"

Sam scratched his cheek. "Shit, this is giving me a headache. I need a drink."

Both finished their cigarettes at the same time.

It took almost 20 minutes for a low-level fed to find someone for the Sarasota PD to speak to. Finally a bewildered young lady with credentials hanging from around her neck approached them.

"Gentleman, I am Agent Pamela Meyer. How can I help you?"

Harry took the lead, "Agent Meyer, I am Detective Harry Seed and this is my partner, Inspector Sam Simpson. We have reason to believe that a suspect in a murder investigation is staying here at the Midway."

"Murder suspect?" She repeated "What is his name?" she queried as she pulled out her notepad.

"Zavitch. Clifford Zavitch," Sam responded.

"Z A V I T C H." Agent Meyer spelled it back.

"Yes."

"OK, guys, do you want to wait? It may be a while, or can we call you?"

They looked at each other, and then Sam shrugged, "We will wait."

"OK," Meyer said as she turned and walked away.

Joe, the off-duty temp metro officer, watched and smiled as Agent Meyer walked away. "Sorry, guys. You better relax. I expect it will be a while."

"Hey, Joe where can we get some coffee?" Joe pointed at the Pepper Mill. "Great java."

"Want a cup?"

"No thanks, guys. I'm good."

Harry volunteered to get the coffee while Sam waited for what or whoever.

LAS VEGAS—INSIDE THE MIDWAY
Friday 9:45 PM

Things inside were not going as planned; chaos was putting it mildly. There had been numerous grabs at chips on the tables; in the confusion, there were several incidents where patrons turned ugly and tried to steal chips from right off the gaming tables. Unfortunately, there were a few injuries, both patrons and employees.

Phil and Mark had been taken to the showrooms to help keep the execs cool while they were being "processed and interviewed."

"What a mess," Mark Karl commented as he was being escorted to the main showroom. Once there, and to their surprise, not one shift manager or supervisor had made his or her way to the showroom.

"Fuck, I would say they are a bit behind schedule," Phil noted sarcastically as he pointed at his wristwatch. Both took seats on stage to welcome the future federal guests.

Meanwhile, in the security center, Roger Mackey was trying to do everything he could to keep the casino on an even keel, if that were possible. Inside the bubble, Steve Lambert was trying to explain what the problems were.

"People are simply not leaving. Most are demanding refunds; some say they won thousands of dollars and want to be paid; people are stealing chips off tables; security guards are hitting people; our people are hitting people; there are about five major confrontations. And we have not processed a single employee yet."

Moments later, Lambert came storming out of the bubble, again red as a beet.

"God damn it, Roger. Get these people the fuck out of the casino."

"Steve, what would you have me do? Start shooting them?"

Suddenly there was complete silence in the center. All eyes were on Lambert, and Roger's heart skipped a beat.

Lambert just broke up. "Nah, don't shoot them, Rog, too much paperwork. " and everyone started laughing.

LAS VEGAS—OUTSIDE THE MIDWAY CASINO
10:00 PM

Sam and Harry were starting to enjoy the craziness around them. The crowd was almost like a New Year's Eve crowd in Times Square. There was anticipation, but no one knew what they were waiting for. Folks were starting to have fun; drinks were being passed through the crowd; and people who were once inside were telling their stories to those outside.

"I couldn't fucking believe it. I was playing the slots one minute and then some asshole has a fuckin' gun in my face," one patron related.

Rumors were flying. One was the state had taken over all the casinos in Vegas and the Religious Right Wing of the Republican Party was going to close them all down.

Suddenly Joe, the metro temp, called for Harry and Sam.

When they arrived at the entrance, Joe introduced them to Agent Frank Gallino and Silas, still successfully posing as Andrew Parker, who cordially shook hands with the Sarasota detectives.

Frank started: "So what is this about a murder investigation?"

Sam replied, "We are investigating a murder of a John Doe. Mr. Zavitch is a person of interest. He also has been reported missing. We suspect your Mr. Zavitch could be an imposter and our dead John Doe is Mr. Zavitch."

"Gentleman this is very interesting, but there is nothing we will be able to do until early in the morning. As you have probably heard, the federal government has taken over the Midway and, frankly, things are a bit confused right now."

Sam queried, "Is he in the building right now?"

"Detective, I don't really know."

"Could you find out?"

Agent Gallino took a second to look at the radio he had in his hand. He could hear the radio traffic through his earpiece, then spoke, "Detective, your case right now is not a priority. I am sorry, but I will assign detective Parker to aid you first thing in the morning."

Silas agreed. "Sam, I can find our Mr. Zavitch and deliver him in the morning for an interview."

"What time?" Harry inquired

"How about 7 A.M.?"

"OK, we will be here then, here at the main entrance."

"OK, here 7A.M. with Zavitch."

"Thanks, guys."

All shook hands and Sam and Harry departed. The crowd engulfed the agents as Sarasota's finest walked back to their hotel.

Silas and Agent Frank Gallino walked back inside to the mayhem that had just started to calm down a bit.

"I'll get with Lambert and let him know you will be letting the Sarasota guys interview their golden boy."

"Think there is anything to this?" Silas asked.

"Who the hell knows?"

Silas could not believe his luck; the fact that the FBI had held the death of Andrew Parker a secret had given him a chance to fulfill his contract.

SAN FRANCISCO
Midnight

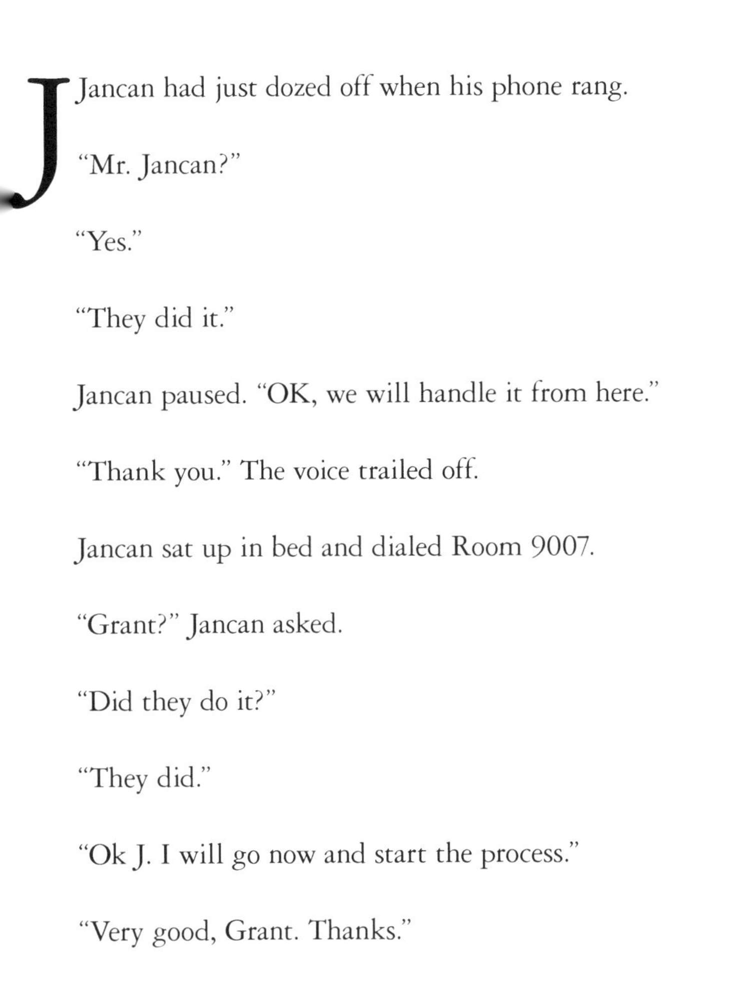

J Jancan had just dozed off when his phone rang.

"Mr. Jancan?"

"Yes."

"They did it."

Jancan paused. "OK, we will handle it from here."

"Thank you." The voice trailed off.

Jancan sat up in bed and dialed Room 9007.

"Grant?" Jancan asked.

"Did they do it?"

"They did."

"Ok J. I will go now and start the process."

"Very good, Grant. Thanks."

LAS VEGAS INSIDE THE MIDWAY CASINO
Saturday 1:30 AM

It was about 1:30 A.M. and Troy and I were getting back to the mayhem of the Midway. We found a somewhat secret entrance to the casino and decided to go to one of the vantage points high above the casino and watch clandestinely. Troy knew that I was best not involved or even seen at this time. We both watched as federal officers tried to herd out 5,000 persons from the premises.

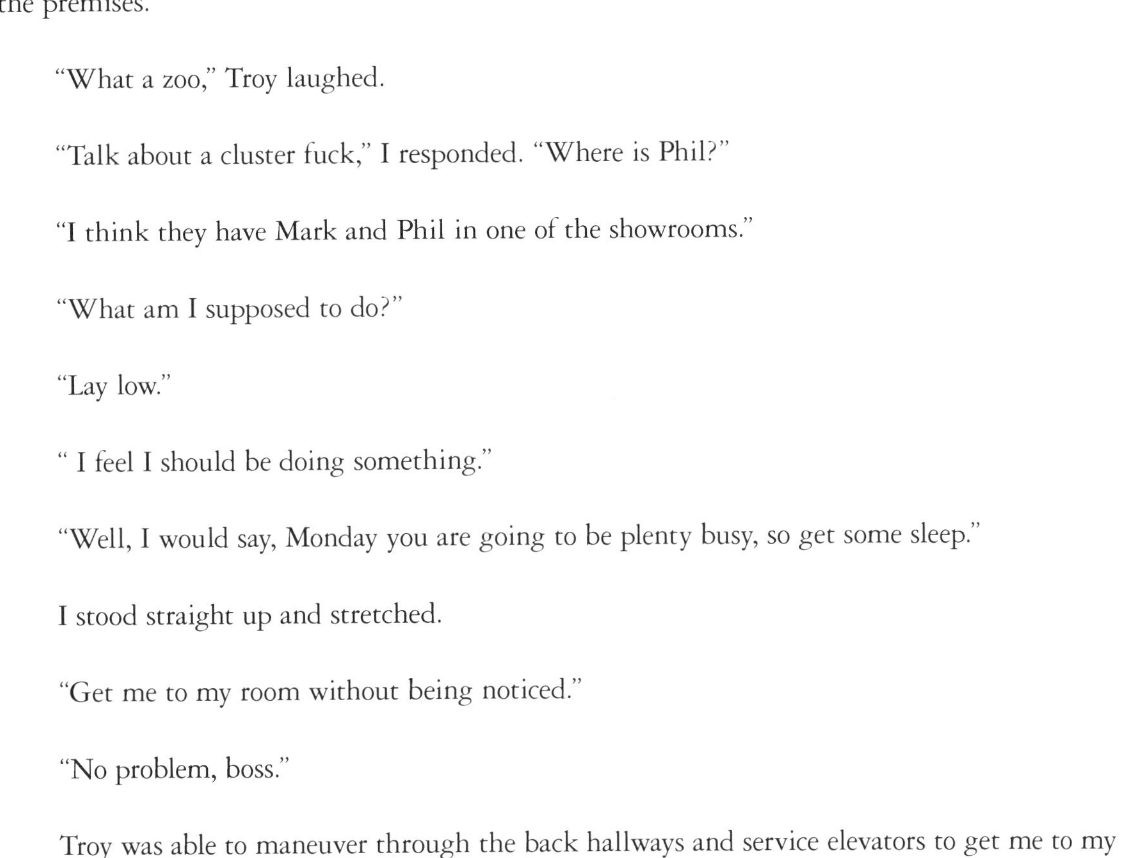

"What a zoo," Troy laughed.

"Talk about a cluster fuck," I responded. "Where is Phil?"

"I think they have Mark and Phil in one of the showrooms."

"What am I supposed to do?"

"Lay low."

" I feel I should be doing something."

"Well, I would say, Monday you are going to be plenty busy, so get some sleep."

I stood straight up and stretched.

"Get me to my room without being noticed."

"No problem, boss."

Troy was able to maneuver through the back hallways and service elevators to get me to my room.

"Get some sleep. I will come get you when they need you."

"Get me up if anything exciting happens."

"OK, boss.".

Phil had actually dozed off when the first arrivals of employees were escorted into the showroom about 3:00 A.M. Things were just not going well with this takeover. There was money to secure, things to be put away, tables to be covered; it was not just herding a lot of people out of a large area. Things were complicated and were getting even more complicated. The original plan was that the Casino would have been secured by 2:00 AM, and now they were just starting the planned process of processing employees.

Phil was a bit tickled with all the confusion, kind of an "I told you so."

But now the bureaucratic talent of the federal government was taking over. Several suited agents took their place behind makeshift desks, made from showroom dinner tables, with a chair in front of each table. Each agent carried a laptop computer, set up in just a few moments, and was ready for business.

Both Phil and Mark Karl were up on stage and gave a wave and nod of support to those being processed; the government would interview each manager for several reasons: to find out what their job was, gather information and match it with the Human Resources records, give them instructions on when to return, and, most important, find out if any of the managers knew about the skim.

Phil watched and realized what the ultimate objective was: find more witnesses, he laughed to himself. His scheme to skim was one of the best-kept secrets of all time. Mark Karl knew, Tommy O knew, and, unfortunately, Cliff knew. Phil had gotten so close to Cliff years ago that after he had lost his son, he wanted him to know everything, to carry on. But things just didn't work out and his tiring mind started to become melancholy as he thought about his dead wife and son, and the son he never wanted. He stared at the coffee cup that had been placed in front of him a few moments ago. Then he was suddenly disturbed from this daydream.

"Phil, hey Phil. Are you OK?"

Phil looked up to see Steve Lambert.

"Yeah, of course. Just a bit tired."

"We all are Phil, but the faster we get everyone processed and out of here, the faster we can get you where you are going, and then you can rest."

"Rest, fucking rest. Sounds like you are putting me out to pasture." In fact they were.

"Look, Phil, we have 25 interview tables and about 350 managers and execs to interview. It's going to be a while, and it appears folks are getting restless. Can you say something to them?"

"Jesus, Steve, what do you want me to say? Just relax while the feds get ready to fuck you?"

Phil opened a pack of cigarettes and looked at Steve.

"Phil, look. God damn it, bottom line I am saving your fucking life. Your past business associates want you dead."

Phil lit his cigarette, threw up his hands, and said, "OK, OK. What do you want me to say?"

"I arranged for some of the kitchen wait staff to stay on. Please tell them to relax and we will be serving coffee and Danish."

"OK, I got it." Phil crushed his fresh cigarette and stood.

An agent standing in the middle of the stage tapped on a microphone to make sure it was working, and then handed it to Phil.

As Phil stood there, the entire room started to hush. After all, Phil had many friends. When he first opened the Midway many years ago he brought with him a reputation of being a real hard-ass, when in fact he was a very fair employer. Many a time he would take care of things for all levels of employee. Once he even paid a large medical bill that a new employee incurred for a child before the Midway's policy went into effect. Phil was truly loved by all. All eyes focused on Phil. Even the processors stopped and turned to see what he was going to say.

"Well, guys, you all have heard about hostile takeovers. Well, hell, you don't get much more hostile than this."

Many started to laugh.

"OK, obviously there has been a change in management. This will be the last you see of me; on Monday there will be a new staff here, some state folks, some feds. All of you will be doing pretty much what you have been doing, except you will just be doing it for another entity. Many of you remember when we opened, a young fellow by the name of Cliff Zavitch worked with us for ten years. Well he…"

Steve Lambert's flailing of his hands obviously requested Phil not to mention Cliff. Phil ignored him

"He left us and got a good education in accounting and finance, and will be second in command here. Some of you old guys knew him; he is certainly a fair person. Now everyone must be processed so you guys can get paid." He stopped. "Everyone wants to get paid, right?"

He got a lot of cheers and response from the crowd.

"Yeah, hell, yeah," they chanted.

"OK then. I am having coffee and some food sent in to eat. So just take it easy and we will have you out of here as soon as possible."

There was a smattering of applause and then the restaurant staff, almost as if on cue, rolled in several carts of Danish and coffee.

Except for the comment about Cliff, Steve Lambert was happy. Phil then sat and lit another cigarette, and the processing continued. After about another half hour, Steve returned to Phil and Mark Karl and had them escorted to hotel rooms so they could get a few hours rest before leaving Vegas.

DOWNTOWN LAS VEGAS—FBI HEADQUARTERS
3:30 AM Saturday

It had been a long night for everyone. Tim Floyd and Bob James—Control 3—had been monitoring all the action from the FBI office downtown. There had been a direct feed set up from the security center, and technically it worked great. The operation, on the other hand, left a lot to be desired.

It was going on 4:00 A.M. and everyone had thought they would be asleep by then. Tim, Toni Cardona's de-facto supervisor, had sent her home earlier and asked her to deploy to the Midway at 7:00 A.M. to check on me.

Steve Lambert was in the bubble reporting to Control.

"Steve, was it as bad as it looked?" Control asked

"Worse. How was it portrayed by the press?"

"I think D.C. and Carson City will be happy. Actually, it made us look good. The press loves chaos and, as one commentator put it, you have to expect some chaos."

Control had been monitoring all the news networks, as well as the live feed.

"What time do you want to move Phil and Mark?"

"We wanted to have them moved by now. Where do you have them?"

"We put them to bed. Phil was dozing off and Mark was drunk."

Control 3 turned and looked at another monitor. "OK, let's get them to Searchlight about 8:00 A.M."

Lambert paused "OK. Just one more glitch. There are two Sarasota detectives wanting to talk with Zavitch and may want to take him back with them."

Tim interjected, "You are kidding?"

"Tim, no it seems that one of the officers was on the scene and saw our dead agent. He suspects that either Zavitch killed him or Zavitch is dead and this Cliff is an imposter."

Tim folded his arms and looked at Control 3, who asked, "What do you want to do?"

Lambert spoke first. "I think we need to keep him away from the police. Hell, what is he going to say? It may blow the whole case. We can't have him saying anything to anyone."

"Agreed," said Control 3.

Steve had an idea. "Look, I know Zavitch, and he probably wants to say good-bye to Phil, let's let them have someone drive Cliff to Searchlight and fly to Kansas with them, and we will slingshot Zavitch back here for work on Monday."

"I like it." said Control. "Do it."

"OK, I will arrange another car and agent to follow in the morning, and we will put him in the air." Steve affirmed

Control 3 added, "I will call Jim, the AG from Florida, and have this thing snuffed. I am sure we can have him call back the Sarasota police. OK, everyone grab a nap." There were sleeping accommodations on site. "Everyone back here at 6:15 A.M."

They all signed off and retired for a few hours of sleep, but Tim Floyd forgot to call Toni Cardona to tell her of the change in plans.

Toni was up first, at 4:45 A.M., so she would be able to meet me at 7:00. She was still on Sarasota time and was still not used to the bed at the Hilton International. Toni put her blonde hair into a pony tail with a rubber band, and she was out and running around the Las Vegas Country Club, almost a five-mile run, which she accomplished easily.

After the run and a long shower, she got dressed in casual but agent-appropriate garb. She hurried down a to grab a bagel and a cup of black coffee, and headed to her car to get over to the Midway before 7:00. She would keep an eye on me, as Karl and Phil were taken into protective custody.

At 5:00 A.M., agents were waking up Phil and Karl to get them ready for their journey. Breakfast was light, bagels and coffee. Phil was the first one ready to go, and he opened the door to find the agent in charge.

"Excuse me, Agent a…er…"

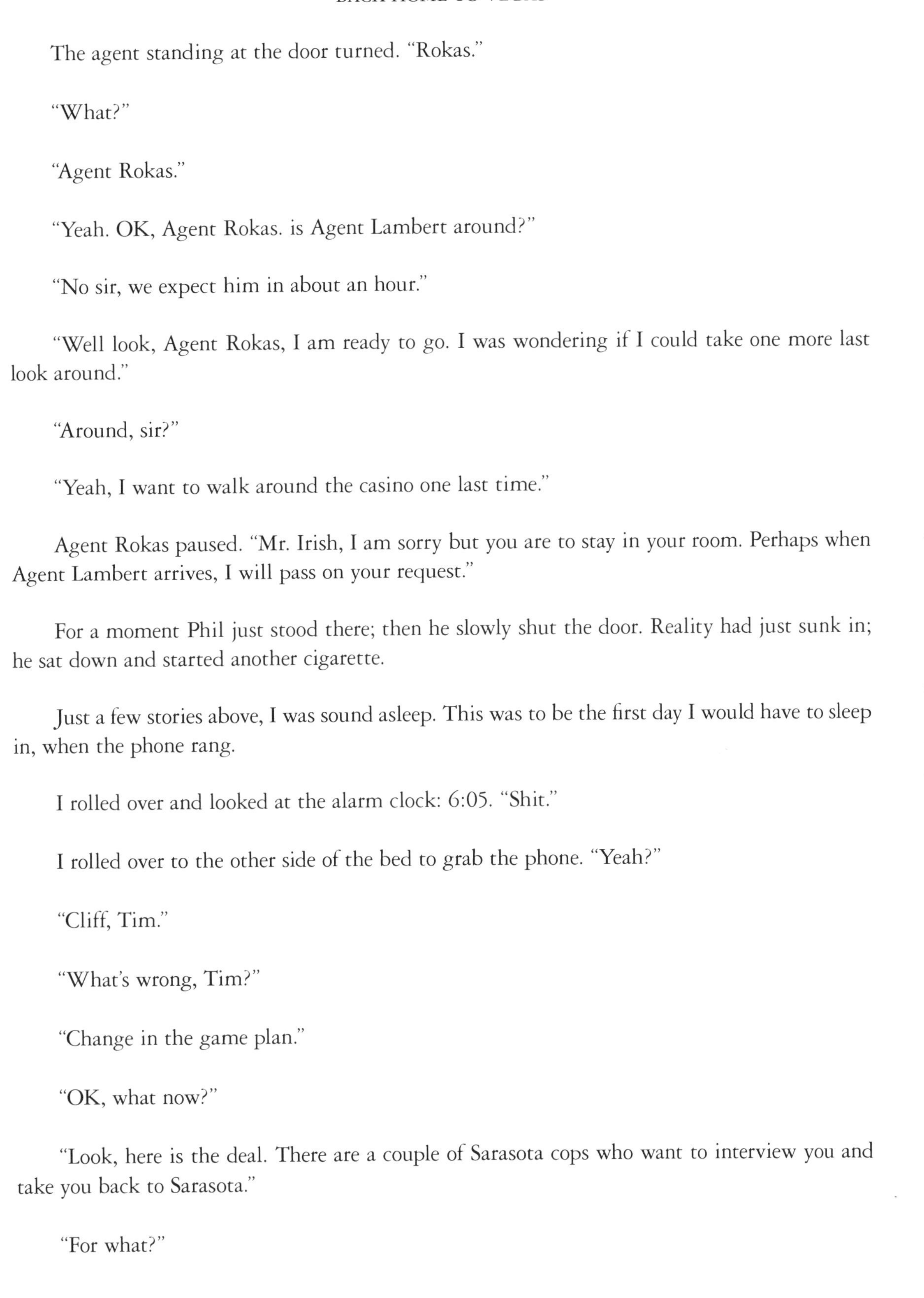

The agent standing at the door turned. "Rokas."

"What?"

"Agent Rokas."

"Yeah. OK, Agent Rokas. is Agent Lambert around?"

"No sir, we expect him in about an hour."

"Well look, Agent Rokas, I am ready to go. I was wondering if I could take one more last look around."

"Around, sir?"

"Yeah, I want to walk around the casino one last time."

Agent Rokas paused. "Mr. Irish, I am sorry but you are to stay in your room. Perhaps when Agent Lambert arrives, I will pass on your request."

For a moment Phil just stood there; then he slowly shut the door. Reality had just sunk in; he sat down and started another cigarette.

Just a few stories above, I was sound asleep. This was to be the first day I would have to sleep in, when the phone rang.

I rolled over and looked at the alarm clock: 6:05. "Shit."

I rolled over to the other side of the bed to grab the phone. "Yeah?"

"Cliff, Tim."

"What's wrong, Tim?"

"Change in the game plan."

"OK, what now?"

"Look, here is the deal. There are a couple of Sarasota cops who want to interview you and take you back to Sarasota."

"For what?"

"Cliff, it is pretty complicated. We don't want you to talk with them, and I thought you would want to see Phil one last time"

"Yeah, that would be great."

"OK, we are going to have an agent pick you up about 7:00 A.M. and you will follow Phil and Mark Karl's car to an airstrip, and you guys will be flying out to deliver them into protective custody. We will get you back right after they are delivered. That will give us about eight to ten hours to get this Sarasota thing straightened out."

"Yeah, OK. When?"

"Now. The caravan leaves at seven. We will send an agent up for you in twenty minutes."

"OK. I'll be ready."

I rolled out and jumped in the shower, in and out in just five minutes, shaved and put on deodorant and some cologne. I then opened my closet, full of every kind of garment, most not even worn yet. I grabbed a pair of light blue denim jeans and a dark blue polo shirt. Neither had not been worn yet, but looked great.

Just as I was admiring myself in the new wardrobe, there was a knock on the door. When I opened it, there was Agent Gallino and Silas.

"Mr. Zavitch?"

"Yes."

"I am Agent Gallino and this is Agent Andrews."

"Andrews? I knew an Agent Andrews."

"Not really an uncommon name, sir."

The agents closed their ID and put them in their jacket pockets, almost like robots.

"I hear I am taking a trip."

"Yes, there are a couple of cops looking for you and the powers-that-be want you out of town."

"I heard."

"Are you ready?" Agent Parker asked.

"Let's go."

The three walked down the hall and waited for the elevator. In just a moment, the right elevator opened. There was an agent running the elevator to shuttle the FBI's VIPS up and down. It was express to the first floor.

We walked down the hall, then turned left into the casino, then walked around the parameter to the front entrance. It seemed very strange there was no one around—no players, no dealers, just a quiet void. In the foyer, Agent Gallino pointed to the couch to the left and asked me to wait there. Time seemed to fly by. It was now 6:50. Mark Karl was the first to stroll by and escorted out the front entrance to a nondescript blue Ford.

As soon as he was secured,, the car was started and was pulled forward. Phil was brought through the empty foyer next and saw me. "Hey, Tiger," Phil waved.

I responded "I'll see you on the plane."

Phil stopped and forced his way over to see me. "What?"

"Yeah, I will be flying out with you."

"That is not in the plan."

"Plans change," Agent Gallino shouted.

"Phil, everything will be OK.I will tell you on the plane."

"Be careful, Cliff." Phil was now herded out the door to the waiting next car. Once in, the car was moved ahead and a black car moved behind it."

"OK, Cliff, let's go." Agent Parker walked out with me and opened the passenger door. He then walked in back of the opened driver's side door, removed his jacket, and put it between him and me, draped on the back of the seat. He shut the door and started the car. As he began, Toni Cardona, with her ID held high, pushed her way across the lines and tape, and shoved her ID in front of the Agent Parker imposter.

"Stop this car."

"Get the fuck away!"

"That person is in my charge. Cliff, get out of the car."

"Look I have my orders, Agent."

"And so do I."

She then opened the back door and got in behind the driver.

"Then drive, damn it."

At the same time Toni was pounding on the window, Detective Sam Simpson and Harry Seed were standing by their car, waiting to have the occupant of the last car to be brought to them for interrogation.

"Sam, I do believe we are being fucked by the FBI."

"Shit, it looks that way. The agent driving was the same son of a bitch who was supposed to deliver us Zavitch. What do you want to do?"

"Shit, Sam, get in and drive. Let's follow the lying sons of bitches."

They jumped into their car and tried to follow the caravan.

Meanwhile, in the last car, Silas had been ready to drive out a few miles, lose the caravan and pop his contract. Now he had to deal with a stupid cunt. So what, he would just have to kill her too; no problem, he had killed women before.

"Just drive. I will make a few calls to find out what the hell is happening." Toni was a bit flustered and I turned to see her. She was certainly cute. She fumbled for her phone and started to dial. After three tries, she started to talk. "Are you aware that Zavitch is being transported?"

"Oh shit, Toni, I'm sorry. We are getting some heat from the Sarasota PD, and Control wanted him out."

"Jesus, Tim."

Tim responded. "Toni, OK, Just hang in with Zavitch. He is going to fly around for about seven hours or so. I don't think he would object to having you as a traveling companion."

"OK, I'll stick with him."

"Sorry, Agent." She paused.

I introduced them. "Agent Cardona, this is Agent Parker," not giving it a second thought.

"Parker?" was all she said.

"Sorry, Agent Parker, but I had my orders to stick with this guy and no one informed me of a change."

Silas relaxed. He decided to follow the caravan since he noticed a car following him. It must be another FBI car. Nothing was said at the briefing, but as he knew things do change. He would take his time. Perhaps when the caravan stopped or slowed down, he would turn and pop Zavitch and then kill the unwanted passenger.

Toni began to relax a bit in the back seat, then noticed Silas's coat draped over the seat. As all good FBI male agents do, he kept his ID in the pocket of his jacket. Her hair was a mess after running to catch the third car, so she leaned on the back of the front seat and put her head between Silas and me.

"Guys, do you have a rubber band for my hair?"

I laughed, "Sorry, don't have any office supplies in the car."

Then I said, "You know what, this may work." I produced an orange-coiled plastic elastic wristband that I picked up from one of the casinos the night before. They were designed for folks to keep their valuable slot cards close to them, but in this case, doubled up, it would make a perfect barrette.

"Thanks, Cliff," she said, as she pulled he arm off the front seat, she purposely pulled Silas's jacket onto the floor of back seat.

"Oops, I am sorry."

She quickly removed and opened and dropped the ID at her feet; then she replaced the jacket and went ahead and put her hair back into a ponytail.

Silas watched her put her hair in a ponytail through the rear-view mirror as he thought to himself: She is cute. I wouldn't mind fucking her before I killed her.

With her feet, she opened the wallet, only to confirm her greatest fear. This was the ID of her partner. She almost became ill but realized she and I were in great peril. She moved around in the back seat and un-holstered her weapon, then slid it under her right thigh.

KANSAS CITY, KS
7:30 AM CST Saturday

It was 7:30 A.M. in Kansas City and Agent Fredrick Vogel was at the front door to pick up Tommy O. Tommy was very calm. He met agent Vogel at the door, kissed his wife, and assured her that in just a few days, they would be reunited at an unknown location.

Agent Vogel opened the back passenger door for Tommy, and once he was in, he slid in right after him. The car pulled away from the quiet neighborhood. They pulled on to an access road which would, after a few stoplights, put them on the freeway. At the corner of 7th Street, a car was stalled at a stop light. The lead car proceeded around the stalled vehicle when suddenly an old blue truck came from nowhere and rammed the lead car. Agent Vogel looked to his left onto the shoulder of the interstate. The last thing he saw was a man with a shoulder rocket launcher. They did not have a chance.

LAS VEGAS FBI HEADQUARTERS
6:55 AM Saturday

In the Las Vegas FBI headquarters, Bob James and Tim Floyd had just hung up the phone after speaking to Toni Cardona. Just as he hung up, Control 3's phone rang.

"Control 3."

"What?"

"What do you mean, you lost Kansas City?"

"Jesus Christ, please give me a confirmation on that."

Bob James held the phone to his ear, waiting with anticipation.

Tim shrugged, "Can I help?"

Bob James said nothing and Tim sat down. There were six others in the room, but no one said anything or even made a movement.

Bob then spoke: "They lost contact with the Kansas City caravan."

He was still and silent.

"Yes." Then there was another long pause.

Bob James went white and he returned the red phone to its receiver.

"Tommy O is dead."

"How?" Tim inquired.

"Bulletproof glass will not stop a rocket launcher."

"Oh, God," exclaimed Tim Floyd.

It took only a few seconds for Bob James to get back to reality and the job at hand. "Mike get me all the cars in the caravan. I want contact with them every five minutes. Pipe us in; I want to hear everything. NOW, Mike. Now, please."

It took about two minutes for Mike Rhomana to connect the radios in the cars with Control 3.

Bob James took control while looking at a large map, and started to bark commands.

"Mike, I want to know everything that is going on. Everything!"

Mike Rhomana was a communications officer in the U.S. Army before his stint with the FBI. Mike was the best on the West Coast., He knew technology and was frantically pushing buttons and tuning knobs while intently listening on a set of headphones.

Then, over the speakers, in came a few crackles. Mike announced, "OK, you are in and on."

"OK, folks. I need reports, what is going on out there? Car 1, talk to me."

"We are good, Control 3."

"Car 2?"

"We are fine, enjoying the drive."

"Car 3?"

Silas queued his mike. "All OK here."

In addition to the three transport cars, there were two other support vehicles. One stayed in front and the other moved front to back checking on the three autos and their occupants.

"Escort 1?"

"We are OK, sir. What are we looking for?"

Bob James: "Be prepared for anything."

"OK, chief," replied the lead escort car.

"Escort 2?"

"Got it, eyes wide open."

"OK, we are going to check in every five minutes. What is your ETA?"

"About ten minutes before the gate."

"OK, the gate will be secured with an agent. Let me know when you are at the gate."

While Bob James was checking on everyone, Tim Floyd walked around the massive platform where he and Control 3 were sitting, and picked up the clipboard, which gave the rundown of driving assignments. When he glanced at who was driving Car 3, his stomach became sick. "Holy shit," he mumbled under his breath.

The caravan was nearly to its destination; an old airfield in the middle of the desert once used by the military, but now used for private pilots and a few warehouses. Tim stumbled as he hurriedly stepped up on the platform, got next to Control 3, and said softly, "We have a dead man driving Car 3." He then pointed to the clipboard with the name of the agent driving Car 3. It listed Andrew Parker, Tampa office.

"Tim, take the chopper, and get out to Searchlight now, please. I will call Nellis and see if we can get some additional help."

"Right." Tim did not take any more time to chat. His longest and best friend, as well as the mission that took almost 20 years to complete, was now at risk.

Bob James looked at Rhomana. "Rhomana, are we off?"

"Yes."

"They cannot hear us?"

Rhomana again checked his controls. "Bob, we are off."

"OK, group, here is the situation. Tommy O has just been assassinated. They used rocket launchers. These folks are very bad. We knew that. And they're well funded. We also knew that. We may have underestimated the means they would use to stop us. Also, we know that the driver of the car with Clifford Zavitch in it is not an agent and is probably an assassin. That's it group. Let us formulate a few ideas how we let our troops knew there is an assassin in Car 3."

When he stopped, there was complete silence, except for the radio.

LAS VEGAS
6:45 AM Saturday

Samantha Terry got to sleep late, although she was not at the Midway when it was taken over. She managed to watch the proceedings on KLAS—Channel 8 news when they cut in to Friday night's primetime programming.

She had just taken her dog Ratso out for a walk, and had finished giving Ratso his breakfast and sat down with a cup of coffee to read the newspaper accounts of the takeover when her phone rang. It was her boss, David Rose, from D.C.

"Sam, we have a problem."

"With?"

"International Recreations and Leisure Adventures Corporation."

"Who are they?"

"They claim to be the new owners of the Midway casino."

Sam, usually calm, stood straight up from her chair, knocking her coffee off the table onto the floor.

"WHAT!"

"Their lawyers are in San Francisco as we speak, and they have convinced Judge Houge of the 9th District to have an emergency hearing for injunctive relief based on the 4th Amendment."

"So fast? That is impossible. Who are their lawyers?"

"Bruggerman, Jancan, Frazier and Scott from Chicago."

Samantha paused, "I know them."

"So do I, Sam." David's voice trailed off. "Their contention is that the Midway was sold ten days ago and that we did this on purpose to foul the deal—and Judge Houge is furious."

"Who the hell is International Recreations and Leisure Adventures Corporation?"

"We don't know yet. We are working on it here. You need to get to San Francisco now. We have a bureau jet at your disposal at McCarran. The hearing is at 4:00 P.M.," her boss informed her.

"That is insane," Sam replied.

"Not really Sam. We have just seized an enterprise that makes over $1,000,000 profit a day. We have closed it down and the ownership is in question. Sam, this case took us almost 20 years. You need to get to San Francisco and do your magic."

The phone went dead.

"SHIT," was all that she said as she dialed her neighbor Tammy Swanson to watch Ratso.

SEARCHLIGHT, NEVADA
9:00AM

At 9:15 AM the first escort car and Car 1 of the caravan arrived at the gate of the Searchlight airstrip. An agent checked them, asked for no ID or papers, and signaled to have the gate opened. Once inside, the gate was secured until the next cars. In about five minutes, the next two cars arrived, and the same procedure was followed. Then the last car carrying me was let through, but after we were granted entrance, the two agents closed the gate with themselves outside the gate. They got into a car and left the premises.

Sam and Harry passed a car speeding coming from the direction of the airstrip.

"Jesus, where is he going?"

Soon they arrived in front of a locked, unattended gate, but could see several cars driving slowly over the un-kept, semi-dirt road.

Toni decided to start some small talk.

"So Agent Parker, how long have you been with the agency?"

"About 10 years."

"Where do you live in Miami?"

"You mean Tampa."

"Do I?"

At that, Silas decided to make his move. He stopped the car about twenty car lengths behind the next car. He raised his right arm to reach for his gun, but Agent Cardona already had hers out, loaded, safety off—and as he turned, Agent Cardona shot Silas right in the face as he turned.

Although I had been taking lessons, nothing sounded louder than the gun firing less than three feet away. I was covered in blood, inhaled a strong smell of iron, and had blood and gray matter chunks in my mouth. I immediately started to gag and spit out the unwelcome chunks. In addition, I involuntarily emitted small amounts of excrement and urine.

"Just shut up get out of the car, and get behind the trunk."

At that moment there were three explosions, too close.

"Cliff, now! Get out"

Suddenly there was gunfire directed at us.

Toni, keeping her head got out of the car, opened the driver's side door, pushing Silas's now lifeless body to the middle, and popped the trunk. She quickly rolled around the car, using the open door as a shield. At the rear of the car, the open trunk revealed a cache of weapons. She then loaded up with two hand guns, handed me two, and grabbed an extra rifle.

About 200 feet away, there were three persons bearing down on us. She indicated to me that we were going to make it to the open warehouse. She then handed me the rifle.

"OK, I'll cover you. Get inside the warehouse."

I nodded, and just like the old west, Toni Cardona rolled to the left side of the car and started to fire at the attacking gunmen. I sprinted, carrying two handguns, a box of ammo, and a rifle. At the warehouse, I stood partly outside and started to fire, to give Toni a chance to get into the warehouse.

Sam and Harry were now out of their car, trying to find a way into the compound. The gate was securely chained with a huge "Master" lock.

Sam told Harry to get back—he was going to try to blow off the lock.

Harry responded, "Are you nuts? Don't you watch TV? You are not going to open the lock."

"Watch me."

Sam carefully judged the angle of the ricochet and squeezed the trigger. After the loud bang, the lock still remained in place.

"See now. What did I tell you? Shit. Hell, I am not climbing this chain link fence. Look, it has razor wire. Forget about it."

It was then they heard the gunfire Toni and I were taking.

Sam shrugged as they turned to get back into the car.

"The car is rented, did you take out the collision insurance?"

"I think so."

Harry got in the car and threw it into reverse, then drive, and floored it—right through the once-locked gate.

The warehouse was full of huge rolls of newsprint some stacked twenty feet high. Toni pointed to what seemed to be a wall of paper rolls for protection. They ran over to catch their breath.

"Cliff, give me the rifle. I am going to try to shoot the chain that holds the warehouse door up. I think if I can cut it, it will fall."

"OK, Annie Oakley." I handed her the rifle with a scope.

Toni took aim, shot, and hit the chain on the left side. The left side of the giant door fell about five feet, but a different chain secured the right side, and the door was hopelessly stuck in the up position.

"Shit." There was not enough time for another try. Besides, two of the gunmen came through the normal—sized door on the north side of the building. Immediately, they took cover behind two large paper rolls, one behind a roll on the left and the other about six feet away on the right.

They fired, and Toni and I returned fire.

"OK, Toni. Where is the cavalry?"

She stood and fired about four more rounds.

"Don't know, Batman. I think we may be alone on this one. Do you see the third guy?"

I peeked my head up, and drew fire.

"Negative."

We heard what sounded like cans rattling. Then we smelled oil. Toni peeked through a crack between two rolls of paper.

"Shit, I see the third guy. He must have gotten in from the roof. He just poured oil; looks like they are going to burn us out."

Toni saw the third man go to strike a match. She stood straight up and fired, hitting him in the head before he could ignite the floor. Unfortunately Toni drew fire while standing up, and was shot and fell. I rolled over and fired my weapon twice, and pulled her behind the paper rolls. I cradled her in my arms; blood was everywhere.

"You are a great guy, Zavitch." She went cold.

I started to cry as I held her and started to rock, but only for a few seconds. Then I got mad. I gently laid her down and picked up two handguns, checked each clip and made sure they were full.

"Fuck it," I yelled and stood up firing, running, and screaming. I had sure footing until I hit the oil slick. Then the gunman on my right side shot and hit me in the knee, as I was slipping and horizontal in the air. The impact of the bullet hit me above the left knee. It spun me around and I fell on my back, landing on the oil slick. One lucky shot from my right had taken out the gunman on my right side before I went into the spin. As I landed on my back, I slid right through the gap in the rolls of paper they were hiding behind and now was behind the gunman. I did not give him a chance to turn. I emptied the last remaining bullets into the gunman's back. Except for what sounded like a loud hum, there were no more shots. Now bleeding and feeling pain, I dropped my head to the floor and started to cry. While my eyes were closed, I heard a click. I opened my eyes to see Steve Lambert, with his perfect blond hair, with not one hair out of place, tan and handsome, still a Redford look-alike.

"Thank God, the cavalry."

"Well, sounds like they are coming by chopper. It will take a moment for them to land and to find your dead body. Cliff, they are all dead—Tommy O, Phil, Mark."

Lambert put a bullet in the chamber ready to fire. I knew both of my guns were out.

"Shit, it was you."

"Of course. Hell, I am amazed I was able to do it. Did anyone really think I was going to give up the glamour, money and the power of the casino for a shitty government job? Oh, by the way, this is the gun of the dead man over there. He is the one who killed you." He raised the gun.

"Drop it," Harry and Sam said simultaneously.

Lambert looked up, "Now who the fuck are you guys?"

"Sarasota, Florida, police."

"Well I am FBI and this is Nevada. You have no jurisdiction here."

"Yes, sir, that very well may be." Harry said. "But drop the gun, please, and we will get this all straightened out."

Harry and Sam, old pros that they were, started to move apart from each other, and Lambert knew that if he had a chance to take both of them out, he had to act.

He relaxed his stance over me and put his weapon to his side. Then he raised it and took a shot at Sam, hitting him in the left arm. But Harry never relaxed, and drove 3 shots into Lambert's heart. Steve Lambert was dead, not I.

There were sounds of several people running from all sides to the warehouse, and in just seconds, people wearing dark blue jackets with F B I in bold yellow letters surrounded us.

Led by Tim Floyd, all drew down on Sam and Harry, making them drop their weapons and lay flat on the floor. They were even cuffed, but neither resisted. Under the same circumstances, they would do the same. Once an agent had taken charge of Sam and Harry, Tim walked carefully on the oil-slicked gray floor to get to his best friend, now in great pain and losing blood.

"Hey there; busy day."

"Toni is dead," I said, sniffling.

"I know."

"Steve said Phil was dead."

At that time, medics who were part of the emergency contingent were hovering over me and injected me with a painkiller that put me to sleep and lowered my heartbeat.

Tim looked around at the destruction and shook his head. He holstered his gun and began to walk out of the warehouse.

While the medical folks were taking care of the dead and me, he walked outside to survey the damage to the caravan. Agent Addison McCall met Tim.

“Rocket launchers from the rooftops.”

“All dead?”

He nodded. “All dead.”

Tim stayed on the scene with the criminalists. There were many questions. Why was Lambert out of the lead car? Why was he dead inside the warehouse? Who killed whom? After about an hour, he met with the Sarasota officers, and then decided to take them back to the Vegas FBI office. Sam had his arm taken care of. It seems that Lambert was slipping on the oil slick and was not able to get off a clean shot.

SATURDAY AFTERNOON
Las Vegas FBI headquarters

When they got to the office, Bob James, a/k/a Control 3, was on the phone with Dave Rose and Samantha Terry.

Bob James now grasping at straws. "What about the gambling license?"

"You are not going to believe this one. International Recreations and Leisure Adventures Corporation hired Alex Logan, who holds the license for the Majestic Casino…er…who held it two weeks ago. He applied for a transfer with the new ownership of International Recreations and Leisure Adventures Corporation for the Midway—and here is the strange part, it was approved without a full commission hearing."

"So this was done and we did not know," Bob James said with his face red and veins bulging in his neck.

Samantha chimed in, "Guys, you are not giving me much to go on."

Dave Rose responded. "Sam, if you can get us a continuance until Monday, that will be a home run."

"I'll try, sir."

Bob James appeared frazzled as he reset the phone. "Tora Tora Tora."

"What, sir," Tim asked.

"Remember our briefing the day before yesterday. Dave Lee said it will be "Tora Tora Tora." Complete surprise. Well it was on us. Where is Lambert?"

"Dead, sir."

"Who killed him?"

"I did, sir," Harry announced loudly.

"What? Why?"

"He was about to kill our murder suspect. He drew on us and I took him out."

"Shit. Lambert. Tim, get his files, lock down his office, get me his phone records, everything.

SAN FRANCISCO
3:45 PM Saturday

In San Francisco, justice was swift, maybe not fair for the state, but quick.

"Samantha Terry for the Department of Justice, your honor."

"Yes, Ms. Terry. You have a motion?"

"We wish to ask for a continuance, please."

J Jancan stood up. " We object. Time is of the essence in this matter. Our clients are losing millions of dollars in profit and goodwill; their business has been illegally seized; and we demand injunctive relief so our clients may reopen their business."

The judge seemed impressed with the plight of Mr. Jancan's client.

"Ms. Terry?" The judge turned to the state's side.

"Your honor, we have proof of racketeering, and are just about to impose the RICO act because of illegal skimming and illegal payoffs and bribes."

J Jancan stood and pounded his index finger into the table. "No sir; no, your honor; not my clients. You have a list of officers who sit on the board. They are upstanding, and there are some prominent people on that list."

The judge took few moments to study the stack of documents he had on the bench.

"Tell me, Mr. Jancan, why was there no public announcement of the acquisition of the Midway Casino?"

"SEC rules your honor. International Recreations and Leisure Adventures Corporation is planning to go public, and the SEC requested we do not publicly announce until we have officially taken over."

"Do you have this documentation?"

"Of course we have it."

"I am sure they do," Samantha retorted sarcastically.

The judge said nothing, but looked up over his glasses and stared at Samantha Terry. No one said anything; the judge did not even blink. Then after about two minutes, Samantha said, "I am sorry, your honor." The judge sat back.

"Mr. Jancan, I have approximately a thousand sheets of paper on this bench. Could you save me the time and find them for me."

In just seconds, Franklin Fraser produced the documents, and they were given to the bailiff to give to the judge.

"Ms. Terry, what evidence do you have that there was corruption, payoffs, skimming, and bribes? Will you be able to produce witnesses?"

Standing at the podium, Ms. Terry folded her hands as if she were praying, sat her chin on her thumbs, and contemplated what she was about to say. "No your honor. They are all dead."

There was an instant rumbling in the room, including on the defense side. The judge, a bit shocked, rapped his gavel and asked everyone into chambers.

Once in chambers, the judge started to ask more questions about the death of the witnesses. "Dead? How?"

"Killed, your honor."

"When?"

"This morning."

The judge turned to J Jancan. "JJ, I have known you for years. Do you know anything about this?"

"Jack, hell, no. Look, just take a look at the merits of our case as it stands. We would not have to kill anyone. Our client is International Recreations and Leisure Adventures Corporation, a company that is about to go public, not some band of thugs."

"Bullshit," Samantha blurted.

The judge raised his left hand, read some more and then looked up. "One more question, JJ. Why has your client waited to take over?"

"Simple. Carson City. Our client hired Alex Logan, who holds the license for the Majestic and has applied to transfer the license to the Midway. Our client could not move on the Midway until the license was officially transferred. We heard it was approved. We were just waiting. It is probably on some bureaucrat's desk."

The judge put his hand over his mouth as if he were thinking. "Please, everyone leave my chambers. I will rule on the motion for continuance and the motion for injunctive relief in thirty minutes.

Thirty minutes to the second, the judge appeared on the bench.

"I have contacted some folks in Carson City, who confirmed that Alex Logan has indeed been approved as the new license holder for the Midway Casino. They also confirmed that this was done several days ago, strangely outside of commission, which I understand is done occasionally when there is a transfer, but not for a new licensee."

The Judge took in a deep breath. "The state's contention is that the owners of the Midway engaged in illegal activities, and it was about to impose the RICO statute. The problem here is complex. When, exactly, was ownership conveyed? Even if it was not sold to the new owner, would the new owner, who by the documents I have before me, paid millions for the property, would it be right to deprive them of the revenue? The documents appear to be in order."

The judge cleared his throat and went on "The RICO violation of the old ownership has absolutely no bearing on the new ownership. Even if there were taxes owned, the transfer of ownership documents have the seller liable for any back taxes, and it appears that here is a large sum in escrow to take care of any back taxes. As for a RICO, we find that the state has no right to deprive the rightful owners of their property. I deny the motion for continuance and order that the federal and state government release all property seized immediately.

"This matter is settled."

LAS VEGAS—DESERT HOSPITAL
Sunday Morning

Physically, I was in good shape. The knee hurt, but the bullet only grazed it. I could be up today, but emotionally I was shot. Watching several people die is not good for anyone's mental health.

The doctors called Tim when I was up and able to talk to visitors without the shadow of heavy drugs impairing my recollections. Tim entered the room with a cadre of people with recording devices and notepads.

"Hey, guy, I know this sucks, but we have to ask you some questions."

"I understand."

A professional FBI interviewer took over and started from the top, from getting the phone call from Phil to Steve Lambert's betrayal and desire to kill me. The effort took almost two hours.

"OK, now I have some questions."

"Sure, go ahead."

"I want to get back to work as soon as possible at the Midway."

Tim looked around the room and asked everyone to leave. Once they were gone, Tim sat on the hospital bed of his old friend.

"You are not going back. While you were getting shot at, and Toni was getting killed, some high-powered lawyers did some fancy maneuvering and gave the casino back to the bad guys, only this time under a different name—a large corporation that will soon be traded on wall street which I am sure they control. Late last night a judge ruled so, and in just a few hours, the place was rockin' and rolling again. FECMAC, Inc., the Federal Emergency Casino Management Corporation," verbally highlighting the long name, "has no standing with the Midway, and unfortunately, you don't either."

Tim got off the bed and sat in the standard hospital chair next to it.

I got up and stood, then picked up a blue plastic water pitcher and hurled it against the wall, shattering the plastic and splashing water everywhere.

I then started to pound the table. "God damn it; God damn." Then I picked up the side table that slides under the bed and flung it across the room. The noise drew a crowd. Tim signaled that all was OK. I then put weight on my left knee and went down. Tim hurried over to help me up, but I pushed him away, and managed to get back into bed myself.

"You are now going to tell me that I fucking have to go back to that shitty job in Sarasota."

"For a while, Cliff. Look, I will help you find something."

"When?"

"Cliff, I want to send you to Bethesda to talk with some people. You have been through a lot."

"Shrinks?"

Tim nodded affirmatively. "Yeah, shrinks. Cliff, I killed someone once. They helped me."

"It may be a good idea. Are you going to tell me now that I can't tell anyone about this?"

"Except for the shrinks and me, yeah."

"What if I say, shit, I am going to write a book?"

"And who is going to believe this, Cliff?"

"Hell, fiction books make money."

Cliff, there are still people who want you dead. When we find Silas's agent, then write your book. But not until we find them."

"Agent?, Who hired him to kill me?"

"Steve Lambert?"

"Steve, shit I thought he liked me?" I said half laughing.

"Cliff he may have but it was all just business. Steve was a double double agent. He was under cover too long and got friendly with the owners of the Midway. Steve knew about Phil, Mark and Tommy skimming and was in contact with the old owners."

"When did you find this out?"

Tim shook his head "Cliff I really did not expect him at all it was a surprise. Control 3, Bob James had his suspicions but could not prove a thing. The old ownership knew everything we did Steve fed them everything. If the heroes from Sarasota would not have killed him and he killed you he probably would have been retained as the New GM."

" We knew we had a leak and Lambert was the one to yell the loudest about it, I should have suspected him too. He let them know when the take over was, let them know our legal strategy so they, the old ownership, were able to hire a high powered law firm and he let them know about you and where Phil and Tommy O were going to leave from. You became key, if they would have killed you I knew for a fact Phil would have backed out and taken his chances with the old ownership."

"When will I be safe?

"Not until we find the Murder for Hire agents, we know they are from Chicago and they are very well connected?"

"How long?"

Tim shrugged, "A year, five, twenty, maybe never." He immediately changed subjects "Cliff. We have a cover story. Your employer has been notified that you were skiing in Aspen and hurt your leg, I had Beth Downs call and act as your aunt who lives in Colorado."

"What else?"

"That is it. Cliff, you were skiing."

"My car?"

"It will take some time, but we will take care of it. Look, I will take some time off and stay with you a while. We will have some fun."

"Cool. OK."

"When can I leave?"

"Are you ready?"

"Yeah."

"I will make the arrangements now and we will fly over to Maryland for a couple of days, and then back to Sarasota.

I sat on the bed and nodded my approval. "Get me out of here, Tim."

As Tim was leaving, he turned, "I'm sorry, Cliff."

"About?"

"Everything—the job at the Midway, the shitty job you have to go back to, Phil."

I nodded.

I spent 48 hours on various couches of high-powered shrinks, talking to them, telling them my feelings about killing two people, having one person's brain sprayed in my mouth, and having a beautiful young friend die in my arms. Yeah, I was OK.

Two of the shrinks wanted to give me drugs, but I declined.

It was Wednesday when I got back. I was just gone ten days. My plan was to take another day off and go in Friday, put up with some bullshit and then get into my regular schedule on Monday.

SARASOTA, FLORIDA
Thursday Morning, 1:17 A.M., April 30, 1987

And this brought us here, right now, me with a Glock and Tim behind a couch ready to blast an intruder.

I saw the lock turn and then the doorknob move. Then I heard a familiar voice.

"Cliff?"

"Kurt, what the fuck are you doing?" I put the Glock on my bookcase and motioned for Tim to roll back out of sight.

"I was partying downtown and drove by and saw the lights on, but no car in the driveway. What happened to your car?"

"I understand it got stolen and burned up. We took a limo from the airport."

"We?"

"Yeah, my friend and I. Hey, Tim."

Tim peeked around the corner. "Hey."

I quickly introduced Tim and Kurt.

"Heard you were hurt?"

"Went skiing with my aunt and cousins, and ran into a tree."

'Christ, lucky you weren't killed. Oh yeah, a couple of cops came by to see me. It seems that not only was your car burned up, but someone was killed inside. And what happened to the Vegas thing" Kurt looking over to Tim. "Weren't you the one who was suppose to take Cliff to Vegas?"

Tim cut in "That, when I got here Phil called and there was no need to bring Cliff to Vegas and coincidentally Cliff's Aunt called and we both ended in Colorado.

Kurt was suspicious and then tried one more time "Heard on the news there was a lot of trouble in Vegas, several guys got killed."

"Kurt seems you know more about this than I do. Hell, I just got back. Look, I would offer you a drink but I just took some pain pills."

"OK, when are you coming back to work?"

"Well, Tim and I are going to go looking at cars, my uncle, Uncle Sam, is going to buy a brand new car for me, isn't he, Tim?" Tim was still standing just around the corner.

"It seems so, it seems so."

"Great, let me know what you get."

"Good night, Kurt."

"OK, guys, good night."

I sat on the couch until we heard the car pull away.

"He doesn't buy the skiing story."

Tim made a tight smile and shook his head. "Nope, he is not buying it a bit "

Tim pulled a few strings and procured a nice used Volvo for me. Work, as I suspected, was hell. Tony was still an asshole and Alexandria was just as cute, but was a real bitch.

On Monday, after the "de-motivational" meeting, I hobbled into my office and sat. A few moments later, Tony and Alexandria visited.

"How is the leg?" Tony asked with fake concern.

"I should be walking without crutches in a couple of days."

Alexandria broke in, "Nelson found many problems with your book of business."

"I am sure he did."

"Cliff, I am afraid that I must tell you that the SEC and the State DOI (department of Insurance) will be here in three weeks, and I think you will need legal representation. I can suggest a few."

"No thanks. I did nothing wrong. I don't need an attorney and if I do get one, it will not be anyone you recommend."

"Jesus, Cliff, you do have an attitude."

"Are we done?"

"WE are" they said in unison.

For the rest of the day, I sat at my desk wondering what I would be doing if I were the assistant GM at the Midway, a dream that would stay a dream.

Friday, the doctor told me I could walk without crutches. It was time for Tim to leave; he did not say a thing to me about leaving. When I came home, he was packed and asked me to take him to the airport in the new car that Uncle Sam purchased for me.

Tim's flight was late, so I thought it would be appropriate to take him to Yoder's one last time.

"Cliff, this has got to be the best home cooking in the world."

"How about I buy you a pie to take with you?"

"Nah, how about we buy a pie and eat it here?"

"OK."

While we were eating pie, we discussed my problems at work. It seemed that Tim had taken an interest in my legal situation.

"Don't worry; things will work out." He said with encouragement.

We finished the entire chocolate peanut butter cream pie and left for the SRQ, Sarasota International Airport.

I still had my handicapped decal so we got parking close in. It was obvious I was still hurting, so we walked into the terminal and found the nearest bar.

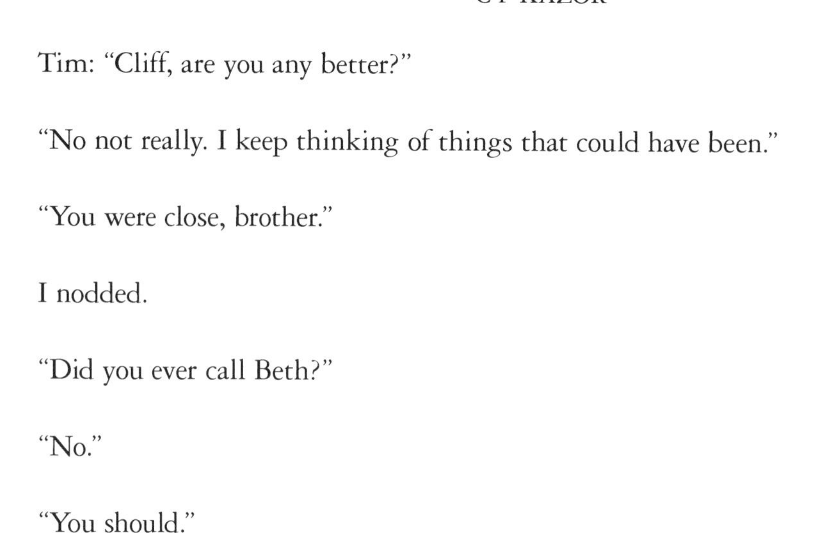

Tim: "Cliff, are you any better?"

"No not really. I keep thinking of things that could have been."

"You were close, brother."

I nodded.

"Did you ever call Beth?"

"No."

"You should."

"Maybe."

Tim looked at his watch. "Better go now."

I gingerly got off my bar stool, gave my lifelong friend a bear hug, and limped back to my car.

The next few weeks were not pleasant, just a week after I got back; Tony had me suspended for compliance violation. When I got back after ten days without pay; I was relegated to answering phones and helping agents make appointments.

SARASOTA, FLORIDA
Friday June 5, 1987

I had interviews with several other companies and was waiting for some kind of response. It was a beautiful Friday morning and I had gone across US 41 to get a cup of Kona at Denny's. When I arrived back on the tenth floor, Tony and Alexandria met me.

"We are sorry, guy, we could not protect you any more. There are feds all over the place and we think you are going to be arrested today. They are in my office waiting for you."

Alexandria then put her few cents in, "You should have played ball with us, Cliff. Now I think you are going away a long time."

I said nothing but turned in the opposite direction and walked to my office. They were right. There were Feds all over, and when I entered my office, there were people going through my desk. I dropped my briefcase on the desk. The fed going through my desk asked, "Are you Mr. Zavitch?"

"I am."

"There are people waiting for you in Mr. Lopez's office."

I said nothing and took the long walk to Tony's office. A gentleman who I did not believe to be a fed met me at the door.

"Mr. Zavitch?"

"Yes, sir."

"May I see some identification?"

I was both puzzled and stunned. "Sure, to make sure you arrest the right guy?"

The man said nothing, just looked at my ID, and made a quick note.

"Can I go in now?"

"Yes, of course."

I walked in the door, followed by the strange man who asked for ID. There were about eight people around Tony's desk going through papers, only at his desk they were tagging and bagging. Someone was sitting in Tony's $1,000 chair with his back to me.

"What a lovely view," a familiar voice said.

"Jesus, Tim, is that you?"

"Actually it is Deputy Director Floyd."

"No shit."

"In the flesh."

Tim walked around the desk and embraced me.

"What is going on?"

"These guys, your boss, his bimbo, and that guy Nelson, they have been running a scam, but they are lucky rank amateurs." He pointed to the gentleman at the file cabinet. "That is Agent Philips; he is AIC for this case, and he will be reporting to me. I told you things would work out."

I turned around. "Who is this?"

"Mr. Zavitch, I am a life agent with Great United Pan American Life Insurance. I need to have a word with you."

Puzzled I said "Sure."

"In private."

Alexandria had an office in the office, which was off to the side. I pointed and led him into the small side office.

"Mr. Zavitch, you knew a Mr. Phil Irish?"

"Yes, sir."

"Mr. Irish has named you beneficiary to one of his life insurance policies." He turned and got his notebook and handed Cliff a check.

"Sir, if you would sign this for me."

"Sure."

"Thank you, Mr. Zavitch."

He stood, shook my hand and left the room, then left Tony's office. I walked back into Tony's main office.

Tim was smiling. "Well?"

"Death proceeds."

"Well?"

"Well it is not as good as $385,000 a year plus bonus, but it is substantial. I really need to ask you something."

"Shoot."

"Phil's son?"

'Josh."

"Yeah."

"Don't worry, Cliff. He has been taken care of. Phil had a ton of life insurance. You know we can't touch those funds."

"I know, so why are you here?"

"Besides here to see my old best buddy?"

"Yeah"

"I figured it out," Tim said like the proverbial cat.

"What?"

"The Scam, almost brilliant, you were too close and could not see it."

I stretched my arms palms up and shrugged, "Do I get enlightened?"

"Absolutely, I told Agent Phillips you would help him out."

"Yeah, no problem. What was the scam?"

"Well while you were convalescing I became interested in your little problem here. Did you know that Tony and the gang would meet at Kinko's in Tampa each Sunday for a Pizza Party?"

"What?"

Tim stretched put his feet on Tony's desk and hands behind his head "Yeah, seemed strange to me until I found out what they were doing"

"OK what were" Tim cut me off by putting hih finger in the air.

"First I had to learn about Life insurance and Annuities, by the way Cliff you got a great library. What do you know?"

"Really only what I had already told you when we got back from Vegas, not too much. I know that, my old partner, 'Chris Bear,' was getting credit for a ton of whole life policies that he did not know anything about, then they would be removed from his commission statement before he got a check. The memo was a 'processing error.' These were high commission policies, but Chris never saw a dime. The 'errors' were always corrected before the comp was released. It was driving Chris nuts, mainly because the computer would lock him out and he could not find out anything about the policies. We knew they were whole life, high commission, and we could only get the person's last name and the face amount—always $50,000.

"We could not get the apps or anything. When Chris Bear died, then I started having the errors on my report. I managed to find some applications that were stored in a closet in a storeroom. They were in bankers' boxes with Chris's name on them. I opened the boxes to find applications that had Chris's name on them and his signature, but it was not his signature."

"Tim interrupted those applications were all whole life applications, right?"

"Correct, all of those applications in the box are all whole life applications, with Chris's and my phony signatures". I conceded

"And how much money or commission does an agent get for one of those policies?"

"Whole life has a first year commission of at least 80 percent. So with a $3,000 premium, the agent would make $2,400 commission. Then if the policies stayed on the books for two years, the company would bonus the agent another 30 percent on the first and second. That would be another $1,800 or…"

Tim interrupted. "$4,200 per policy. But they were supposed to be annuities. How much does an annuity of $3,000 pay?"

"Well, as you know, an annuity is like a savings account. On a $3,000 deposit, maybe 5 percent."

All were looking at me now. One agent whistled, "Only $360 commission for an annuity. What about Kinko's?" I added

While you were under the influence of one of your pain pills I followed them one Sunday or I should say one Monday morning and witnessed Tony, Alexandria, Nelson, and nine other agents in the Tampa Bay area, from Naples to Clearwater and over to Tampa, were meeting at Kinko's regularly.

"OK and what were they doing?" I asked with a completely bewildered tone.

"Eating pizza"

I was really stumped now, "Pizza?"

"and made hundreds of copies, forging policies!"

"Changing the face pages?" I asked still not exactly getting it. At that point I finally got it, it was so easy but like Tim said I could not see the proverbial forest, "How many agents did Tony have running the scam?"

"About thirty." Tim went on "Yep, the face page that tells the consumer what they bought. Each life and or annuity policies comes with a first page called a "Face Page." It describes the policy. The whole life policies were issued by the company and sent to agents. Then they had a party and would print annuity illustrations, then take the policies apart using the tools at Kinko's and then again using the large staplers Kinko's provides to re-staple the policy."

"How many policies?"

"About 200,000 policies over five years"

"Average $3,000 per policy?"

"Almost to the dime, they were targeting nurses and medical personnel under 35"

"So no one would have to sit for a medical" I broke in. "Let's see that would be about $48,000,000 in commissions "

"Cliff, do the math again. You dropped a zero."

"Jesus Christ! Almost a half billion dollars."

Tim started to laugh. "It was a closely knit, highly motivated group."

"What about our home office?"

"Say they didn't know a thing. They say Tony and the gang are fabulous agents. See me to the elevator?"

"Not going to go for pie at Yoder's?" I inquired

"No, but I left you something at the house, and put the key through the mail slot."

"What did you leave me?"

"It is a surprise. If you don't like it, send it back."

Tim walked out and his entourage filed around him, with Tim and me in the middle. Spectators thought I was in custody. They waited at the elevator, then the elevator door opened and to everyone's surprise, Tim gave me our customary bear hug. Tim and six others entered the elevator, leaving me on the tenth floor.

"Take care, brother."

"Take care, Timmy." And the elevator door closed.

Everyone seemed bewildered. Then Agent Philips appeared from Tony's office. Tony stood at Alexandria's side. She was completely befuddled about what had just happened.

Several agents followed Agent-in-Charge Philips as he approached Tony Lopez.

"Are you Tony Lopez?"

"Yes."

"Mr. Lopez, you have the right to remain silent. Anything you say can and will be used against you in a court of law. You have the right to speak to an attorney, and to have an attorney present during any questioning. If you cannot afford a lawyer, one will be provided for you at government expense. Do you understand these rights?"

When they started to cuff him, he lost it "You fucking assholes. Nelson, call my attorney."

Tony was taken onto the elevator.

Agent Phillips pointed to Mr. Nelson and said, "Mr. Nelson, you have the right to remain silent. Anything you say can and will be used against you in a court of law. You have the right to speak to an attorney, and to have an attorney present during any questioning. If you cannot afford a lawyer, one will be provided for you at government expense. Do you understand these rights?"

"I want to make a deal. It was them, Alexandria and Lopez, who did it all."

Agent Phillips then turned. "Ms. Alexandria Butterfield, you have the right to remain silent. Anything you say can and will be used against you in a court of law. You have the right to speak to an attorney, and to have an attorney present during any questioning. If you cannot afford a lawyer, one will be provided for you at government expense. Do you understand these rights?"

She started to weep wildly as two female agents took her away. She would have preferred guys manhandling her, I thought.

Agent Phillips asked me to follow him back to Tony's office were agents were ransacking the office. I was ushered into Tony's old office and sat in his $1,000 chair.

Oh, and by the way, your buddy Tim Floyd owes you big time."

"He is now deputy director?"

"Because of Las Vegas?"

"Hell no. You know that was a cluster fuck, but you turned him onto this and he followed up on it, so now he is a number one. If you had not gone to Vegas, we would not have uncovered this scam for another couple of years."

I smiled.

I could see the elevator opened on the now quiet tenth floor. Most of the agents were sent off and an embarrassing message was put on the phone. "We are sorry, the office of Great International Global Life and Casualty has been seized by the U.S. Federal Department of the Treasury."

I wondered if they put that on the Midway's phone.

I saw my old friend Kurt Elwood trying to peek in to see me. I asked if Elwood could enter, and he was given permission.

"You really look good behind that desk. Are you the boss?"

"I laughed. No, as a matter of fact, I am retiring, quitting, getting the fuck out! Help me clear out my desk."

"Are you serious?"

"Yep."

I pulled out my check and teased Kurt by showing that it contained six figures.

"Jesus, you are serious."

"I am. Gentlemen, am I needed here anymore?"

"No, thanks for the help"

Kurt and I walked down the hall, stopping to pick up a few banker boxes on the way. I immediately started to toss things into the boxes willy-nilly.

"What is happening, Cliff?"

"Well, my friend, the defecation hit the cross blade. Tony and his beautiful cocksucking companion have been running a multimillion dollar scam and they got caught."

"And you?"

"An innocent bystander."

"Why are you quitting?"

"Retiring."

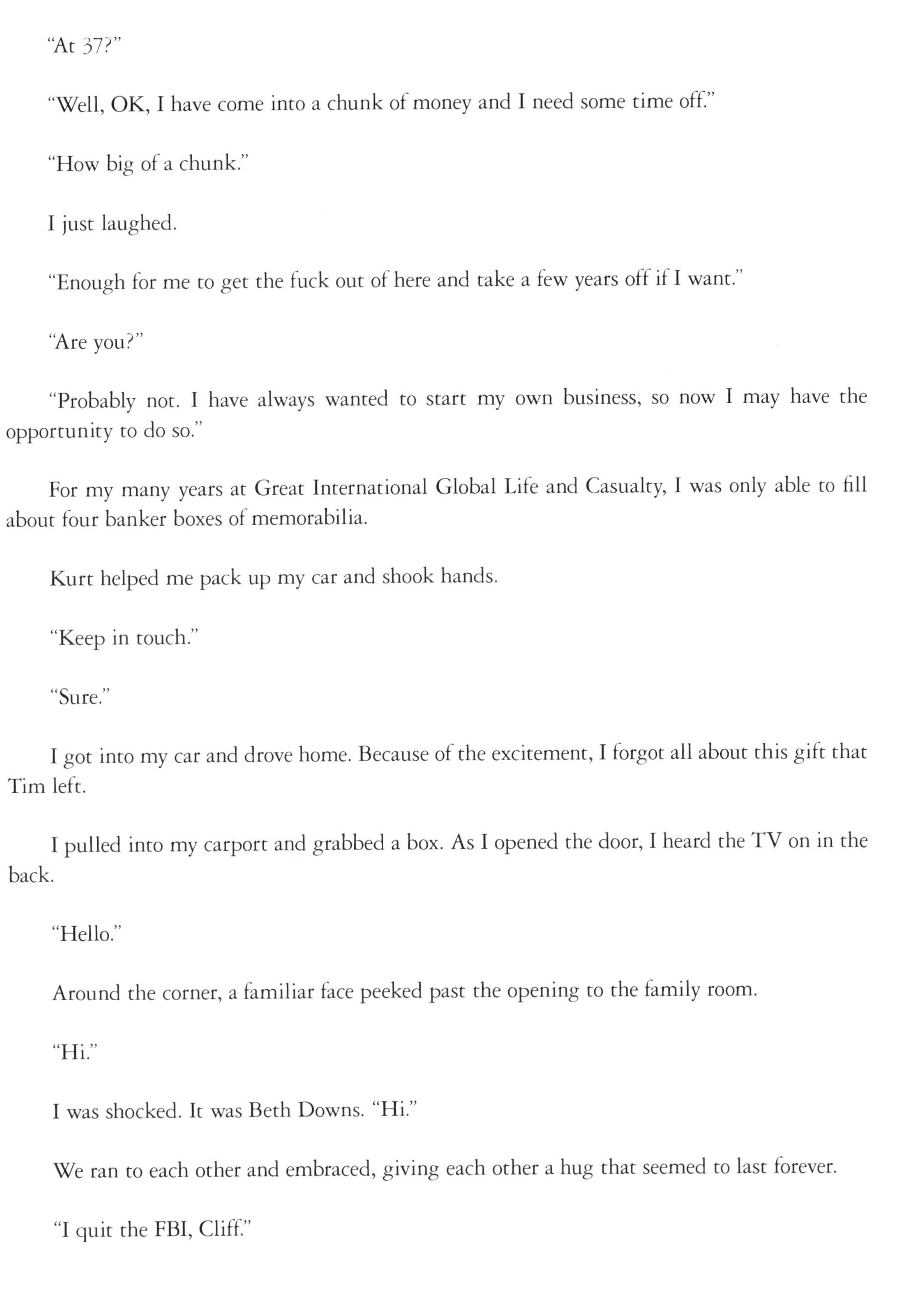

"At 37?"

"Well, OK, I have come into a chunk of money and I need some time off."

"How big of a chunk."

I just laughed.

"Enough for me to get the fuck out of here and take a few years off if I want."

"Are you?"

"Probably not. I have always wanted to start my own business, so now I may have the opportunity to do so."

For my many years at Great International Global Life and Casualty, I was only able to fill about four banker boxes of memorabilia.

Kurt helped me pack up my car and shook hands.

"Keep in touch."

"Sure."

I got into my car and drove home. Because of the excitement, I forgot all about this gift that Tim left.

I pulled into my carport and grabbed a box. As I opened the door, I heard the TV on in the back.

"Hello."

Around the corner, a familiar face peeked past the opening to the family room.

"Hi."

I was shocked. It was Beth Downs. "Hi."

We ran to each other and embraced, giving each other a hug that seemed to last forever.

"I quit the FBI, Cliff."

"And I quit my job, too."

"Shit, we are both unemployed. Want to take a trip or something?"

"Or something." I planted a big old sloppy wet kiss on her, picked her up and carried her to the bedroom.

Beth said, "Or something is good."

TAMPA, FLORIDA MONDAY APRIL 25, 2005 – 10:30 P.M.

I was driving home late from a seminar I had conducted when my phone rang. I glanced at the Caller ID and saw a strange note: "SECURED CALL."

"Cliff Zavitch, may I help you?"

"No, not really but maybe I can help you. It's Tim."

"Jesus, are you in town?"

"No, as a matter of fact I'm about 5,000 miles away from you."

"What's up? Are you all right?"

"Yeah, how is Beth?"

"Great, ah, you called to tell me you are getting married."

"No, no."

"Wait, how did you get my cell number if you didn't first call Beth."

"Come on Cliff. Directory assistance calls me for numbers. I know everyone's number." He paused, "You need to get the paper tomorrow. Look in the National and World section—there is news."

"News?"

"Got to go, Cliff, Love ya, brother." The phone went dead.

TUESDAY, APRIL 26, 2005

14 indicted in anti-mob move

CHICAGO—Federal prosecutors yesterday indicted two former Chicago police officers and 12 reputed mobsters, including the man the FBI says ran the Chicago mob, in connection with 18 murders nearly three decades ago.

The murders include the unsolved death of Tommy O'Sullivan, Mark Karl, and Phil Irish, managers of the Midway Casino, who purportedly had turned state's evidence and were about to testify against many high-ranking mob bosses.

END

Made in the USA
Columbia, SC
23 June 2023

18792343R00139